Death of a She Devil

Fay Weldon, one of the most successful advertising copywriters of her generation, is now recognized as one of our most important and distinctive literary voices. She published her first novel, *A Fat Woman's Joke*, in 1976, and has gone on to write over thirty novels, as well as short stories and screenplays. In 1983, she wrote *The Life and Loves of a She Devil*. The story of Ruth, taking delicious revenge on her cheating husband Bobbo, has become a modern classic, adapted for film and television and recently serialised on Radio 4.

In 2001, Fay was awarded a CBE for services to literature. In 2015, her short story collection, *Mischief*, celebrated four decades of her witty, engaging and socially observant writing. She teaches creative writing at Bath Spa University and lives on a hilltop in Dorset.

ALSO BY FAY WELDON

FICTION

The Fat Woman's Joke
Down Among the Women
Female Friends
Remember Me
Little Sisters
Praxis
Puffball
The President's Child
The Life and Loves of a She Devil
The Shrapnel Academy
The Heart of the Country
The Hearts and Lives of Men
The Rules of Life
Leader of the Band
The Cloning of Joanna May
Darcy's Utopia
Growing Rich
Life Force
Affliction
Splitting
Worst Fears
Big Women
Rhode Island Blues
The Bulgari Connection
Mantrapped
She May Not Leave
The Spa Decameron
The Stepmother's Diary

Chalcot Crescent
Kehua!
Habits of the House
Long Live the King
The New Countess
(The Ted Dreams)
Before The War

CHILDREN'S BOOKS

Wolf the Mechanical Dog
Party Puddle
Nobody Likes Me

SHORT STORY COLLECTIONS

Watching Me, Watching You
Polaris
Moon Over Minneapolis
Wicked Women
A Hard Time to Be a Father
Nothing to Wear & Nowhere
to Hide
Mischief

NON-FICTION

Letters to Alice
Rebecca West
Sacred Cows
Godless in Eden
Auto da Fay
What Makes Women Happy

Death
of a
She
Devil

Fay
Weldon

HEAD
of ZEUS

First published in the UK in 2017 by Head of Zeus Ltd

Copyright © Fay Weldon, 2017

The moral right of Fay Weldon to be identified as the author
of this work has been asserted in accordance with the
Copyright, Designs and Patents Act of 1988.

Extract from *There Are Bad Times Just Around The Corner*
by Noël Coward, © NC Aventales AG by permission of
Alan Brodie Representation Ltd / www.alanbrodie.com.

9 7 5 3 1 2 4 6 8

A catalogue record for this book is available from the British Library.

ISBN (HB): 9781784979591
ISBN (TPB): 9781784979607
ISBN (E): 9781784979584

Typeset by Adrian McLaughlin

Printed and bound in Leck, Germany,
by CPI Books GmbH

Head of Zeus Ltd
First Floor East
5–8 Hardwick Street
London EC1R 4RG

WWW.HEADOFZEUS.COM

Death
of a
She
Devil

PART ONE

The Past Is Never Over

1

My Children Will Not Speak To Me...

These days, when the She Devil wakes she must remind herself who she is.

I am in my eighties now and I see no one fit to follow in my footsteps. Who can be trusted to come after me? My children and my children's children will not even speak to me. Who will take over when I am gone, will leap out of bed every morning to look after and improve the world? Who will rule in the High Tower?

But I am Lady Ruth Patchett, the She Devil. I am the one who has dominion over the High Tower and all its satellites. I am President and Chief Executive of the Institute for Gender Parity. Once upon a time Mary Fisher, a wicked purveyor of romantic fiction, a teller of lies, ruled here in the High Tower, but she is well dead and gone. Where once she sipped champagne, lit her scented candles and slept with other women's husbands, notably mine, now I, Ruth Patchett, She Devil, rule the roost. I am as good as any man, and crow the triumph of the true, the proud, the honest working women of today, the ones that we set free. Gone with the wind are Mary Fisher's simpering ninnies, raising their doe-eyes in adoration of lusty dinosaur men, and thank the Gods for that – though gone too, come to think of it, are the lusty men. Lusty is so out of fashion.

But still I wake uneasy in the mornings. And aching too, as one does at eighty-four. All is not well. Is it conscience that troubles me? When I step out upon the ground it seems to tremble – is it that the sea batters the rocks on which the High Tower stands, or is it just that my limbs are old? I always did the best I could, surely, within the limits of my own nature. I am without guilt. So why am I so hated? Why do I hate myself?

Why does no one bring me my coffee? Surely it's time?

Morning light seeps round the edges of the blinds. I have work to do. The nation needs me.

Women need me.

2

Now Let's Look In On Bobbo...

The She Devil's husband is ninety-four, bedridden and has Alzheimer's.

Ruth keeps the foul-mouthed old goat alive in the Lantern Room of the High Tower, if you ask me just so she can gloat. She's still his wife but she never visits. To think that I, the ghost of Mary Fisher, weeping and wailing in the wind that blows around the High Tower, was once so in love with this stringy, nasty old jailbird! It's beyond belief. I catch his thoughts as they fly. They're more a jumble of bad feelings than thoughts, of course, but let me translate them for you. What's he muttering now?

'What a fucking fuss about nothing! Any red-blooded man would have done what I did. Why would I stay with Ruth when I could have Mary Fisher? It was a no-brainer. Ruth was the hulk of a wife, an ugly old bat with a wart on her lip. Mary was the slim, tender mistress, the willing bird, eye-candy on the arm. Ruth was a nagging housewife, Mary a romantic novelist, wealthy, earning millions with her stupid novels. Ruth and the kids just sucked money out of my purse. Ruth was grateful when – if – I fucked her, Mary played hard to get. And she said she loved me. What a little bloody liar. Women think men are only interested in sex, but they're wrong: men want love as well as sex. Of course I went.

'True, I had to walk out on the kids to do it. Fucking ungrateful brats they turned out to be. But scientists say it's in a man's nature to look after women and kids when they're helpless. As soon as the wife can help herself, and the kids grow older and start answering back, he sods off to spread the selfish gene elsewhere. Quite so. That's all I did. But you'd have thought from the row that resulted, the bleeding noise and fury, that I'd done something unthinkably, unnaturally wicked. I never got it. I'd certainly done it to the wrong fucking wife and kids, triggered off more than I ever reckoned.'

'Look at me now, living out my days between a bed and an armchair, so old I don't even have the strength to get it up any more. Even Viagra won't do it, not even Nurse Travers, my hot-tottie little nurse, skirt up to her arse when she bends over. It can't be me. I reckon it's Dr Simmins' pills doing it, murderous old lezzie slag that she is. They're all trying to finish me off. They won't succeed. And by the way I don't have Alzheimer's. I just pretend for the fucking tests...'

Yes, that's Bobbo. Once my true love. Sorry about the language. Oh dear... 'I lean'd my back against an oak, thinking it was a mighty tree, but first it bent and then it broke, so did my love prove false to me.'

The past is never over. I am the ghost of Mary Fisher, weeping in the wind.

3

The She Devil Tells Herself Lies

'I did the best I could, within the limits of my own nature.'
A likely story!

It wasn't as if I hurled Mary Fisher to her death, down to the craggy rocks on which the High Tower stands, battered by the fury of wave and wind. Much as I longed to. Just a little push from me, I thought, and over she'd go, champagne flute in hand, through the open picture window of the Lantern Room, long blonde hair streaming as she fell. That, I thought, would put a stop not just to the romances spewing from her seductive pen, but to the little trill of a voice, half giggle and half erotic gasp, that so enthralled my husband and drove me mad with rage. But I didn't. I held my hand.

I did not love Bobbo as she did, I can admit that, but Bobbo was my wedded husband, father of my children, my great achievement, the most precious thing I owned or hoped to own, and Mary Fisher stole him from me. He was my status and my income, the one and only notch on my bedpost. I'm not someone who forgives easily.

But I didn't push. I was too cunning. Rather I let a little worm of doubt and dread grow in her silly mind until she realised life was not worth living and only then did she die, slowly and horribly from a cancer that devoured her from within. I allowed her to live that day, as she stood laughing and trilling at the window, but I gave her my children. 'Where your father goes, you go,' I said to Nicci and Andy, and left.

That day I hated Mary Fisher more than I loved my children. But the day passed and I lived to regret what I had done. Too late. And now they will not speak to me, nor will their children.

Ah, thank God, here's my coffee. Valerie Valeria, my PA, brings it in. I am early waking, not she late in bringing it. Seven-thirty on the dot. Such a pretty, clever, competent girl, and ambitious too. My shield and support. And she's brought a red rose in a long-stemmed vase. The world is such a changed place, that a rose can be brought to me in November. The more people moan about carbon footprints, the more they create them.

4

According To The Family Therapist

The She Devil caused a great deal of damage.

I'm sure women in general have a great deal to be grateful to the She Devil for, equal pay and all that, and as a force in society she is an admirable person and the Queen had good reason to make her a Dame, but she was a bad, bad mother, running out on her children the way she did, dumping them on her husband's mistress, Mary Fisher of all people.

If the She Devil's children won't speak to her it's not surprising. What did she think would happen? As so often with these narcissistic mothers – self-absorbed, brittle, easily angered and 'always right' – the only thing their children can do is either cut the ties that bind and run, or stay and placate. Anything other than face the anger. Adored by others, hated by her children, Ruth Patchett is typical of the powerful, charismatic, narcissistic mother. And as ever, the therapist, that's me, is left to pick up the pieces.

Every week the little family visits me, Matilda Eavens, for family therapy. Nicola Finch Patchett, the She Devil's daughter, brings along her three children, the girl twins Madison and Mason, and her boy Tyler. Nicci is a staunch feminist. They have been coming for at least ten years. Nicola likes to get value for money and the sessions are paid for by Nicola's nameless benefactor, who fathered the twins on her when she was fifteen. (The girl had low self-esteem, which is hardly surprising, considering her background.) I like to think that these family visits give all of them much needed stability.

The girls, at thirty-two, are inseparable and employed as supervisors at the local call centre. Tyler, at twenty-three, is a beautiful lad, but resentful and unemployed. His mother, who currently works for the Women's Right to Choose movement, does not suffer fools gladly especially if they are male. All three children have difficulty leaving home.

I suspect Nicci may have a tendency towards maternal narcissism herself, the condition tending to pass from mother to daughter, as epigenetics tells us these traits often do. I may have no formal training in Freudian analysis but I have read deeply and widely and know enough to guide others through life towards happiness. I charge for my intervention. One has to live.

So many ghosts, so many unexamined and unexplored traumas in this little family! I am, as it happens, currently writing a book, commissioned by my publisher, entitled *The Narcissistic Mother and Her Inheritance.* My observation of Nicci and her children's struggle to get out from under have been most enlightening. Something of this struggle, alas, seems to be manifesting in Tyler's reluctance to turn up for sessions. Tyler currently has a most unwholesome goth girlfriend, one Hermione. She deals in drugs locally.

5
Signing-on Day

A reality check at the Jobcentre Plus.

Tyler Finch Patchett looked at himself in the smeary mirror of the men's toilet of the Shapnett Jobcentre Plus and wondered what he could do to make himself look less beautiful. Since the surgical procedure on his strabismus eye misalignment a year ago his good looks had become something of a problem. He now looked super-normal and not disfigured. Friends, family and teachers no longer called him Cyclops, or (more understandably) Walleye. He'd always had two eyes. Only one of them had wandered, making him look shifty and sly.

Girls had flocked to him in greater numbers when he had been unsightly, hoping to comfort him before discarding him – or so he was convinced. But the epiphany to male beauty was also beset by problems. Girls preferred men with money over men with looks, men with cars over men who couldn't even afford driving lessons. HR took one look at his photo, rejected him as a troublesome pretty boy, and took on a pretty girl instead. Girls always won. He had been signing on for ten months: soon he would become long-term unemployed, and the Jobcentre would have even more control over his life. Humiliation after humiliation.

Tyler's brow could be seen to be wide and smooth, his bright blue eyes, large and black fringed, to function perfectly normally, his nose to be as straight as David Beckham's, his mouth as sensuous as Justin Bieber's, his shoulders broad and well muscled as the young George Clooney, his waist as slender as Bowie's. Tyler, indeed, was now so gratifyingly good-looking he made women first swoon and then dismiss him as gay, which he was not. Other disadvantages to being a male beauty had become apparent.

Today Tyler was number eleven in the queue to see his Jobcentre Plus advisor. He would try to divert Miss Swanson's attention by enthusing about the voluntary work he was doing, sweeping up at Mrs Easton's store in St Rumbold's village, but were she to check and find out he hadn't turned up for his interview at the Brighton Beaux model agency he'd be on course for a sanction. That meant no money for at least two weeks, and that was if his advisor was feeling kind. Possibly three months. That he'd thought twice, fearing for his virtue, and turned back on the step would not be sufficient excuse.

But something had to be done. Tyler had applied for the job, one of the ten a week job applications he was obliged to make to earn his £57.90 jobseekers' allowance. He'd actually been called in for an interview, which was good, but the nature of the firm involved, he'd discovered, was not good. This was not likely to weigh upon Miss Swanson's conscience. Under threat of sanction for breaking his 'preparedness for work' contract, she could pressure him until he consented to attend the interview. Pointless for Tyler to argue that the sister agency – Brighton Belles – had been struck from the official situations vacant lists for being gender specific, advertising for bright and beautiful female 'escorts' and making no bones about the nature of the work; Brighton Beaux was on the Jobcentre Plus books and that was that. There Tyler would be interviewed, weighed, measured and photographed and with luck end up on a catwalk somewhere. Or more likely be trafficked for the sex trade – being only six feet and not the six feet two male models were expected to be – and so end up a rent boy.

He could pull out a front tooth, he supposed, and thus spoil his looks and meet Miss Swanson bloody but unbowed, and she might well take it as an excuse for non-attendance. But his front tooth was so perfect, so white, and strong, lining up so satisfactorily with its thirty-one companions, it seemed a pity to lose it. And besides, it would hurt. And life as a rent boy might not be so bad. You could end up in a penthouse not just a gutter. One must look at the bright side. The half-empty cup must be seen as half-full, as Miss Swanson so frequently reminded her depressed and desperate clients.

His name was called; 'Tyler Finch Patchett?' Double-barrelled, so there was a sneer in the voice that called it. But Tyler had always rather liked his name. He stood up and went up to the bullet-proof screen.

6

Matilda Likes To Have The Last Word

It is her job to defend her client.

Tyler himself is a strikingly beautiful boy with an agreeable nature and a devil-may-care attitude, which I suspect masks an inner rage. His masculinity has been under attack from the beginning by mother and sisters who are firmly convinced that women are the superior sex. He is a graduate but has not been able to find employment, always beaten to the post by some girl better qualified or more submissive than he. Employers tend not to employ attractive young men if they can help it. They get above themselves and cause trouble. And pretty girls tend to shy away from them. Too much competition.

Tyler's father is one Gabriel Finch, a very good-looking plumber who ill-advisedly married Nicci only to leave home the day Tyler was born. He ran away to join a male revue group, Bronze Gods International, the better to delight the hearts and fire the loins of hen parties and such like, probably because it had seemed impossible to achieve the same things with Nicci at home. Nicci does not like sex with men: the idea of penetration is abhorrent to her: this very reluctance seems to make her attractive to a certain class of men.

Nicci has many qualities, and is working hard with me to improve her mothering skills. She has toiled hard and stoically for women's movements all her life, often in the area of reproductive rights. Interestingly enough, she continues to live in St Rumbold's village in the shadow of the High Tower. As some crave to be near the love object, others crave to be near the hate object. This too needs to be worked through in our weekly sessions. I am well aware I have a duty of care and confidentiality to my patients, and try not to abuse it if I can help it. But it can be difficult.

It was on my advice that Nicci broke off all contact with the She Devil in case she sought her grandchildren out and destroyed yet another generation.

I do feel that all Nicci's ills can fairly be laid at the door of the mother who first abandoned her, and then disinherited her and her twins when she was fifteen, when the poor girl declined to have a termination. Ruth Patchett – they call her the She Devil for good reason – had the nerve to blame the stepmother, Mary Fisher, for putting ideas into the girl's head. As it happened, going through with the pregnancy was the most sensible thing Nicci could have done, she being under-age and the father a wealthy pillar of the community and married at that. A meal ticket for life.

7

Hooowoo-h, Wooo-h, Wooo-h, I Am The Ghost Of Mary Fisher

I circle the High Tower on stormy nights, which I love. But I too can feel quite angry.

Hear me moaning in the gale that whips around the High Tower on stormy nights and be afraid. Pull the blankets over the head. The dark is frightening; anything could happen. The electricity goes off, the candle blows out, the torch battery has gone missing. *Hooowoo-h, wooo-h!* The wind howls. Just you and the dark and your guilt between racing clouds; perhaps the glimpse of a blood moon. And what is that scrabbling sound on the windows, that strange shape in the moonlight? It is me, Mary Fisher, come to haunt, come to remind you of your sins (*wooo-h, wooo-h!*), and possibly punish you for them.

Oh why do I waste my time? You don't believe a word of it, do you, you don't even notice me, you just carry on as usual and turn up the central heating. I'm a figure of fun, a suffering soul turned comedic, no longer serious. Once I was, now I'm not. That's what death does for you if you miss the boat to heaven. Which I seem to have done.

Once I lived here in the High Tower, scene of so many glorious fucks with Bobbo. (I reckon there's not been another one for the past three decades.) Now I'm dead I have become part of its very bricks and mortar. There's dry rot in the woodwork, fungal tendrils creeping sideways: the She Devil is not as secure as she thinks. Of course the ground trembles under her feet. Centuries of pride and endeavour may any day just crumble: one further battering from wind and tides may bring the whole structure tumbling down. I encourage the dry rot as best I can, fanning spores. But my ability to affect the world of now is shockingly limited.

Once I stirred a cosmic rage in the She Devil and she in me. Called a She Devil by Bobbo, her poor provoked husband, that's what she became. Ruth Patchett, deserted wife and mother, the feminist, the ultimate victim, came to rule the world, sitting smugly on the moral high ground in all her squalid bulk (Lord, was she plain!), casting lightning bolts of disapproval and condemnation wherever she goes.

Ruth had all the powers of reason, social justice and Satan to back her up. All I ever had was the power of love, and that was not enough. She is still alive, and I have passed away. She won. I, poor little Mary Fisher, lost. The women of the world gave up romance, subservience and submission, and once empowered, took to hard work, truth and reality. Much good has it done them. The pain of love might sometimes seem unbearable, but oh, oh, what fulfilment, what riches, what pleasures women have lost! A generation of millennials sunk into callously copulating, digital gloom.

8

Valerie Valeria May Be Too Full
Of Good Ideas

*She's very pretty and pleasant, but is she as good a feminist
as the She Devil supposes?*

'Diavolessa,' said Valerie Valeria to the She Devil, 'we have
three things to celebrate: the winter equinox, forty years since
the Institute for Gender Parity was founded, and your eighty-
fifth birthday. All on the same day, the 21st of December. A great
day and one for great opportunities! How about we inaugurate
an annual ceremonial Widdershins Walk round the High
Tower? The equinox! The IGP's birthday, and yours too, the
President heading the procession, a flood tide lapping round
our feet, symbol of the inexorable rise of female power across
the continents! Great copy. A PR wet dream!'

Valerie was at her laptop as she talked, concentrating, her golden
head bent over the keys, the tip of her tongue showing between
scarlet lips. She was all of twenty-five years old, sixty years
younger than the She Devil. She had a bold taste in lipstick.
Now she lifted her head and met the She Devil's rheumy eyes
with her own clear bright blue glance.

'A rather unfortunate male analogy,' said the She Devil.

'Oh not at all,' said Valerie. 'Women have them too. But delete, delete. Just PR dream, not wet dream, if you prefer.'

The She Devil let it go, as seemed only prudent. One had to resign oneself to the lack of sexual inhibition in the young, and go with the flow.

'The twenty-first of December!' Valerie said. 'Midwinter's day. We'll make it our own. Widdershins Day. We'll invite the great and the good: the staff will have a day off! We'll make it a party to remember! Oh, Diavolessa, this is so exciting!'

Ruth quite liked being called Diavolessa. It seemed affectionate yet not over-familiar. To be known as the She Devil was all very well – suggesting as it did it might be wiser not to tangle with her – yet the Italian sonority of Diavolessa both acknowledged and softened her reputation. She hoped it would catch on.

And she liked the way Valerie Valeria did not question, but announced, with built-in exclamation marks. She supposed she could take the girl at face value – and it was, Ruth couldn't deny, a very attractive and unusual face – all cheekbones, planes and angles, topped by golden curly cropped hair, enlivened by quick, brilliant blue eyes, and with the skinny flat long-legged figure of today's ambitious young female. In the She Devil's young day legs had been shorter and altogether bulkier. It was as though the patriarchal society had managed to squash them down and inhibit their normal growth, stop the female body stretching towards the sun.

Valerie had turned out to be an exemplary employee of the

Institute – a competent, literate, dedicated feminist with a PhD from the University of Sydney – just full of rather misjudged enthusiasms: of which the She Devil feared this Widdershins Day might be one. It was nearly a year since Valerie had applied to be the She Devil's PA, and since then she had become indispensable: an efficient, sensitive and pleasant help and companion, but perhaps not as level-headed as the She Devil had hoped. But one had to be conscious of the paranoia which came with advancing age, though, and not let it take hold.

'But the twenty-first of December, midwinter? It will be so cold!' protested the She Devil. 'And since, as you say, it's a very high tide the rocks will be far too wet and slippery for any sort of procession. And why on earth Widdershins?'
'Because it sounds so good,' said Valerie, 'and it will catch on! The Widdershins Women's Walk! And it's fun. It's not like you to be so negative, Diavolessa,' said Valerie, the bright eyes briefly clouding over. 'In these days of the Internet, markets as conversations and so on, feminists can't afford to be negative and lag behind. Today's price of progress is eternal vigilance and a catchy phrase! I shall be there, oh Diavolessa, to hold your arm as you lead the Widdershins Women's Walk, the High Tower's Own. I will not let you fall!'

The prospect of a nasty, wet, cold equinox didn't disturb Valerie Valeria at all. But then she didn't seem to feel the cold herself, going round winter and summer in jeans and striped t-shirt, with a skimpy waist-length cashmere cardigan on top if the temperature fell below freezing. The She Devil had to shroud herself in woollies, and maintain a room temperature at 70 degrees Fahrenheit in order to be comfortable.

Once excessive heat or cold had annoyed her yet not curtailed her actions. Now they did. She must remember that midwinter was not such a source of fear to others as it was to her. But Widdershins? Really? Widdershins was unlucky.

'Wipe the twenty-first of December from your mind, Valerie,' said the She Devil briskly. 'I am old I know, but growing older is nothing to celebrate, let alone remind others about. Age is bad for business. So no party. No Widdershins. Concentrate on the IGP brochure. It's more than a week late and the Board is getting restive. I'll take a look at it tomorrow.'

'Very well,' said Valerie Valeria, meekly. But really, meek was not in her nature.

The wind got up and howled around the High Tower; the buzz of the central heating changed its tone; the She Devil went to warmer quarters and Valerie reached for her skimpy little red cashmere cardigan.

9

A Life Of Constant, If Misguided, Endeavour

The old lady tries to sleep, broods, and feels sorry for herself.

Well, what is to be done? The past is what one made it. '*The Moving Finger writes and, having writ, moves on,*' as the poet said, though I can't for the life of me remember which poet it was. I left school when I was sixteen, my parents not favouring education for girls. I would have a hard enough time in the marriage market, they thought, without having learning added to my other shortcomings. How did the poem go on?

> *Nor all thy Piety nor Wit,*
> *Shall lure it back to cancel half a line,*
> *Nor all thy Tears wash out a Word of it.*

And death is death however it comes. I haven't long to go. No doubt the curses of the living help it on its way, and I've had curses enough. But let them curse away. I am old, old, old, I would quite like to die. I am tired, my business is done, I am satisfied. The world is as I want it: women triumphant, men submissive.

There are plenty who praise me for what I have done. I, Ruth Patchett, She Devil, honoured by Her Majesty the Queen for Services to the Community, now Dame Ruth Patchett of St Rumbold's. I took my name from the little village at the foot of the High Tower. I seldom visit the village. It's small, depressed and boring. I prefer to sweep through it in my armoured S-Class Mercedes, bought at dear Valerie's insistence. I am President of the Institute of Gender Parity, a major incorporated charity, a community of women living and working in the High Tower. Our mission is to bring about equality of dignity and wealth between the genders. I wear the royal badge with pride, the only jewel a feminist can legitimately wear. And still my children will not talk to me.

There is a man living in the High Tower, spoiling the perfection of our all-female community. Bobbo. A male-free environment seems so difficult to achieve! Not because Bobbo is the husband who walked out on me and in so doing set me free. Not from any lingering fondness, I assure you, but because in their bureaucratic folly the Charity Commissioners decided that to justify a claim for gender parity there must be at least one male on our Steering Committee. My old husband Bobbo was a suitable cipher so I recommended him. He was a monster but these days he's no trouble. He suffers from dementia but is legally fit to sign a form. He no longer recognises me when he sees me, or else he mistakes me for Mary Fisher (which still has power to hurt, as though I were a girl again). He just dribbles and looks vacant.

So I take care not to see him more than I have to. I hired a carer to look after him, Samantha. She refuses to live in but comes in daily. Security looks in on him by night and Dr Simmins visits once a week. Old Bobbo, once so vigorous, now this wretched scrap of living flesh! *Timor futuri perturbat me.* And *custodum*, come to that. My carers, my guards. Dr Simmins says I must prepare for the worst.

Too late for remorse; all, all too late. I am eighty-four, so old, so tired, so weak that tears of grief start to my eyes unasked, and at the slightest provocation. I will weep at the sight of an apple tree in bloom, or the beauty of clouds lit by a rising sun, but most of all I weep for what I was, for what I did. Mary Fisher is dead, Bobbo is all but dead, and my children will not speak to me.

10

A Dream Turned Sour...

Bobbo, confined to his bed in the High Tower, has no distraction but his own disagreeable thoughts. Serves him right!

I reckoned, when all those years back I left Ruth and the kids and moved into the High Tower with that slag Mary Fisher, I'd be able to do a bit of gene spreading. Kids, even. But when it came to it, the willing bird got less and less willing. She was too old: she'd lied about her age: nothing like deceit to put an honourable man off. She put one over on me with all that make-up, and I twigged her game too late. Got all lovey-dovey and never enough sex. *'Don't mess my hair, don't smudge my lipline. I have a deadline. Please no, Bobbo, not now.'*

Bitch. I should have been warned. I came to hate her. Things began well, but after Ruth burst in on us, me and her together on the white velvet sofa, and handed over her kids, the lovey-dovey dream began to turn sour.

I'd think about that, ladies, if I were you. Sneer away all you want, but you're not going to have it your way for long. You think you've put us men in our place, but we're having you on. We let you have a go for form's sake, but everyone can see that the more you take the top jobs the more you make a mess of them. We're stronger and taller and have better brains than you, and we're a good deal more ruthless. Revolt of the bloody dinosaurs? It's on its way.

I heard you! Old trout of a dried-up slag, Dr Simmins, I'm not as deaf as you suppose. '*We must prepare for the worst.*' You can fucking well prepare all you like, I'm not ready to go. There's life in the old man yet.

11

Actuality Becomes Irrelevant

Valerie Valeria does her best for the brochure.

Next morning, and Valerie Valeria is working on the brochure when the She Devil, refreshed and enlivened by a good night's sleep – she took sleeping pills in the end – and a good breakfast (porridge, no salt, no sugar, no cream, but freshly squeezed orange juice), creeps up unseen behind Valerie to see what she has on her screen.

'The High Tower, an ancient and important Heritage site, is a fitting home base for IGP's varied charitable activities. And what a history it has! Built in 1646 to act as a lighthouse to warn mariners when they were too close to the rocks – but also, it is said, as a sumptuous hidey hole for the beleaguered King Charles I.'
'A good attempt,' says Lady Patchett. 'But your sentences are too long. Keep it brief and snappy. Readers of funding pitches have a very short attention span. And I am not sure of your historical accuracy.'
'I put in the "it is said" to be on the safe side,' says Valerie Valeria and grits her teeth. She is accustomed to praise, not criticism.
'In 1664 the tower was destroyed by male parliamentarians, who razed all spires, pinnacles and gilded balustrades to the ground, including the metal reflecting mirrors. Two ships went down as

a result. In 1815 Ada Lovelace, wife to Charles Babbage and inventor of the first computer, designed an ingenious array of mirrors so the light could be seen five miles away.'

'But Ada Lovelace and Charles Babbage were not married,' says the She Devil. 'You will have to change that.'

'I have done my research,' says Valerie, 'and I'm sure they slept together, so it's much the same thing. We must see these ancient partnerships for what they were. "*His*-story" is so often the male account of the past that it becomes important to redress the balance. Actuality becomes irrelevant. Or so I was taught at uni.'

The She Devil scrolls further down the page: '*It was not until 1832 that the High Tower was decommissioned as a working lighthouse and fell into private hands. And more recently, ironically enough, into those of a famous writer of romantic fiction. After her death the striking steel and glass structure, which now abuts the High Tower and is known as the Castle Complex, became the headquarters of the Institute for Gender Parity. Here we comfortably house some fifty resident sisters, dedicated as they are to the improvement of society, and up to thirty temporary guests in the inspirational IGP Women's Retreat [see accompanying leaflet].'*

'Better,' says the She Devil. 'But your sentences are still too long and I don't think Mary Fisher should be described as famous. Notorious, perhaps, using her ill-gotten wealth to turn a ruin into a love nest where she freely seduced the unfortunates who fell into her web. I don't see the point of mentioning her at all.'

'Because I was going on to talk about the way her ghost still haunts the High Tower,' says Valerie, 'and why. That's more interesting than any amount of history!'

'This tower is not haunted,' says the She Devil. She is very angry. 'Serious people do not believe in ghosts. Write such rubbish and we will be beyond contempt. You need to remember that the Institute pays your wages and deserves your loyalty, and that you work for me.'

It is turning into quite a quarrel.

'OK,' says Valerie, 'though people love a good ghost story. And what do I say about the Lantern Room which is closed to visitors though it's the room everyone always asks to see?'

'If my ex-husband Bobbo lives his poor demented life out in the Lantern Room,' snaps Lady Patchett, 'where he has all the medical care and consideration he needs, it is thanks to my good graces. And he will not be with us for long. What you will say, Valerie, is absolutely nothing!'

'Very well,' says Valerie Valeria. 'If you say so. Nothing about the ghost. But tomorrow can we get back to the Widdershins Walk and the equinox? It's so important not to be negative!'

Valerie knows well enough that to give way on a small thing is to get your way on the one big thing that really matters. And what does the She Devil know about publicity? Nothing. Long sentences indeed! Valerie has evidently touched on a very sore spot indeed. Now is clearly not the time to bring up the subject of the Widdershins Walk. Valerie Valeria smiles sweetly and holds her tongue.

12

She's Not To Be Trusted

Valerie just so happens to run into Ms Bradshap.

Ms Flora Bradshap, aged sixty-five, who was one of the five founder members of the Institute for Gender Parity, was on the walkway that led from her bedroom (2CC/23: second floor of the Castle Complex, room 23 in the flashy glass and steel edifice that abutted the High Tower) to her dark, dank office (3HT/12: third floor, High Tower, room 12) when she was accosted by young Valerie Valeria.

Valerie was a pleasant sight. Today she was wearing heels with her cropped jeans and her shins were slim, taut and bronzed. Her little red cashmere cardi – it was November, after all – was worn over a long-sleeved t-shirt, striped navy and white, her lipstick more pink than scarlet and her hair blonder and shinier than ever. On such a dismal day Valerie seemed a welcome source of youth, vitality and light.

'Ms Bradshap,' said Valerie, 'I've had such a wonderful idea!' And she explained the concept of an International Widdershins Day, in which women throughout the world would be reminded that the old concepts of feminism were over: men and women both must walk anti-clockwise: 'the other way'.

'That sounds very nice, child,' said Flora Bradshap. 'By all means work on it. But isn't that what witches do – widdershins: walking round churches and stone circles?' And she tried to get by, because she was in a hurry and others depended upon her. But Valerie stood in her way and was gazing up at her with such bright happy eyes that Ms Bradshap stopped, though her instinct was to get through the glass walkway as fast as she could, the weather being so bad today.

Outside seemed too near inside; the skies were dark and menacing as though it were dusk not mid-morning; wind whistled in spite of the double-glazing and lightning played about in rolling black clouds. The High Tower was having one of its 'bad hair days', as one of the girls had described it, though more sensible people knew well enough it was the unique configuration of coastline and hills, land and sea which made the High Tower attract weather conditions unknown elsewhere.

Valerie, having lived in Australia, seemed impervious to extreme weather conditions: or else she preferred to ignore them.
'No, take me seriously,' she beseeched Ms Bradshap. She explained that though young – indeed probably because she was young – she had friends and colleagues in high places, in both UNESCO and the International Conference of Homophile Organizations, and could probably get Widdershins Day formally listed.
'I am sure you could, my dear,' said Ms Bradshap, soothingly. 'And I am glad you have such important friends. But we do have other things to worry about. The gender pay gap is now 13.9 per cent. There is real work to be done.'
'But you do think *Widdershins Day – Walking the Other Way* is best? Or perhaps *Walking the Other Way, Widdershins Day* would be better?' persisted Valerie.

'Either, I suppose,' said Ms Bradshap, with a hint of asperity. 'And quite brilliant. Like so many of your ideas, my dear. But no mention of women? *Widdershins Women's Day* has a real swing. But perhaps you should give your attention first to the *Tower on Top* brochure, which the Board is eager to see, and as soon as possible? Is that gum you're chewing?'

'Yes, sorry, but it does say it's sugar free,' said Valerie, unfazed, and, removing a tissue which she kept in her bra, wrapped the gum in it and put it back.

'But not sweetener-free,' said Ms Bradshap. 'Sweeteners can be worse than sugar.'

'I'm already working on the annual brochure as fast as I can – so it's in time for our very own Widdershins Walk,' said Valerie. 'I was thinking of changing the title *Tower on Top* – it has rather unfortunate sexual connotations for our gender-fluid friends – to *Women Walk the Other Way*. What do you think?'

'What do I think? It's change, and who likes change? The point is, as with so much these days, what does Lady Patchett think?'

'The Diabolissima? I did try and discuss it with her,' said Valerie. 'But she went to take her rest. These days she seems tired a lot of the time. And it does rather hold things up and then it's left to me to take up the slack.'

'That is what we pay you to do,' said Ms Bradshap, quite sharply. 'And the IGP does not tolerate discrimination against the old. Though I must say it's quite a good name for her, Diabolissima!'– which was as far as she was prepared to go in open opposition to the She Devil.

Valerie, satisfied, took her lightness and brightness away down the walkway, taking a little hop and skip as she went. She then rescued her chewing gum and put it back in her mouth.

13

Fear Of The Future

A desperate measure.

Tyler, the She Devil's grandson, had taken the felt-tip pen he kept in his pocket the better to fill in the Jobcentre Plus forms – biros on the end of string were provided free but had no ink – and had tried blacking out his front tooth. But as soon as he closed his mouth it all washed off, the fantasist in him faded, and he became aware only of the smear on the mirror and the stench left by so many angry and deliberately careless visitors to the men's toilets, and was shocked back into as near to rationality as you can get in a Jobcentre Plus.

He joined the others slouching in the waiting room, where he was still sixth in the queue for Miss '*I'm here to help you*' Swanson, and where the cloacal stench was somewhat modified, but only somewhat. The door to the toilets hung open, wrenched at some stage from its frame.

Miss Swanson and her colleagues worked behind toughened glass windows, presumably from fear of assault. Certainly notices informed clients, as those claiming benefits were known, that the Department for Work and Pensions took physical and verbal abuse against their staff very seriously indeed. Miss

Swanson called him Tyler, and seemed friendly enough that day. If you were relegated to Long Term Unemployed (LTU) you lost the privilege of a given name, and got called by your surname without even the benefit of a Mr, Mrs, Ms or Miss. Things weren't looking too bad.

Miss Swanson had said Tyler's dubious objections were unfounded and he was not in a position to refuse his interview with the Brighton Beaux Agency. If he did he would find himself financially sanctioned for at least two weeks. Moral objections to working for any listed firm were seen as frivolous. 'Just go along like a good boy,' she said. 'Use your ingenuity. Tell them you don't approve of gay marriage and you'll be out the door in five minutes.'

'You want me to starve?' he asked, raising his wide and innocent blue eyes to her rather rheumy ones, but Miss Swanson had just laughed merrily and loud, showing metal fillings and one missing tooth near the back, and stretching her green cardigan tighter over her bosom. Today there was a grease stain over her rather low left nipple. Miss Swanson's laugh was quite loud and at a pitch which could be dangerous: Tyler had watched marvelling once as a plastic ceiling tile, fluorescent tube and all, had trembled and fallen to the floor in the waiting area, catching a Security guard's shoulder as it went – Security staff usually outnumbered those in the waiting area.

Hermione, Tyler's on-off girlfriend – as some would say bed-buddy, there being lust and affection between them, but no love – was sure that Miss Swanson was in love with Tyler. For the short time Hermione herself had been an official jobseeker at the Jobcentre Plus, Miss Swanson had required her to call at the office three times a week and produce evidence of five job applications on every visit. Miss Swanson was letting Tyler off very lightly and it wasn't fair, Hermione maintained. Tyler should report the woman for sexual harassment, or at the very least unconscious bias. Tyler pointed out that the fairly sensible distinctions were made because Hermione was an early school leaver with a drug problem, while he, Tyler, was a graduate student with a future, but Hermione would have none of that. Insulted, she stopped going to the Jobcentre Plus, became a drug dealer instead of a drug consumer, and kept her dignity.

It certainly seemed true enough that when Tyler was called to her cubicle Miss Swanson would lean back in her chair and put her hands behind her head, a sure sign, according to Hermione, who read the tabloids, of a heightened sexual awareness – Tyler himself read the *Guardian*. But then it wasn't as if Miss Swanson had managed to put any employment his way. She always seemed rather pleased that she hadn't.

'You won't starve,' said Miss Swanson. 'Even if I do sanction you. We're starting a food bank out the back to help everybody. It'll cut down on the actual assaults. This is a dangerous job!'

Even as she spoke there was some contretemps behind them – an unshaven middle-aged man in flared trousers – no doubt from a charity shop – was shouting 'Legalised slavery! Arsehole! Cunt! Scum! Give me my fucking money!' and banging his fists against a closed window until two large Nigerians in Security uniforms descended upon the wretch and eased him out the front door to an assortment of cheers and jeers.

'Typical male!' observed Miss Swanson calmly, when all was

quiet again. 'That'll be a two-year sanction for him, I imagine, and a gold star for his supervisor. But I tell you what. There are minimum wage jobs going for catering staff up at the High Tower. Why don't you apply? You have family connections, I believe. Why you graduates prefer to sponge off the State rather than your families I cannot understand. However.'

'There are family reasons,' said Tyler. The State seemed to know more about one than one did oneself. Facebook, he supposed. They'd know all about his wicked Gran.

'There always are, I find. Just apply,' she said. 'You're quite safe. They'll reject you because you're not a girl.'

'They're not allowed to do that.'

'Employers have their little ways,' she said. 'And you're such a pretty boy. I suppose you could always dress up as a girl.'

Sometimes, it was perfectly true, he liked the feel of fabric between his legs, and the sound of the swish of a skirt. What else did they know? But he was male, male, male, male. He said as much.

She said she'd be kind and let Tyler off a sanction this time. He went off to find Hermione.

14

The Power Balance Is Altering

Valerie drops a bombshell.

'Lady Patchett, I'm so sorry to keep returning to this point, but decisions have to be made about our Widdershins Walk. We really do need to have a man in the procession. Perhaps Mr Patchett, Bobbo, could parade with you? He is on the Board, after all.'

Was the girl out of her mind? Did she understand nothing? Feminists did not 'need' men. There were such depths of miscomprehension here. Valerie had been working for the She Devil for almost a year, editing lectures, articles, writing leaflets, arranging festivals and so on, travelling with her, bringing her wake-up coffee. She must surely know what her employer felt about husbands, not to mention marital law: how marriage was a fraud and a wife no more than a sex slave, how fraudulent the very concept of 'family' was. How Bobbo was a ghost trustee, no more than that, because of the OTT requirements of the Charity Commission. At least he now lacked fleshly wherewithal, too old and withered to do much harm. Had the girl sat through a hundred such lectures and learned nothing?

Valerie Valeria waits for a reply, her lovely little face eager with hope and expectancy.

'Bobbo is far too ill to walk anywhere,' says the She Devil, less sharply than she might have. After all the girl is young. Her feminism is still only skin deep, an academic study. History, now fashionably related in the present tense, has deprived the past of its reality. Any sense that what had happened once could happen again, that the cost of liberation actually was eternal vigilance, simply hadn't occurred to her. Horror at the lingering of patriarchy was yet to dawn upon her. If ever she had children she would learn what submission was, and helplessness, and dependency.

'But I've seen him up and about,' says Valerie. She tells the She Devil how she had been coming upstairs with the She Devil's good-night cocoa when she encountered an old man running down the stairs from the Lantern Room in bare feet and pyjamas. A nurse had come down after him and wheeled him back.

'I take it that was Bobbo? He seemed perfectly lively, just rather old.'

'He's nearly a hundred, he won't be with us long. But it shouldn't have happened. Those stairs are so steep! I'll have a word with Nurse Samantha. She'll have left the door unlocked and he's off like a shot. The girl's rather a fool. He has Alzheimer's and keeps trying to run away, it's a common symptom. Did he try to expose himself?'

'He didn't really have time, Diavolessa. But it's true his flies were undone, and it hung out like a little grey pencil. Ugh!'

'You get the picture now?' says the She Devil. 'No Bobbo. No Widdershins procession, come to that. I thought I okayed a small party with a few guests, nothing more.' Valerie seems not to hear her.

'Ellen says the light will be best for us at midday, so we're in luck, it's a very high tide,' is all she says. Ellen is the official High Tower photographer, aged seventy-three. 'She hates those low-tide shots when the foreground is all seaweed and washed-up plastic. A big tide covers all faults. So we walk widdershins before lunch, with the sun behind us so we look our best. The twenty-first of December, your birthday, and the IGP's, and the winter equinox, all in one. Oh, wonderful!'

What sun? the She Devil refrains from asking. Valerie had arrived in a mild winter and didn't know how rare a fine day was; how savage the midwinter storms could be; how high and strong the seas; how up on the higher floors the wind howled like the wrath of God: how the lightning ignored all diversionary tactics and kept on hitting other bits of the High Tower. Conductor rods, the contractors claimed, were neutralised by the sheer number of aerials and antennae which, alas, these days sprouted from the top of the tower to keep in contact with the outside world. And how cold!

The She Devil is frightened of the cold. All she thinks about at night is not the sins of man or the folly of women, but how her children will not speak to her, and how will her poor old bones keep out the cold? Or is it that her heart is cold?

'Okay, no Bobbo,' says Valerie Valeria. 'But you keep going on about having no family, when you have a grandson down in the village. Perhaps he could process with you? We simply must have a man. No longer war between the sexes but peace! Glorious peace!'

The She Devil has no idea she has a grandson. Her first instinct is to deny it.

'I have no grandson. Whoever it is must be an impostor.'

'Yes, you have a grandson. Your daughter Nicci has a boy called Tyler. He lives locally. I've seen selfies on Facebook.'

'Nicci is no daughter of mine. I disowned her and her misbegotten twins decades ago. Ruined by romance, by her stepmother, by Mary Fisher's silly ideas. Nicci was only fifteen. Those poor babes should have been aborted. I know I am being hard but it was a matter of principle. And I've heard nothing about her having a son. Obviously an impostor. Someone after my money.'

Her own vehemence quite startles her. So much could be blamed on Mary Fisher, left in charge of Nicci, just a young girl, and then failing to live up to her responsibilities.

'Anyway she's had a boy since,' says Valerie. 'Today's feminist cannot afford to be seen as opposed to family life. Diavolessa, try and understand. Men are no longer the enemy.'

'That's news to me,' says the She Devil, regaining her composure.

'And it would look so good in the brochure! Age and youth hand in hand leading the Women's Widdershins Walk! Feminism comes of age, male and female together, forward into the New Age! We can have Fancy Dress (optional) on the invitations.'

'Are you joking, Valerie?' asks the She Devil, incredulously. 'The IGP is a serious organisation. I suppose you'd like me and this alleged grandson, this potentially criminal impostor, to dance around the High Tower wearing crowns and ermine trim. Backwards, if we're to go widdershins.' Now, she is even laughing.

'Wonderful!' enthuses Valerie. 'Glorious!' The She Devil realises that Valerie, like so many of today's young, has great determination and ambition but absolutely no sense of humour.

As for Valerie, she finally notices that the She Devil is looking at her askance.

'I can see,' she says kindly, 'all this must be rather sudden for you. Supposing we go down to the village and see him in his native habitat. It isn't far.'

'Supposing,' says the She Devil grimly, and then grudgingly, 'perhaps.'

At least it isn't a decided 'no'.

'Though I quite agree,' says Valerie unexpectedly. 'It is a pity Tyler isn't a girl. I really only like girls. He's really fit, and I say that even though I'm gay.'

15

Ms Bradshap Is Riled

Real or unreal, the ghost of Mary Fisher scores a little victory.

After speaking to Valerie Ms Bradshap went on into her office, 3HT/12, which looked out on a panorama of dismal rocks and dank seaweed. She hated the room, and today it seemed darker than ever. Ms Bradshap brooded over the She Devil's short-comings.

Lady Patchett had blocked all her attempts to switch offices. Ms Bradshap needed one in the Castle Complex where it was light and bright and had a good atmosphere. She could no longer endure the High Tower. It was an unforgivable humili-ation to be so denied. Was she not, Flora Bradshap, a founder member, a trustee, in effect High Tower Quartermaster, to borrow a male military term? Quartermistress? The She Devil, CEO and President though she might be, and loved for so long as inspiration and leader, had gone too far.

Months back in July, on Visiting Day, the annual occasion when the High Tower was open to the public, Ms Bradshap's great-niece Irene had visited her great-aunt in 3HT/12 and commented that it was not only damp and smelled badly of dry rot, but was haunted. Indeed, Irene had had to run out of the room, the atmosphere was so malevolent. Irene, granted, was very new-agey, was hung about with crystal gewgaws and talked of unquiet spirits, so was perhaps not to be taken too seriously.

'All her crystals clanking as she ran?' the She Devil had observed rather meanly when told of Irene's reaction.

Irene had brought her two toddlers with her, boys of two and three who had fussed and cried all the visit through thus upsetting the other guests. Irene had a degree in Industrial History (which the She Devil had derided after Irene used the present tense when talking about the past) and had asked to visit the Lantern Room on the ninth floor which had the most spectacular views and had once housed a historic range of parabolic mirrors. On finding it to be out of bounds she had made quite a noisy and unnecessary scene. The ninth floor was where Bobbo lived and was nursed.

'I suppose the great-niece thinks I'm keeping him prisoner,' the She Devil had said in Ms Bradshap's hearing. 'Hasn't she ever heard of Alzheimer's?'

Well, it had occurred to Ms Bradshap that it might be the case: that the She Devil needed Bobbo's signature on the frequent forms that came from the Charity Commissioners and so he wasn't in a care home where he certainly ought to be. Most business these days was conducted by email; only the government sent letters. Bobbo's signature was always already on such forms as the She Devil put before her.

Emboldened by Irene's earlier comments on the haunting, Ms Bradshap had told the She Devil that she wanted to change offices.

'It's not only the damp,' she said. 'It's the atmosphere. I am quite an orderly person and like to keep the seven rainbow marking pencils arranged on my desk in Isaac Newton's spectrum order, but someone keeps disarranging them when I'm not in the room. I do not believe in ghosts as a rule and am not an impressionable person like my great-niece, but since I keep my door locked I can only conclude that some entity such as a poltergeist is trying to tell me something. I need another office: in the Castle Complex preferably, or somewhere else where I shall not be disturbed.'

The She Devil replied brusquely that she was sorry but there simply wasn't any 'somewhere else' available: it was considered an honour to be allowed to work in the High Tower. She personally did not believe in ghosts any more. In her experience belief in the supernatural was a sign of low intelligence, not enough sleep and a troubled conscience combined. She was sorry Ms Bradshap had found her coloured pens in the wrong order but perhaps in the great scheme of things it didn't matter very much?

Flora Bradshap backed down and agreed that perhaps she was being foolish: her great-niece was naïve and ignorant and must not come to Visiting Day again having once been crass enough to bring two sons. Poltergeists were in the neurotic head and not a reality, and she understood the privilege of being housed in 3HT/12.

But then Ms Bradshap had no savings and could see that living with Irene and the boys – for there was nowhere else for her to go – might be very difficult.

44

16

Blood's Not Always Thicker Than Water

...so the She Devil concludes.

How can Valerie know all this and say all this about a relative I didn't even know existed? And what has her being a lesbian have to do with anything? Millennials do so like to bring their sexual proclivities into everything. Being a lesbian is not something to be proud of, or ashamed of, merely a rather inconvenient fact of life in the search for a partner, narrowing one's field of choice.

It's surreal. Valerie knows what the lad looks like from selfies and sexties. This brave new world keeps coming up and hitting me: slap, slap, slap around the face. And Nicci – still after all these years harbouring grudges against me, training her child to dislike me! That upsets me. Is Valerie so insensitive that she doesn't understand this?

'Okay, then.' Valerie continues to talk to me as if I were a child, not improving my temper.

'If you won't do the processing around the High Tower with either of your menfolk, how about this: you and Tyler both set off in opposite directions and then meet in the middle and then stop to greet one another as family?' Ms Bradshap and

Ms Laura, she went on, had seen the provisional ads for the *Walk the Other Way* brochure and were very excited.

'Feminists can't afford to be seen as man haters any more. Feminism is not at odds with happy families, just the old-fashioned traditional unhappy kind. The smiling man, the pretty woman, and a pigeon pair of happy kiddiewinks is out! That's the way you started out, Diavolessa, and I know it upsets you that the kids ended up with Mary Fisher. I've heard you talking about it in your sleep.'

I feel totally traduced. My privacy has been invaded. She's been listening to me talk in my sleep, she is interfering with my dreams! What else does this girl know, paddling around in the Archives as she does? There are things I would rather were not made public. The reason why Bobbo went to prison: certain things that I did – all justified, but even so. And my kids did not 'end up' with that whore Mary Fisher – I gave them to her as an existential act. I realise that I have to be careful. I try not to show my upset.

'I'm hardly sure a granny image suits me,' I say as lightly as I can. 'I need time to come to terms with this suddenly shifting ground beneath my feet. And the last thing I want is people being sorry for me.'

It does not suit me one bit to have my family back in my life. It was absurd sentimentality on my part to think I did. I prefer the idle mournfulness of missing them to the trouble, bother and confusion of an actual reconciliation. True, I hurt dreadfully when the existential act took place. No one warned me that would happen when I gave my children away. I felt as if I had been deprived of a limb, I remember that: I wailed aloud, as if with a physical pain. But just as a cow will bellow and moo in panic when its calf is taken away for the slaughter, the distress lasts the shortest of times. A new bale of hay drops onto the shed and all is forgotten; the cow chews placidly on. I prefer the melancholy of 'my children will not talk to me' to the actuality of some young, selfie-taking, sexting, socially-mediated yob of a grandson who at best disapproves of me, and at worst will tell me he loves me in the hope of an inheritance.

As for Valerie, this chit of a girl who turned up out of the blue in response to an advertisement in a newspaper for a 'good feminist with secretarial and social media skills', got the job over a hundred and twenty others, mostly because of her looks and youth – how can I have been so naïve? She has wormed her way into my confidence, thinks nothing of eavesdropping on my private thoughts and cynically calls me Diavolessa because she knows my weakness – that I want to be liked. Anger surges up in my gorge. I have a fit of coughing. Valerie runs at me with a glass of water.
'Oh dear,' she says, when I've recovered. 'I shouldn't have said that. I'm so sorry. I can be very tactless.'

The afternoon is too much for me. I tell Valerie I am going to my room to take a power nap.

I am much beset by difficult memories. I shut my eyes. The older you get the more inviting sleep becomes.

17

Falling in Love Again (Can't Help It)

The ghost of Mary Fisher explains her assignment.

Woo-ooh, woo-ooh, woo-wooh... Me again, the ghost of Mary Fisher, wailing in the wind that swirls round the High Tower. Listen! I am so, so excited about the beautiful but troubled lad who is Tyler Finch Patchett. He has quite re-energised me, you know. He is my step-grandchild. I've never had one of those before. I looked after his mother Nicci when the She Devil dumped her kids on me. I packed them off to boarding school and the first thing the girl did was get herself into trouble. She must have had wiles; she certainly didn't have looks. But love is blind. She went ahead with the pregnancy – love twins – and then vanished from sight. I got the blame, of course. '*Putting ideas into her head,*' as if I would. If I taught her anything it was that a girl's best weapon is her virginity. The twins turned out to be, well, dreadful, but Nicci's son Tyler is a different matter. Not only beautiful in body but in temperament too – generous, open, kind, strong. What a man should be. But he needs direction. He's so young. I have fallen in love with him. He is Bobbo the Beautiful's grandson and young and virile, and it shows.

Yes, I am the one who wronged the She Devil. I freely admit it, and perhaps I am being punished for it now. I no longer have a body to go with my spirit. I, Mary Fisher, believer in truth, beauty and romantic love, once stole Tyler's father Bobbo from the She Devil's long, overlarge and muscly arms and I am now, it seems, condemned to make amends, poised forever between life and death, circling this dratted High Tower, observing what goes on – the dereliction of the Bobbo whom once I so loved.

But I have faith. In my lifetime I was a romantic novelist and as such was a devotee, with other writers, of The Great Fictional Religion. It is Momus, the God of satire and comedy, whom we worship. Momus, The Great Writer in the Sky. I have faith that Momus, blessed be his name, will decide in his glorious wisdom that the plot has been properly resolved and allow me to get off to heaven where I so obviously belong. This endless fidgety wailing is getting me down. I do not honour it with the word 'restless'. Fidgety is what it feels like. Irritating.

I think my sin might well have been dying out of turn; I have to come back in one form or another to alter the outcome of the story. Praise be to Momus. If only I had teeth I would be clenching them as I say it, but however: Praise be to Momus.

What I really need is a great storm, a great explosion of lust, rage and finality, but all I can muster is this pathetic little wail – 'remember me, remember, Mary Fisher dead and gone'. Once I lived here, loved here, conformed the coastline to the sweep I wanted, now at least I haunt here. Better than nothing. I suppose. Is that what I'm meant to feel? Grateful for small mercies?

Up there on Mount Olympus Zeus and Venus still haven't made peace. The gender war rages there the same as here. Sisyphus

49

still rolls his rocks uphill. Crows still tear at Prometheus' innards. Momus, a lesser God, I daresay, but one important to me, shelters in the lower foothills of Olympus from whence he directs so many of the plots and plans of mankind. He has no standards. He rejoices as much in the sudden turns and twists of celebrity living as in those of great movements, vital politics. Sometimes I suspect he is not as good a writer as he's cracked up to be. He'll do anything for a good headline; if things get too complicated he's quite capable of cutting the story short with an earthquake, an epidemic, a sudden resignation or even death. Think of Princess Di – of the shock when the narrative stops. Momus was there in that tunnel – a demiurge of a writer, not the true God. But to see the writer of life on earth as a bad writer, a demiurge of a novelist, a Dan Brown not a Dostoevsky, an E.L. James not a Jane Austen, why, this smacks of apostasy – forget it. Heads might roll. Delete, delete. Rewind, as we used to say.

And oh! my Bobbo was once so beautiful! I try to forget but I can't. His golden limbs, his golden hair, his smile like Adonis – but that was before the She Devil broke him, had him imprisoned, punished him for the sin of being male, for preferring me to her. I do not think Bobbo will lurk around the High Tower as I do. He is old, old; soon he will be dead and gone – the crows tell me – gone with the wind which circles the High Tower, it will whisk him away to somewhere I can't follow. When it came to it, he did not love as I did. The truth is, like Clark Gable in *Gone with the Wind*, he didn't give a damn.

All the songs and stories of the past I knew do not go away; they play havoc with my memories. I hear Jerry Lee Lewis and he's singing, *She Still Comes Around (to Love What's Left of Me)*.

In Bobbo's mind I became one of the siren women, another of the destroyers. And now the song *Delilah* comes fluttering in; could I have been a Delilah, lying in wait for decent men? How very unfair. I am Mary Fisher, sweet, beloved and beautiful, the ghost of true love, singing *All You Need Is Love*, the song of my generation. Love, love, and more love.

I do my best. It is in my nature. I go singing in the rain or howling in the gale. I see what I see. I hear what I hear. Bits and pieces. I'm all ghost, no substance at all.

18

Walking The Other Way Walk

Valerie's so sharp she almost cuts herself.

I am not in a good mood. I am with young Valerie down in the meeting room, 1HT/2 – a windowless chamber where the howl of the wind cannot be heard – and it is at least warm, and Valerie is still going on about her dratted equinox.

'Tyler could take Bobbo's place in the procession, I suppose,' says Valerie. 'If his grandpa really is totally troppo, as you say he is.'

What does she mean, '*as I say*'? He most certainly is. Let alone 'totally troppo'. Which is Australian, I gather, for 'round the bend' or whatever one is meant to call the mentally disabled these days. Poor Valerie spent years in Sydney, picking up all kinds of outlandish words and ideas.

'We're meant to be working for gender parity,' she goes on, 'and surely the odd male turning up in our literature would not go amiss.'

'We struggle for gender parity,' I say. 'To suggest we have achieved it would be dangerous. Don't even think of it.'

'I thought you and Tyler could both wear crowns,' she says next. 'Be Frosty King and Queen of the Widdershins Winter Wonderland. Do say yes, Diavolessa, it would be such a PR coup, and a hoot too!'

A hoot? I am the She Devil, the liberation feminist queen of all I survey. And this Valerie, this chit of a girl who dares to call herself a feminist, suddenly wants to make a crown for Tyler, descendant of Bobbo, that senile dinosaur, that foul-mouthed bully whom given half a chance she would have made King to my Queen and made us walk widdershins hand in hand round the High Tower. Like the two old people bent double over their walking sticks on the road-crossing signs. Humiliating. Someone needs to take those signs off the streets.

'The public would so like it,' she persists. 'A lovely shot – young and old, heads together: "My favourite grandchild, says the She Devil", all that.'

'No way,' I say. 'I'm sorry but no way.' And my face must betray my feelings.

'Oh dear,' she says. 'I keep getting this wrong, don't I!' She smiles so sweetly that these unsettling emotions swirl away as quickly as they crowded in. One of the penalties of growing old is that paranoiac fears come thick and fast and one has to guard against them. I remember how young she is, how inexperienced, how little she knows for all her PhD from Sydney in Feminism in Development. God knows what they taught her there.

'You're young,' I say, 'so you will get things wrong. But it doesn't matter, if you can learn from those older and wiser than your-self that it is a bad idea to be seen as frivolous, lightweight and unimportant. The IGP stands for equality, parity and dignity, not the joys of family life. For heaven's sake, Valerie, get that into your head.'

It might be a very pretty young head, but perhaps not as clever as I had assumed. I am beginning to feel rather annoyed with her.

'But a big party would be so good for morale, don't you think? And I'm happy to get it all together. A bit of excitement and good cheer? It can get to feel cut off and boring for everybody out here, and the food here can be a bit sad. We could have canapés and champagne for our Widdershins Walk, our equinox party! And the media would come in droves. Oh do let's, Diavolessa, do let's!'

High Tower food is perfectly serviceable. I'm not interested in food. Canapés are a wicked waste. One mouthful and all that time and effort gone for nothing. But I weaken. I can see the advantage of such publicity. Equinox, parity, equality; an Institute anniversary; my own birthday. All on the one day. Media fodder. The girl is probably right.

'Very well,' I say. 'Start the ball rolling. We have something to celebrate, and we need to remind the public what the IGP has achieved.'

'Oh wow!' she says. 'A party!'

19

For The Small-Minded, Small Things
Are Important

Flora Bradshap nurtures her grudge.

Ms Bradshap thought that, in the great scheme of things, alive or dead mattered very much indeed. She hadn't heard from let alone seen her ex-husband Roy for at least twenty years. Perhaps he had died and the disordering of her pencils was some kind of message from him from beyond the grave, the best a ghost could do? Was Roy saying he forgave her? But surely it should be the other way round? He was the one who needed forgiveness; she had been right to go. She had been in an abusive relationship, and it had taken a consciousness raising group to point it out. She had seen what she had seen; she did not make mistakes.

The She Devil had then made Ms Bradshap feel far more foolish than she deserved. For a full five mornings after her request Lady Patchett had come up tip-tapping with her stick, following Ms Bradshap to check the arrangement of her pencils when she opened up. There had been no disturbance, though the mushroomy smell of dry rot had got worse morning by morning. This the She Devil had failed to notice.
'Strange smell, Flora? What smell? Oh, that! That's just some

seaweed gone mouldy outside, I daresay. The next high tide will wash it away. You are becoming rather odd, Flora. Perhaps you should see Dr Simmins about your hormones?'

Flora Bradshap found herself reflecting that with Alzheimer's one of the first symptoms was loss of the sense of smell – when an old person can't tell the difference between a freshly cut onion and a freshly cut apple they need to take medical advice. She herself had a keen sense of smell. Should so important an organisation as the IGP be left in the hands of someone who could not even detect the smell of dry rot? Someone whose age, as Valerie would put it, meant others had to take up the slack? Perhaps Ms Bradshap had been too short with Valerie and her latest bright idea. She must take care to make amends. Valerie was very popular with the Board and might even be drafted onto it. The She Devil had an unreasonable amount of power, being self-appointed Chairperson of the Board, CEO and President, all three. Everyone must see that. Elections would be in February: for four decades they had been a foregone conclusion. This time others must stand, at least for the Chair. The median age of the Board was seventy-two. At sixty-five Ms Bradshap was one of the youngest. The IGP needed new younger blood: someone not forever in need of an afternoon nap.

Even now as Ms Bradshap looked at the neat row of rainbow-coloured pencils on her desk she could have sworn she saw the indigo and violet pencils lift up and place themselves before the green. She struck her forehead with her hand and when she was able to look again the pencils were back in their proper order.

These things were happening in her own neurotic head. She

couldn't even smell the mushroomy dry rot smell any more. Banging her head so hard with her own hand seemed to have shaken her out of some kind of paranoiac episode, which albeit unreasonably she blamed the She Devil for provoking in the first place.

20

Samantha Stands By Her Man…

…old and demented though he might be.

Samantha had a good job up there at the High Tower. The Institute for Gender Parity paid above the odds, and she was saving up to afford a degree course in Social Care she planned to take when old Mr Patchett moved on. It was bound to happen but she would be sorry when it did. She had become almost fond of him. He said dreadful things sometimes, and most would dismiss him as a foul-mouthed dirty old man, but he spoke the truth the way he saw it.

There'd been a certain amount of unpleasantness when she broke it to Human Resources that she was going to get married and would live henceforth down in St Rumbold's village. She'd been upset enough that there'd been not a hint of congratulation from the all-female staff, let alone a whip-round. So much for sisterhood. She'd known better than to send out wedding invitations. Even so, someone had muttered *androphile* after her on the stairs. She'd looked up the word on Google. It meant *lover of men*. Well, so she was and so she did: she loved Chris and that was that.

But now she was not just married but pregnant too. HR would

really hate it if they found out – marriage was disloyalty; procreation wicked and irresponsible. She'd resolved to keep quiet about it as long as she could, at least until the time came to start worrying about maternity benefits, and she'd managed for five whole months. But she couldn't keep it secret forever. Forget HR, she wouldn't put it past the old biddies on the Board to try to make her abort if the baby was a boy. She did seem to remember there'd been a clause – along with a confidentiality agreement – saying she had no intention of getting pregnant for four years. But she didn't think she'd ever actually signed it and, even if she had, HR were always in such a muddle they wouldn't have checked, and it hadn't been intentional anyway: a condom had split.

And what could the Institute do about it anyway? They weren't going to find anyone prepared to look after old Bobbo Patchett in a hurry, let alone anyone who actually cared about him. She'd recently smuggled in an iPad so he could keep up with current porn while he was awake, and she, Samantha, could keep in touch with her many Facebook friends on it while he slept.

Lady Patchett's eyesight was bad and she wasn't likely to cause any trouble, let alone notice Samantha's figure. She hardly ever came up to see the poor old man, anyway – once it had been for a photo shoot when the concept of 'the compassionate feminist' had been all over the media, with the She Devil at Bobbo's bedside, explaining to the cameras how upsetting it was to see the husband she had once so loved in his present mindless state, a soul trapped in a derelict body, not even able to recognise his nearest and dearest, and so on. Samantha thought Bobbo recognised his wife well enough.

On that occasion he'd certainly found his tongue.

'*Get away from me, She Devil*,' he'd cried, and they'd had to turn the camera off. '*Bring out the garlic, the wooden cross! It's the bat-mistress from hell herself.*' And another photo-op had been spoiled when Bobbo leapt from his bed and opened the window. '*Off they go! The black bats, the black bats! The shadow of lies darkens the land. Male the villain, female the victim. Avaunt thee, foul she-demon!*' and so on and so forth, until the She Devil left, weeping crocodile tears for Ellen the photographer to catch.

Bobbo was confused and mad but he had the gift of the gab and was not stupid. Sometimes Samantha could almost see the bats flowing out from the High Tower, spreading darkness through light, like some scene from *The Lord of the Rings, Part 1*, her favourite film.

And whenever the wind started howling, Bobbo would start up in his bed. '*Frigid bitch!*' he'd cry out. '*Lying, frigid bitch!*' and then lie back in bed again and sob as if his heart would break and the wind would howl and howl as if to keep him company. It was a good thing Samantha was not the superstitious kind or she would have said the Lantern Room was haunted.

As it was, Samantha, on reflection, decided her continued employment was secure enough, at least until Bobbo's death or the baby's arrival, whichever came first. She knew where the bodies were buried, as it were. And she had a kind of fellow feeling with the ghost, if that was what it was, and that would keep her safe.

21

Surely Someone Else's Fault?

Memories can be so elusive.

My power nap has failed to empower me. I am too disturbed. This girl Valerie seems to know more about me than I do myself. She must have been snooping round in the Archives. A grandson! I suppose I have to accept him as real. Forget the impostor story. Nicci had a son? Did I ever know, or have I just forgotten? One forgets so much. Things in the past fade out.

I'd actually tried to get hold of Nicci lately. One gets milder and sorrier as one gets older. I'd even gone on Facebook, against my principles – I leave all that social media stuff to Valerie – and been instantly unfriended. So she must know of my existence, and does not choose to get in touch. It still hurts, though I daresay I deserve it. But surely it was up to Mary Fisher to look after the little by-blows she had been so keen to bring into the world. Abort, abort, I had said to Nicci, what about your future? But she hadn't listened. Just keep out of my life, she said. At the time I wanted nothing more to do with her and hers.

And now, apparently, after the girls, who I believe were not a success, a grandson! And so like Nicci, with her appetite for ugliness, landing the child with a vulgar American-sounding name. Tyler. But getting in touch with the boy as Valerie is so keen for me to do? I am not sure. Wearing a crown and walking backwards with the lad as mythical family? Absurd.

But Valerie is so persuasive. I have scarcely been in my bed twenty minutes or so when there is a knock on my door and it's Valerie saying she has a bunch of party invitations which she needs me to sign if they're to catch the post, the personal touch being so important – I thought I'd said no to this party of hers but it seems to be going ahead: I must have misremembered. And also, the dear girl, she is bringing a cup of the extra strong coffee she brews especially for me, Ms Bradshap serving only decaf in the canteen. I put on my red dressing gown and let her in. She is still going on about happy families and myself and my grandson hand in hand. I quite like the sound of 'your grandson', I have to admit.

'I am not sure a granny image suits me,' I say, cautiously. 'I need time to come to terms with all this. A boy, you say. It would be so different if he were a girl.'

'Feminism is evolving, Lady Patchett.'

'Feminism will never change,' I say, automatically: how many times have I not said it? 'The battle for equality is eternal, and its price is vigilance.' Valerie doesn't seem to hear: just goes on with her riot of exclamation marks.

'We need to be young and cheerful! To show the world that feminist men are welcome! Too long we've been identified with the old, the humourless and the drab! Tyler knows you're his grandma but his mother won't let him speak to you. She's in therapy. But Tyler's so lovely! And I'm supposed to be a lesbian!' She will go on about it so. Of course she is a lesbian. Who isn't, these days? It is such an obvious simple step out of the clutches of the patriarchy. If only I had been told about a granddaughter, not a grandson. A Tanya not a Tyler. If she was halfway intelligent I could have trained her up. She could have been the one to take over.

'This Tyler,' I ask. 'Is he heterosexual or gay?'

'A very second wave question,' she remarks. 'Fluid, I daresay, like so many of us.'

It's all too much. Don't wish for family in case you get it. The last thing I really want, I realise, is for Tyler to speak to me. 'My children will not speak to me,' has created a kind of runnel in my brain through which a whole lot of universal complaints and emotions have got diverted.

The Board had chosen Valerie Valeria from a hundred and fifty-two applicants, all of them with good feminist credentials – her insistence on wearing lipstick overlooked because she was so bright, competent, quick and cheerful, full of ideas, understood social media and, not least, how to charm and manage their CEO and President, the She Devil, and keep her on her toes and up to date. And now she is certainly keeping me on my toes with the Widdershins Walk.

Valerie had built a successful funding campaign around the fact that the High Tower had once been a lighthouse. '*Light into the Life*,' her mantra went. '*As once it shone as a beacon for shipwrecked mariners, now the High Tower shines into the lives of women and men and guides relationships to safe harbour.*' The High Tower, as a phallic symbol shining through stormy, foamy waves, was now a logo on all Institute publications and had certainly attracted funding. Donations had come pouring in.

It had seemed somewhat crude to me at the time but I had been outvoted by three-quarters of the Board, Valerie assuring them that for once the end justified the means.

'Nothing,' she had said, 'must stop the drive towards gender parity. The end justifies the means.' That had gone down well with the Board. One has to suppose she knows what she is doing. She is so young, and we are all so old.

'Only in the northern hemisphere is widdershins unlucky,' Valerie exclaims as if to a public meeting. 'We are all globalists now! Other cultures, other customs! Our feminist struggle overall is to upset the status quo, overturn the apple cart!'
'In black masses witches walk widdershins round the church,' I say, 'and then go inside to summon up Satan. I'm the head of an international charity, not a witch.'
'Never a witch, Lady Patchett!' cries Valerie Valeria. 'A seer, yes, perhaps! If you won't do crowns and ermine trim, you shall wear the purple velvet coat, the laurel wreath of the Cumaean Sibyl of ancient times, as you process widdershins round the High Tower! Leader of women the world over!'

It is an unfortunate comparison. I remember lessons in classical mythology where a Sibyl soothsayer had angered some God or other, and had ended up moaning in a jar hanging from a tree on Mount Olympus with little children taunting her. '*Sibyl, Sibyl, what do you wish for?*' And the Sibyl replies: '*All I wish for is to die.*'

In my youth I'd invoked all the powers of cosmetic surgery and wealth to turn myself into a simulacrum of Mary Fisher,

Bobbo's mistress. It had been a very painful process and had never quite worked. My shortened legs still ached unpleasantly. Cosmetic surgery more than thirty years old is not a pleasant sight. Bits swell and other bits shrink. Little by little original features return, as if the mind insists on finding its true reflection in the body. I avoid mirrors as an unpleasant reminder of reality. In my old age, I prefer not to look at or be looked at. My once *retroussé* nose droops down to meet my chin, and my eyebrows shoot in different directions. It is not the icy cold I fear, or stumbling on uneven ground, so much as having my photo taken.

'Anyway, the High Tower isn't a church, it's an old lighthouse,' Valerie protested. 'And widdershins can be good luck not bad. In Mecca it's how they go round the Kaaba, in Judaism it's how the bride circles the groom, and if we set off at the right time from the right place the light will be right for a photo-op. Ellen will get the shot she wants. And we've bought the latest in photoshopping software. Very expensive.'

So that's all right, then. I am suddenly very sleepy. Valerie gets my permission and forges the rest of the invites for the Women's Widdershins Walk, while I snuggle down under my blanket again. I do so like sleeping.

22

Free At Last

A warning to wantons.

Tyler leapt on to the back of Hermione's Harley-Davidson and the young couple roared off into Brighton to withdraw his £57.90 from Barclay's Bank on North Street. That safely done, Hermione, the rather alarmed Tyler clinging on behind, whisked round the corner to the Dome and the Pavilion. They thundered illegally down a newly opened pedestrian tunnel, low, bumpy and underground, built in 1804 by the Prince Regent to meet his lovers (or so it was said). A notice flashed by which read 'Not Safe for Baby Buggies' as walkers scattered in alarm and a cloud of petrol fumes. Hermione shrieked with joy as they emerged. They roared back to the cliff-top road and made off for the dullness of St Rumbold's and home.

Hermione had been at school with Tyler, but had left at sixteen. She was now prosperous, even rich. After a disastrous spell at the Jobcentre Plus, she'd gone on to make a living selling drugs and legal highs from a remote cottage up the coast. She was dyslexic and anorexic, dressed in vintage goth, had long black hair and hollow eyes, a twenty-two-inch waist and a one-inch thigh gap, and when Tyler was on the back of her motorbike his beautiful hands could clasp round her middle. As Miss Swanson had suggested, she was always good for a meal, but was more free with her favours afterwards than Tyler (a nice lad but easily influenced, as his headmaster once described him) thought appropriate. So 'free' was perhaps not quite the right word.

Tyler and Hermione had been friends since they were fourteen. Both were understood by their mates to be outsiders, Hermione by virtue of her independent way of life and frequent conversations with the police, Tyler by virtue of his wonky eye and easy nature. Hermione was sexually easy and a frequent sexter, Tyler more scrupulous in his dealings with the other sex. Other than Hermione, there had been only two others (one male, one female) in seven years – which made Tyler almost a hermit amongst his peers, but at least one who had the kind of respect and affection once awarded in the old days to a saint.

It was true enough that when lit from behind his hair would make a halo round his head, and his smile was benign, though his eye so wandered it was hard for others to recognise quite what sort of emotion lingered there. People tended to avert their own eyes, so that his full beauty was not instantly evident. All the same his nickname was Archangel, after St Raphael, whom a teacher had told them was patron saint of eyesight. He had the blithe confidence of one not bullied at school, though it could be easily punctured by casual insult. Tyler might be Archangel to his school friends, but at home in Seaview Cottage he had been at the mercy of his twin sisters Madison and Mason, nine years older than he, who delighted to refer to him (usually in the third person) as Cyclops, and despised him as of right for the brute arrogance and boorish insensitivity of all males the world over.

Today Hermione called by Somerville House at Kingsdean, a mile from St Rumbold's, just to deliver a small package and collect some money. Somerville House had once been a hotel for posh holiday makers, but since a road had been built between it and the sea it had fallen on hard times and now catered for benefit claimants and a handful of asylum seekers. Hermione stopped the bike in an alley and suggested Tyler stayed with it while she made the delivery.

'No need for you to be involved, Angel-face,' she said, 'and better for all of us if you're not.' And she stalked off, booted legs long, thin and glorious, thigh gap obvious, into the unknown.

After ten minutes or so, in which Tyler rolled a joint and puffed on it, he noticed that the petrol tank of the Harley-Davidson was leaking; more than just leaking – fulsomely dribbling its contents from a seam onto the sandy soil of the ground below, where it quickly disappeared leaving nothing but its smell behind. There must be some kind of rational explanation which would eventually become apparent. Perhaps the bumpy ride through the secret tunnel, Tyler wondered idly, had set off some kind of metal fatigue? There seemed little Tyler could do about it.

Hermione came back without her parcel, looking happy, and Tyler told her about the petrol tank. Hermione said that was totally impossible, it was a brand new machine. They both looked at the tank and there was no leak any more and no smell. He'd been smoking, hadn't he? It was really strong stuff, she should have warned him, she said. So they set off without more ado, Tyler prepared to accept that what he'd witnessed need not correlate exactly with what had happened. But after they had gone a few hundred yards the engine spluttered and died. The road was long and empty and a cold wind was blowing.

'I could have sworn I filled her up,' said Hermione, and indeed, on checking the receipt she had stuffed into her pocket, she found she had done just that. Hermione said the world was like this, these days, the oddest things happened but the answer was not to fuss and marvel but just to accept. They pushed the bike half a mile until they reached the Auto Solo Garage outside St Rumbold's where the man checked the tank, found nothing amiss and filled it up again. They went back along the main road to Hermione's rose-covered coastguard cottage, with no trouble at all. The wind had got up and was making howling noises. Hermione said when the wind was from the west it tended to do that, she didn't know why. She microwaved a fish pie, which they shared. She said she'd just paid her mortgage off.

'If you hadn't been so stupid and gone and got a degree, Tyler, you too could afford a love nest. Now look at you, long-term unemployed, schmoozing up to an old lady in a pink cardigan.' Miss Swanson had once been Hermione's supervisor in the days before the Jobcentre had a plus at the end. 'What have you come to?'

'I rather like her,' said Tyler. 'She could be much worse.'

'You're such an angel-child, Tyler,' said Hermione, peeling off greasy black and purple garments to reveal an anorexic white body beneath. 'You'll forgive anyone anything. Bloody unbelievable!'

She remarked upon the beauty of his body, and suggested that since he was so hard up it might be a good idea if he did as Swanson had suggested, put on a maid's uniform and got a job up at the High Tower, but Tyler became quite angry and said he was not a transvestite, he was a man. Had she not just noticed? She said he was all right, but lacked finesse. 'Lacked finesse?' He was shocked. He had thought he was all finesse. Nevertheless he handed her the £50 note he'd got from the bank that afternoon – usually she charged four times as much but serviced Tyler as a *prix d'ami*.

There was a sudden thud as a tile fell off the roof and landed in the garden. Nothing would do but that Tyler went out into the dark – 'prove your manhood,' she said – up a ladder (at least she held the bottom), slipped the tile back into its home and put a nail through it. The rain held off while he did it. Then she said she was expecting 'a friend' at midnight but she would give Tyler a lift home. Tyler had rather expected to spend the night but no such luck. Perhaps 'the friend' had more 'finesse' than he, or more money. The rain had begun again, and Tyler, usually so good-natured and happy, was feeling rather upset and anxious by the time he got home to Sylvan Lodge, as well as being soaked to the skin.

23

'There Are Bad Times Just Around The Corner
There Are Dark Clouds Hurtling Through The Sky...'

Bobbo scares himself.

'Last night a black gull crashed into my window, broke its bloody neck and fell onto the rocks down below. If that's not a sodding omen I don't know what is! But I don't want to fucking die; I'm not fucking ready. Fetch that doctor! On second thoughts, nurse, don't bother. I don't want to set eyes on that old battle-axe, not a hormone left in her. But I look out the window and there's this poor bird lying flat as a bloody pancake with blooded feathers and a broken neck, and it lifts its head and its face is Mary Fisher's. With smudged lipstick!'

'It was only a nightmare,' said Nurse Samantha.

'Only! What do you mean, only? When I bloody looked again it was the She Devil's face – with snakes instead of hair on her head, writhing and squirming. And she says to me, "You're going to die."'

'Your poor old mind's playing tricks again, Mr Patchett.' Samantha took his hand. There seemed no end to her kindness.

'Parody of a beautiful woman, her indoors, that wife of mine, a Mrs Frankenstein, all cut about and re-stitched to turn herself into Mary Fisher. All that pain, the money (my money) and all that trouble, and all for love of me. Why couldn't she have just shut up and waited? I'd have gone right off Mary Fisher in time, conceited, shallow bitch of a woman, and gone back home. But Ruth bloody jumped the gun.'

'Mr Patchett, don't distress yourself. What is the point of going over and over these things? It's all so long ago.'

'How could someone like her turn into a beauty like Mary? Ever. It did Ruth no good. Look at her now! Her chin covered with warts, the nose drooping to meet the chin, then the fake bubble breasts burst… God, Mary's real ones were pretty!'

'Is it Botox that's sent her left eyebrow higher than the right?'

'How should I know? What a joke! Ruth Patchett's a fucking joke, an insult to God and man, especially man. How can you bully a man into love?'

'Oh dear,' said Samantha. 'You are cross! Couldn't you both find it in your hearts to forgive each other? Don't let the sun go down on your anger, that kind of thing? Or life itself go down, come to that.'

'That's what you think, Miss Pollyanna Bubble Breasts! I've got enough anger to keep me going 'til the end of fucking time. My wife fucked a judge to get me put inside for ten years and that's not a thing a man easily fucking forgets. Just keep the cow away from my deathbed. Use anything you like – wooden cross, clump of garlic, whatever it takes – just keep her away from my door. And don't you worry about my hate. It's love that weakens us. Hate's what keeps me alive. I'll sing you a hymn to the death of love, like Ruth did before me. Hate's catching. Will that satisfy you, cunt? Now just shut up and let me sleep.'

24

All Change!

The new, energised ghost of Mary Fisher.

Wooo-h, remember me? Yes, you're right, me again. It never rains but it pours. There have been more convulsions lately on Mount Olympus. A coup. Momus is challenging the role of Zeus, attempting to form a new religion – The GFR: The Great Fictional Religion, in which all men and women must join in worship of Momus, The Great Writer in the Sky, and strive towards happenings and happy endings in which a moral element must be contextualised and normatised, that is to say, the good rewarded and the bad punished in everything printed or viewed. No more moral ambiguity: no more sitting on the fence.

Suits me! I find I have a little more power to my ghostly elbow, a little more play on my tether. I can travel inland: I can even get to Brighton in the service of the Great Momus. But all this is nothing to do with you, dear reader, just life after death stuff. Forget it.

Enough that I was there when Hermione – a girl whose lifestyle I am now obliged to abhor but used rather to admire – came roaring and blaring down the bumpy underground tunnel at the Brighton Dome, startling and terrifying helpless tourists, and careering off with poor Tyler clinging on behind. Such a shocking blast of noise!

I never had a lot of time for Nicci, Tyler's mum. She was my stepdaughter for a while – when all was well between me and Bobbo. I tried for his sake to hide my dislike of her, but she was a difficult, unprepossessing, unforgiving child at the best of times – and her mother dumping her on me did not help, I suppose. Overweight, too. She took after her mother in her dependence on cosmetic surgery and got a gastric band – but once a fatty always a fatty, at heart if not in body – and managed to marry a Bronze God: but it didn't last.

Her two daughters were plain as pikestaffs. I'd look through the window of their cold little house – she would never turn the heating up, the miserable cow – and entertain myself making howling noises. But Tyler, oh Tyler! The best of my Bobbo and Mr Finch combined – how generous of spirit, how loveable, how beautiful! Bobbo had his nasty streak and that in time won out with him as nasty streaks are inclined to do – listen to poor Bobbo now. But I love Tyler as best I can, unearthly creature that I am, with no fleshly attributes, just an undying spirit – at least so far. Trust me, trust me.

Hermione roared back home on the A259 with Tyler clinging on behind, and with a little more pressure from me on her left hand than her right I could have steered her straight into a pothole, unseated them, and killed them. But I refrained and so altered the course of history. I am the spirit of love, which however irrational still has its powers.

The Great Fictional Religion can't have it all its own way. The bad must be punished, but I couldn't have my innocent Tyler done to death as along with Hermione. And the Harley-Davidson was such a beautiful machine I must admit I was reluctant to damage it, make it skid along the road driverless and on its side. Some of my happiest memories are of clinging to Bobbo as we roared round the paradise of my young life.

But I had the strength to prise apart the seam at the bottom of the petrol tank for a short time while she went to indulge in her drug deal and probably a little selling of her skinny female charms to some low bidder. Honestly, Somerville House! How low grade can you get? A truly wretched place. I'm surprised they could afford a cup of pot noodles! And later – though thwarted in my desire to hamper Tyler as he made a fool of himself with Hermione by his sexual thrust, which though enthusiastic and strong, did without doubt, as Hermione described it, lack subtlety – I did at least manage to loosen a tile on the roof and tempt him out of the house to put it back. I helped him adjust the ladder and stopped the wind from simply blowing him off it.

I stayed around to see if Hermione's midnight visitor turned up once she was back home, but he did not come. Perhaps she was just tired and wanted a rest and made him up, the slut, or perhaps Tyler had been a little inaccurate in his thrusting; she was too bruised and she called it off.

Oh *wooo-h-ooh* to you too. I'm going back to bed. I too am tired. It's been an exhausting day for a poor little frail thing like me.

25

Samantha Tries To Make Things Nice

...but Bobbo isn't having any of it.

'Water, water! I want water, nurse! Where are you? Christ! What are you doing? Now you've spilt it, slag, idiot! All over me, all over the sheet. No, I did not move my hand on purpose. Do you think I'm that sort of person? You're the one who spilt it. Gone back to the old "Care Pathway" to death, have you? Food and water not allowed. I know your tricks. How about a shot of fucking Viagra? I'd soon show you who's alive, and who isn't.'

'You won't bloody react, I give up. Nurse, darling, sweetheart, any way you can get me out of this hell hole and into an NHS nursing home? Anywhere where the rules of common sanity apply? Why am I kept here? I don't understand it. Dr Lezzer calls, I have an injection, I sign a document shoved under my nose, you take my fingerprints, the Monster herself appears weeping crocodile tears down her travesty of a face, some cunt takes a photograph of her and me together? If they want my signature why don't they just forge it? What are they trying to prove? That they don't hate men? That human blood, not bile, runs in their veins? Are they bloody joking?'
'You're very lively today, Mr Patchett.'
'It's because I didn't take my sodding pills. Hid them under my

tongue and kept them there while Dr Lezzer pulled my neck up from behind to make me swallow like you do a sick cat.'
'I think you must have imagined that, Mr Patchett, and her name is Dr Simmins, do try and remember that. You'd get on much better with her if you were nice to her. And please try and think nice thoughts about your wife.'
'Oh nice, nice, nice, Miss Pollyanna Big Tits! When I think of my wife all I ever think of is the day she ruined my life.'

He does, too. Bobbo remembers hammering his fists against a bathroom door long, long ago, and telling Ruth she was a bad mother, a bad cook and a worse wife, how she was not a proper woman, she was the She Devil incarnate. Then she'd pursued him to the High Tower, hunted him down, and that was the beginning of the end. Now the She Devil lives where Mary should still be living by rights, and hellish black bats stream out of its windows, spreading doom and desolation as they fly, to the detriment of man and beast. Ruth's doing.

'Bats, Mr Patchett?' He had been mumbling.
'Clap of lightning, roll of thunder and off they go! Flapping black leathery wings. See 'em stream from the windows,' he said, or thought he said. 'Hate and destruction, that's all they do.'

She nodded placidly. She was a good girl. He asked if she had noticed how bad the storms were getting? How the very rock on which this Tower was founded quaked and shaked, and she said she had noticed but tried not to give it too much attention. Mr Patchett drifted off to sleep – perhaps he'd forgotten about the pill and ingested it by accident – and Samantha went over to admire the view.

'Only those with a very low IQ believe in ghosts,' Dr Simmins had said one night, leaving in a hurry before some threatened storm or other broke. She'd tripped on the stone stairs and Samantha had heard her cry out in pain and rage, but when the footsteps soon restarted Samantha resisted the impulse to go and see if the doctor was okay.

Now lightning aimed for the High Tower; it shook slightly. Something had been hit; perhaps one of the many masts. Well, Security would look after it. Four seconds after the thunder the sheet lightning came, playing along the hills on the far side of the harbour. The wind got up and howled some more and a full moon briefly showed itself from behind racing clouds and made a silver line of the great sweep of the bay. It was a wonderful sight.

26

A Thoroughly Sensible, Rational Person

Dr Simmins grits her teeth.

Talk of love disgusted Dr Ruby Simmins. She lived alone and liked it. It was thirty years and more since she had been jilted by Stephen, the young student she had braved scandal to live with, and supported from her grant through medical school. On the day of their graduation Stephen had come up to her hand in hand with her best friend Lucy and said he and Lucy had announced their engagement and wanted Ruby's congratulations. Lucy was very pretty and not very clever: Ruby was very bright and not very pretty. When they picked Ruby up from the floor (literally – she had fainted, her big white knickers showing, and how they had all laughed about that) they were all apologies. Hadn't she realised? Hadn't she known? They were both grateful to Ruby for looking after Stephen so well, but it was not as if they had shared a bed. (Ruby could scarcely believe it: didn't the sofa count?) This thing was greater than they were, and so on and so on.

Trauma such as this is hard to recover from, and the truth was that Ruby never had. Perhaps she didn't really want to, and it suited her well enough not to. She could despise the stupid in peace for the rest of her life, and be spared the cost and annoyance of courting and creating a family; and just get on with being a doctor: a profession which left one with little time and energy to waste on the useless emotions of youth.

No, Ruby Simmins did not think well of 'love', a word that could be so loosely used, and had been so used such a lot by Stephen and indeed her own mother, who through Ruby's childhood had been an avid reader of Mary Fisher's novels. They'd been a familiar sight on the counter of every corner shop in the land at the time, with their cheap pink and gold covers and always Mary Fisher on the jacket with her long hair flowing against a background of foam, rising up as waves broke at the foot of a phallic tower. 'Love me, love me, love me,' they had gushed. 'All you need is devotion, and a hairy tweed jacket to snuggle up against.' Dr Simmins' mother had not prepared her daughter for the exigencies of life as a plain girl, and Dr Simmins very much held it against her. The idea of a ghostly Mary Fisher haunting the place where she was fated to work quite agitated Ruby Simmins. Would the past never be over?

Samantha Travers got on Dr Ruby Simmins' nerves. Those with the wide-eyed innocence of the over-hopeful always did. Nurse Travers believed she was living in Munchkin Land where the Wizard of Oz was king, in the land over the rainbow where good intentions and a soft heart cured all human woes. Nurse Travers seemed impervious even to her own plight. She spent her days with a mad old man who leaked disgustingly from every orifice, in a lighthouse where if you fell down steep stone stairs you would crack your head and die, and when her baby came – five months, Ruby Simmins reckoned – hubby would soon be down the pub, not by her side. It happened to the over-trusting, the over-empathic.

'Only very stupid people believe in ghosts,' she had once remarked to Nurse Travers, but she didn't think it had sunk in. Ruby was packing up and leaving as fast as she could to get home before the storm broke, and because the wind was beginning to rise and sounded really strange, as if some hysterical actress was weeping and wailing and trying to speak at the same time as she died; Dr Simmins had once treated a road accident victim in the street who'd done that.

She was mindful that the High Tower was known to be prone to lightning strikes, and she was unusually fearful of lightning, as she was of any sudden unexpected blow from fate. More, she had perhaps given a rather strong dose of morphine to the revolting old man; anything to shut him up. It would be touch and go, and she didn't want to be around if it turned out to be go. Let Nurse Travers see to it. She, Ruby Simmins, had done what the ethics of the matter, and indeed her salary, required her to do. She had kept the old man alive far longer than his allotted span would suggest, and that at the request of his relatives. But the point when medical science could do no more had surely been reached. She had to get back quickly to St Rumbold's, where she lived and had her small practice. She was much disliked locally, but she was used to that and liked to be left alone whenever possible. She had no desire to 'join in' village life just for the sake of it.

'He may last a week,' said Dr Simmins to Nurse Travers as she left the room. 'He may last a couple of days, but he's failing fast. It would be wise to notify the family. You wouldn't want to be alone when he croaks. His ghost might grab you!' and she laughed as she went off down the steep stone stairs. There was a sudden roll of thunder and Dr Simmins, taken unaware, stumbled and had to grab the handrail in case she fell.

27

Valerie Goes To Her First Board Meeting

Nothing can stop her now.

The Board meeting was in 2HT/3, one floor below ground level, and was windowless but at least warm, well ventilated and draught free. It was a pleasant room to work in, which members of the Board put down to the fact that down here you couldn't hear the sound of the wailing wind.

Valerie was asked to present the brochure, and it was met with general enthusiasm. There were already long waiting lists for bookings in the Retreat thanks to Valerie's earlier efforts, and her revisions were much appreciated. Lady Patchett, who was feeling rather sleepy, sipped from a Thermos of coffee brought along by Valerie, which did nothing, alas, to make her more alert. Indeed, she drowsed gently and occasionally snored throughout the meeting, and no one liked to wake her. The average age of the Board was seventy-two, and everyone realised the value of sleep. And the She Devil was, after all, CEO and Chairperson.

But apparently Valerie had presented the brochure and it had been well received. Nobody noticed the Babbage/ Lovelace timeline error, still in the text, and there was gentle applause when Valerie herself pointed it out, and even gave an entertaining little lecture on how in the digital age actuality could be seen as irrelevant. The end justified the means. Valerie put it to the Board that *Tower on Top* as a title had unfortunate sexual connotations in a gender-fluid age, which since the IGP logo was so obviously phallic, was an argument which now did indeed have some force. The title must change to *Walk the Other Way*, to tie in with the Women's Widdershins Walk. The proposed change was not just approved but won her applause. Only Ms Octavia walked out, complaining about the tone of the proceedings, but she was a sweet, muddled old thing and was always walking out. Valerie, everyone agreed, should take no notice.

All were looking forward to Widdershins Day on the 21st of December. Luxuriette Caterers had been engaged and a programme of events had been arranged. Ms Bradshap proposed a vote of thanks to Valerie for all her hard work. Young blood was certainly needed to move the IGP from its old fuddy-duddy ways into the new digital world. The vote was carried with no opposition, and a very positive meeting drew to a conclusion.

28

The Servant Of A Strange God

Mary Fisher's in full self-justifying flight.

Wooo-h, wooo-h! and all that. But what a fuss about nothing! All I did wrong was to fall in love. I acknowledge my fault; I did harm in the name of love, I damaged Bobbo's children and thereby his children's children, and so on and on through the generations. Though darling Tyler doesn't seem all that damaged to me. But it all seems so endless, and perhaps I deserve this fate. Momus has been very informative lately and I seem doomed to know what it is that Tyler thinks and feels, to see what he does, to hurt as he does. To my mind he does not suffer nearly enough for love. It's so boring that young men think so much about sex, and so little about love.

But what can I know? I am a restless spirit stranded between realities. Fit only to be exorcised with bell, book and candle, instructed to depart this world and enter the next. Only who would do the exorcism? I would exorcise myself, but I have so little faith in my senses nowadays. There is nothing any more to root me to reality. I just exist, only consciousness, no body; with memories that come and go, feelings that shift and drift, as suits remorseless Momus, I suppose, to serve whatever plot he's working out. Drat him. I can't follow his rationale at all. It isn't fair.

Last night a light glimmered from the Lantern Room, and I thought '*that's Bobbo, dying, or partly dying*', and I sent a seagull crashing into the glass. It's the only kind of thing I seem able to do – make little unimportant things worse. It's very frustrating. The bird died but Bobbo didn't. I've always disliked seagulls, nasty things. One snatched an ice cream from my hand when I was a child.

But oh, I loved him so, loved him to the point of death and then beyond. What did I say his name was? Bobbo? Really? Are you sure? That horrid old prisoner in the Lantern Room? It can't be. But love is so much stronger than the person it attaches to: it's Tyler I love. Tyler Finch Patchett. He is so beautiful!

And that's Jerry Lee Lewis I keep hearing in the howling wind. I love that song, *She Still Comes Around (to Love What's Left of Me)*. That's every man's declaration of trust, blowing in the wind. I'll never let Tyler down, ever.

I am the ghost of Mary Fisher, a lost soul, a woman despised. That's what death makes you if you miss the boat to heaven. At least now I have Tyler to love, praise be to Momus. *Wooo-h, wooo-h* and all that.

29

Dr Simmins To The Rescue

The sleeper awakes.

The storm had passed. It was a beautiful day: a gentle breeze, a clear blue sky, a blissful ocean; sea birds wheeling and calling. Dr Simmins called by the She Devil's rooms to hand over her weekly medical report. The She Devil remarked that Bobbo's vital signs seemed to have taken a turn for the better: his blood pressure was normal and his heartbeat no longer fluttery. Dr Simmins agreed, saying that the path to death could be long and bumpy. By rights the old man should have been dead five years ago, but just as some people seem able to put off death in order to see a daughter married or a baby born, so some others seem able to put death off out of sheer malice. Which she was sorry to say seemed to be so in Bobbo's case.

The She Devil did not comment, though she thought that perhaps the doctor should get on with her job and keep her opinions to herself. Asked how she herself was, she admitted to feeling a little last-legs-ish and mentioned that she had fallen asleep at a Board meeting. Dr Simmins said yes, she had heard, and prescribed wake-up pills to be taken before such events to keep her alert. The She Devil, worried that news of her failure had got around and might be used against her, took one of the pills on the spot.

She and the doctor drank green tea together, made in her little kitchen, with its tiny fridge, microwave and dishwasher – main meals were taken over in the modern refectory of the Castle Complex, commonly called the canteen. The place was always abuzz with conversation and comment, and on good days laughter and good cheer, although run by Ms Bradshap, a founder member, who had strong views on healthy nourishment. Very soon the She Devil began to feel livelier, and found herself talking about anything and everything that came into her head.

She told the good doctor how sleep was becoming difficult, that she had to get up to go to the loo in the night ('normal for your age', said Dr Simmins, who the She Devil noticed always seemed gleeful when imparting bad news) and was woken again and again by a tapping on the window for which there seemed no cause. It was all very well for staff to talk about the High Tower's 'ghost' – though the howling sound was apparently produced by the configuration of wind, the new coastal defences against erosion, and the sharp rise of the downs, as Femina Electrical, responsible for the aerials on the roof had confirmed – but now Flora Bradshap was talking about a ghost with kinetic ability roaming wild inside the High Tower. Lady Patchett did not want staff getting hysterical and leaving. Sometimes it seemed to the She Devil that she was running a boarding school, not an institution for mature and intelligent women, dedicated to a great cause. Parity.

The dry-rot smell had been quite strong in 2HT/3, though no one else had complained. Perhaps this was what had made her so sleepy at the Board meeting? She would have to find some building firm to look into it, and see about more damp-proofing on floor 1 down in the basements. Perhaps Femina Electrical would be able to recommend someone? It was IGP policy to employ only women contractors and it could lead to difficulty and expense.

Dr Simmins said it would be difficult to find women pall bearers: their shoulders were not strong enough to bear the weight of conventional coffins, though she believed there were cardboard ones available these days, which were lighter to carry, so the IGP's quest might not be in vain.

'Oh dear,' said the She Devil. 'One forgets. Bobbo. But there's not so much of him to carry as there once was.'

She asked if the doctor could find the address of the funeral directors, and if she thought Bobbo would still be with them by Christmas. Dr Simmins said it was touch and go. She herself wished Bobbo would just get on with it: the stairs to the Lantern Room on the ninth floor were intolerable.

The She Devil was asking what was in the pill she had swallowed, because whatever it was had made her feel a lot better, and Dr Simmins was saying it was new on the market, sodium pentothal and a new form of amphetamine, out of the body in six hours.

Just at this moment Valerie tapped on the door with some reports from the Expenditure Committee and the She Devil asked her to join herself and the doctor in a cup of tea, and she said that since it was green tea she would, and did. Valerie said she had good news. She said she had been looking at the long term weather forecast and today was the beginning of a long spell of exceptionally good weather and the 21st was going to be a crisp bright day and not too cold. The She Devil said if Valerie said so it probably would be, since actuality seemed to adapt itself to the new Board member's expectations.

Valerie said she had found out where the grandson Tyler lived and they must pop down to see him very soon. Only a week to go before the great day.

'The family seems to be coming up in the world. A brand new-build house. Sylvan Lodge – sounds nice.'

'A great day?' remarked the She Devil. 'Sounds suspiciously like champagne. I do beg you no champagne. It's greatly over-rated, very expensive and gives me acid indigestion. And do come and see me tomorrow about those invitations. I need to look them over before they go out. '

'But they've gone out, Lady Patchett,' said Valerie. 'The party's only a week or so away. You signed the invitations.'

'Oh did I?' said the She Devil. 'Fancy that!'

Valerie finished her tea, left her expenditure reports and walked out of the room with a little hop, skip, jump and a click of the heels.

'I must have a word with that girl. She's far too excitable,' said Dr Simmins, and followed her out.

The She Devil looked at the reports, decided they were too boring to read, chucked them in the bin and passed out.

30

'We Hold These Truths To Be Self-Evident...'

...but doctor and nurse argue as to exactly what they are.

'Mr Patchett can be quite lively with his pinches,' said Nurse Samantha Travers to Dr Simmins, 'and I can't forever be dodging out of his way. There's bed baths and so forth. But I suppose sexual disinhibition isn't unusual in the very elderly, and at least I am trained to deal with it.' Samantha, at twenty-three, was newly married, five months pregnant, had a Grade 3 qualification in end-of-life care, and was proud of it.

'He's better than some,' she added, in defence of her patient. 'He's still got at least some of his marbles left, he's not incontinent, deaf or blind. He can even be quite funny. Of course his behaviour can be inappropriate and disproportionate – but he's a leftover from the past. He can't help it. I have a good job here. I even enjoy it sometimes.'

Dr Simmins, on the other hand, didn't at all enjoy visiting Bobbo Patchett. The old man's sick room was towards the top of the High Tower, on the ninth floor, and the lift only went to the third. His language was appalling, his manners were worse and his views out of another century. Bobbo would not be much of a loss to the world when he went.

'His pulse is very weak and fluttery,' she said. 'I can hardly find it, and his blood pressure is falling. We must prepare for the worst, or as some might see it, the best.'

'Just like the air pressure,' said Nurse Travers, who was, Dr Simmins feared, a victim to the pathetic fallacy – that the weather was informed by human emotion. 'It's falling. There's going to be a terrific storm. See the black clouds gathering? I love it up here in the tower when the weather's wild and the wind gets up and howls around like the ghosts of the dammed.'

'I can see that caring for Mr Patchett can be quite a confusing experience,' said Dr Simmins, 'as nursing Alzheimer's patients often can be. But I must point out there is very little relation-ship between blood pressure and air pressure.'

As it happened, as well as her Grade 3 in end-of-life care Samantha did have Grade 3 in Alzheimer's nursing, though she could never see many signs of the condition in Bobbo. He slept quite a lot, but his memory when awake seemed unimpaired. If anything he remembered all too much.

'Old women can be just as bad as old men,' she said mildly. 'I nursed one for my Grade 3 and how she cackled and flashed all over the place!'

Samantha asked Dr Simmins what Bobbo's ETA in paradise might be.

'Still a week at the most,' said Dr Simmins, gritting her teeth. 'Passed on' was bad enough, but 'ETA in paradise' was an even worse euphemism. Dead was dead, brown bread.

Samantha further annoyed Dr Simmins by telling her that the previous day a gull had flown into the Lantern Room's window and either stunned itself or fallen dead. That she hoped it hadn't been a portent of approaching mortality. The High Tower could be a spooky place. Sometimes she thought she heard voices in the wind.

'Some say the voices are in my imagination,' she said, 'but I hear them clearly enough. It's the ghost of poor Mary Fisher, who lived in the High Tower, and stole Mr Patchett from Lady Patchett, in the days when everyone was young and beautiful.'

'We all know the story, nurse,' said Dr Simmins, grimly. 'Just shut the bloody window. And more fool Mary Fisher. Look at Mr Patchett now!'

'But Mary Fisher loved him just as much as his wife did.' Samantha was overcome by emotion. 'But he turned away from her too and so her heart was broken and now she can't rest.'

Old Mr Patchett was sleeping again and Dr Simmins took the opportunity to plunge a needle into the withered old arm. Bobbo woke up briefly with a vicious protest of 'Cunt, cunt, cunt!', but quickly fell silent again.

Samantha opened the sash window just a crack, the better to let the words 'Cunt, cunt, cunt!' drift away.

31

Me, Me, What About Me?

Mary Fisher draws attention to herself.

Wooo-h, wooo-h, wooo-h! Me again, the ghost of Mary Fisher! I do like that girl Valerie! When I lived and loved in the High Tower it was all roses, moonlit nights, champagne and loveliness. Not a whiff of dry rot. My novels were lessons in love, in the glory of adoration, of surrender. I was a successful writer of romantic novels; how beautiful then, my life! It was here in the High Tower I entertained publishers and sometimes slept with them – but then I fell in love with Bobbo, and his wife took such great offence. I thought I could afford to be sorry for her. I was wrong.

Through millions upon millions of human couplings evolution strives towards its goal – and that goal is the grace that is perfect beauty. Call me conceited if you like, but it was in that striving that nature found its apogee in me, the perfect woman, beauty and grace itself. Ruth Patchett was just another of nature's failed experiments, ugly, almost deformed. Of course she envied me. Seriously, though, the She Devil has no idea why she does what she does. She too is driven by forces she does not understand. When Asclepius sends in his minions to keep Bobbo alive, they take the form of one Dr Simmins.

Perhaps it was that in her rage, in her incantations, Ruth managed to invoke Asclepius, the God of Medicine? So he obliged, giving her the powers that She Devils have, but in so doing angered Venus, Goddess of all evolution. And on a whim – these Olympians are so whimsical! – she had me, humble Mary Fisher, devoured by her pet demon, Cancer. But I so loved Bobbo. Venus saved me in this half form so I could go on loving him until he died and joined me. And Asclepius won't let him die, so now he's grown into this disgusting old toad. I daresay a kiss would take him back to normal.

No? Too fanciful? Probably. Anyway, I can't possibly kiss him now, because I love another. What's his name? Yes, that's it. Tyler! Tyler Finch Patchett, young and strong and lovely. The new love of my life.

And now Momus has entered the fray and I wait for directions. Me, a small too, too innocent, delectable pawn in the war between the Gods. At least that's the best sense I can make of it, as I swirl around the High Tower, all my sins forgiven me, poised between life and death, in love, in love, in love, waiting for Bobbo to die. Come to think of it, my rightful place is probably on Mount Olympus, amongst Elysian Fields, lotos-smoking with my beloved Tyler. I was always one for a bit of hash. Oh the too, too totally gloriousness of me, of just sheer existence in whatever form you choose! Thank you, Momus, for this relief, this blessing.

Wheee-h, wheee-h, wheee-h! Look at me, remember me, the one, the true, the only spirit of romantic love!

32

Alone And Old And Very, Very Cross

Bobbo's back from the brink yet again.

The old man was mumbling and protesting as Samantha bent over to bring his tonic drink to his lips. She did her best as ever to understand his train of thought and interpret what he said as meaningful.

'I could die of thirst. No one cares. I talk, no one listens. Are you nuts, nurse? Of course I spilt the fizzy pink stuff. It's poison. When I say water I mean water. Yes, spilt in the bed. Take a little look. Come a little nearer, nurse, do. Oops, that made you hop! What's the matter? You a lesbian or something? Well, don't worry, cunt. It's only a dying man's finger – you're quite safe with me, I'm just an old man, I hardly have the strength to raise my eyelids, let alone anything else.'

Dr Simmins let herself into the room and he seemed to sense as much as see her. Bobbo mumbled on:
'And here comes bloody Dr Simmins from the jaws of hell. She'll lean over me, all wrinkled dugs and foul breath, and spread the word that by next week I'll be bloody gone. She's got a hope. Men like me don't die. We're the Straddlers of the Universe. Curse Dr Lezzer and curse her children if she has any,

which I doubt, may they boil in oil, the lot of them. Curse her mother too, come to that, for giving her birth. Old bat of a dried-up female: grey hair, not a laugh left in her. No bloody use to me. A bloke's body may grow old, but the spirit burgeons. Leave love to bloody women. Hate energises man, lust weakens him, love destroys him. Be my Boswell, nurse, write that down. I sing a hymn to the death of love. Will that satisfy you, Samantha bloody Travers, with your itsy-witsy tits, your waggling little girly bum and your short, short skirt? Love me, love me do, I'm such a bad, bad boy.'

A sudden gust of wind blew through the Lantern Room, and that was odd because there were no windows open. An acreage of heavy, dingy rose-velvet curtains rippled and shivered. Dr Simmins did not seem to notice. Bobbo sat straight up and said quite clearly, 'I see you. Mary Fisher. Won't you for fuck's sake give up?'
He lay back down again. The wind died down, the curtains fell still. Dr Simmins filled her syringe. Samantha didn't feel frightened. These events had become rather normal and life – at least for some – went on as usual.

She bent over Bobbo, who seemed suddenly in a good mood, and was singing in his cracked voice an old country and western song called *Stand By Your Man*.

33

The She Devil Holds Valerie To Account

...and clears a few matters up.

The She Devil finds Valerie at work in her office in the Castle Complex, making one of her unexpected and not always welcome forays into the working life of the IGP. Valerie sees her coming along the corridor, a witch-like figure with a hooked nose and unmatched eyebrows, and thinks that all she needs is a peaked hat. But the She Devil seems amiable enough and even congratulates her on having joined the Board so quickly and so young; says she deserves it for such good work, and that Valerie is to receive a welcome rise in pay as from the coming year. So far so good.

Then she wants details of the Widdershins party and it is not so good. Valerie says she has asked two hundred guests and had a 70 per cent acceptance rate, which is very good, considering it was on short notice and just before Christmas, but then everyone is intrigued by the thought of the Widdershins Walk.

The She Devil says it is perhaps more because of the line on the invitation which reads: '*Surprise Parity Party Bag: a Widdershins laptop, an iWatch, or an iPhone, which will be yours?*

Give yourself a happy Christmas!' Which was hardly within the IGP ethos and who had authorised it?

'Actually, no one,' Valerie feels obliged to admit, but adds, 'It's going to be a splendid party, and we only need to give away one of each. I've got a friend in Apple, and she'll give us a really good deal because we're a charity.'

The She Devil asks if Valerie has ever organised a big party before and Valerie has to say no, but she is qualified: she has done an Events course at uni. Then the She Devil asks who exactly is on the guest list.

'All the usual suspects,' says Valerie blithely. She can see a little blithe confidence is necessary. The She Devil's face is like thunder. Valerie's own mother would sometimes look like this, before Valerie found her hanging from the tall marital four-poster one day, swinging in the breeze. 'Women from Education for Choice, Anti-Trafficking Concern, Women Against Violence, Fem-Fight, the Ministry for Women and Other Minorities, and we expect the Minister for Women herself to come along.'

'My God,' says the She Devil, and her face relaxes, so she looks quite normal. 'This party had better be good!'

Valerie presses home an advantage, or what she thinks is an advantage, and says that Tom Brightlingsea, head of De-Gender Now, would very much like to be asked.

'But he's an arrant heterosexual,' says the She Devil, shocked. 'Not even gay. What could you be thinking of?'

'Tom's a very sound feminist,' says Valerie Valeria.

The She Devil opens her mouth to protest but closes it again. Valerie is maddening. You couldn't expect a wise head on young shoulders, but she was so lively, dedicated and hard-working, so attractive and popular with everyone including the Board that it might be foolish to gainsay her. Things changed so fast in the gender wars it was hard to keep up. Rather like in 1984, today's enemy could become tomorrow's friend within the hour and vice versa. One mustn't be seen to be behind the times. The tide of opinion might change again and these days the tides changed very rapidly indeed. She has seen it all before.

'Well, we will all live in hope,' the She Devil says. 'And let us pray to St Medard that the winter equinox is a beautiful photogenic day and not snow, gales and lightning strikes and that the guests don't get pneumonia and we get sued – you'd better do a risk assessment.'

'I shall, Lady Patchett,' says Valerie. 'Who is St Medard when he's at home?'

'The patron saint of good weather,' says the She Devil, 'and just a figure of speech.'

'Odd, I thought you were an atheist,' says Valerie. Things between them are getting a little strained, and the She Devil has no appetite or energy for theological discussion. She falls quiet. 'Should we make a date to go down and see your grandson?' asks Valerie into the silence.

'I am rather busy,' says the She Devil. 'So are you. Can any of us afford the time?'

'Oh, but Lady Patchett, that's not how we think of you at all! Not old! You're so young at heart, and if you rediscover your family you'll set such an example to feminists everywhere. The IGP needs now more than ever to change course and take men on board to fight the good fight. Men can be very good feminists too. Like Tom Brightlingsea of De-Gender Now.'

'I hope you didn't send him an invitation.'

'Well, actually I did – but it was by mistake. Ms Laura sent out the wrong pile. The other hundred and ninety went out perfectly.'

It is just about conceivable it was an accident – Ms Laura being seventy-nine and with bad eyesight, even though head of the Expenditure Committee – but the She Devil suspects Valerie, the little minx, just wants her own way. Again she says nothing. She doesn't have the energy she once had.

34

Rescue Comes From On High

No sanction today!

Miss Swanson's PC pinged even as Tyler approached her bullet-proof window.

'It's all go today,' she said. 'Lucky you, you're off the hook. That's the Brighton Beaux window closed. They've filled the vacancy. One has to be so quick off the mark these days.'

'So no sanction? Even though I failed to turn up?'

'No sanction,' agreed Miss Swanson. The vacancy was still showing up on Tyler's iPhone. But he wasn't going to argue.

'At this rate I'll be an old man before I get a job.' He'd been right about La Swanson. She was certainly on his side. Perhaps his Best Female Friend Hermione was right and La Swanson didn't want to lose him? Was he then to be trapped in a Jobcentre forever by bonds of love? But it wasn't exactly an Orpheus/ Eurydice situation. Perhaps he should be more like Hermione who had taken herself off benefits and onto drug peddling along the Sussex coast instead. She had the new Harley-Davidson Softail on which she sometimes picked him up from the Jobcentre Plus on it so he didn't have to wait for his bus.

'When you get to be twenty-five,' was all Ms Swanson said, 'your weekly rate will go up to £73.50. Pity you don't have the get-up-and-go of your girlfriend, who doesn't put on airs. She just gets on with life. Your Hermione would have been round at the Brighton Belles like a shot, and sold a few drugs while she was about it. Why don't you just live off her immoral earnings, not off the State?'

Miss Swanson knew too much. Tyler wondered what else she knew. And this latter statement was obviously out of order – he could drop her in total shit if he'd recorded it on his iPhone. Why would she say something like that? Could it be she was goading him into a complaint, that she wanted to be fired, was hoping to muster as many complaints against her as she could? It was possible, but why? Better to be fired than wilfully unemployed, in which case she too would be unentitled to benefits?

'I'm sure you're not meant to say things like that,' he said. 'Do you want me to complain or something? Isn't there someone called a Job Resolution Manager?'

'I am your Job Resolution Manager,' Miss Swanson said. 'They've got me whichever way I turn. Enough of this mucking about. If you get a job which lasts longer than three weeks you realise I get a commission? Also if you get a sanction. It's small but it's something. You're a nice lad but you're virtually unemployable. Nobody wants you. Too clever for manual, not clever enough for middle management. Not even gay.'

'Is that a problem?'

'Of course. Gays help their own. Always ready to give each other a leg up.' She laughed, rather crudely. Tyler shuddered. Miss Swanson looked at him sympathetically. She had nice eyes. If you ignored the grease stain and the cardigan and the double chin and the obvious depression, she was quite a good-looking woman.

'If you really want a job,' said Miss Swanson, 'I suggest you dress up as a girl and apply in person up at the High Tower for cleaner's work. No one would tell the difference, you're such a pretty boy. No?'

Tyler was on his feet and shaking his head. Enough was enough 'Then you're in real danger of a sanction. Four weeks.'

'But what exactly for?'

'Oh, anything.' Her voice rose and rose. 'Try: dumb insolence, raising your voice, failing to keep appointments with your coach without proven good reason – lost in the post is not one – failing to apply for the number of positions agreed by you in your contract with the DWP. Your new address is Sylvan Lodge in the Endor Grove estate – very fancy – and you haven't informed me. Male layabouts like you just drive me round the twist. You're so picky! Give me a girl any day.'

The whole Centre could hear her now. She laughed. In the waiting room a plastic tile fell off the ceiling. She lowered her voice and leaned forward.

'And because that'd be four, towards my target of twenty sanctions a week.'

Tyler met Hermione outside the office and they zoomed off together to Brighton to collect his stipend and perhaps they'd have an assignation afterwards. Life wasn't all bad.

35

The Girl Does Good

Samantha lends a hand.

Bobbo groaned and stirred a little on the bed and fell quiet again. Whatever the doctor had injected him with would work for hours. Nobody in the village ever went to see Dr Simmins if they could help it. Samantha moistened old Bobbo's lips with a damp cloth as she had been taught, and felt a terrible responsibility.

Death was such a peculiar thing. First you were there and then you weren't. She'd miss the old man. The wind would howl unheard around the High Tower. They'd probably use the room for storage after he was gone. The Historic England listing wouldn't allow alteration above the third floor, and that meant no lift for ever and a day, just the awful steep stone narrow stairs. The next storm was breaking. She'd better get home. Security would look in on him during the night. She supposed Bobbo would be there and still alive in the morning.

But Samantha thought of herself as a trained nurse, if only in the care and sustenance of the elderly. She had her training to support her and give her confidence. She still had her notes from Grade 3. '*If any of the relationships with people important to the dying are strained or broken, they may feel a deep desire for resolution and healing while there is still time.'*

Should she warn the family? But what family? All of Bobbo's relationships were strained and broken. Samantha lived down in St Rumbold's and so knew quite a lot about them. Bobbo's children, Andy and Nicci, lived no one knew where; the grand-children were grown and flown the nest or the nest had flown them, more like it. None had even visited the old man, and were not, so far as Samantha knew, going to be welcome at the High Tower. A family divided, shattered.

Unless she, Samantha Travers, *did* something, Bobbo must die alone. No one deserved such a fate. The She Devil herself might eventually turn up, but only if it were a photo-op, and would probably be unwise to do so. Yet it must be possible to effect a family reconciliation. Hate must not be allowed to triumph. Samantha knew she was a fragile vessel to stand up against evil, but who else was there?

It struck her as a bolt from the blue that she had actually been to Ashford High with Tyler Finch, a boy who ran with the fast crowd and had a wall eye, so you could never meet it even if you felt sorry for him and tried. Some said he was actually a relative of Dame Ruth Patchett though others said he wasn't. If he was, he might be up for the deathbed scene. Tyler was okay. They had sexted each other often enough in their schooldays, so they were not exactly strangers. They'd lost touch but she'd call by the Jobcentre Plus and leave a message for Miss Swanson whom she knew of old, and ask her to pass it on. Tyler had been away at uni but someone had said they'd seen him recently sweeping up the dead flies – either unemployed or doing community service – in the village store. Poor Tyler. But at least he'd have the time to attend a deathbed. Not everyone these days had. And she could probably smuggle him in. He might have to dress up as a girl, of course, and claim to be a granddaughter.

36

Mary Fisher Remembers Her Place In Momus'
Script

and how once she was so loved and admired.

Wooo-h, wooo-h, wooo-h, etcetera, etcetera. I am the ghost of
Mary Fisher. I am long since dead, fairly insubstantial and I
daresay more frivolous in death than life. I used to take myself
more seriously, I think, than do I now.

I am expected by Momus to use Tyler – how I love to say that
name – one way or another to bring about the destruction of his
grandmother, the usurping She Devil, still alive and wrongfully
dwelling in the High Tower. But I get so distracted. Tyler is
such a joy to look at – Bobbo reborn, but nicer, kinder, one
of today's metropolitan men with a touch of rural gentleness.
He takes after his grandfather, but less macho, less aggressive,
less testosterone-ridden but still so very male and proud.

The clear, smooth, almost girlish complexion, the curved lip,
the wide and grave blue eyes, the untidy fair hair, the broad and
rippling chest – he gets that from his Bronze God father, no
doubt. But what does Momus intend me to do? Nicci was such
a surly ungrateful child, part of the baggage that Bobbo swore
he would leave behind. Except he didn't. And then his sexual

desires became excessive when he was in jail – lust is part of love but not all of it – and now I am with Tyler lust can be none of it. It's all pure love. Then I had my career to think about and of course there was soon the fraud part and prison – the She Devil stitched him up, Bobbo was perfectly innocent – and I stood by my man – was that Tammy Wynette or Dolly Parton? I can't remember which. But I looked like a mixture of them both. I think.

And then Bobbo went right off me. I've often wondered if it was that dull plain girl who ran the occupational therapy classes in the prison who was to blame. One has to have someone to blame. At the moment in the High Tower it's me; they're threatening me with bell, book and candle. I don't think in this digital age it will work. Me, I'm happy drowsing here in the lotus fields of Elysium loving Tyler Finch Patchett. I am your greatest devotee, oh Momus, but I need a rest. The future of mankind may be at stake but I'm tired.

And I'm a bit upset, to tell you the truth. I looked in on Bobbo the other day. You'd have thought he'd be glad to see me, old times and all that, but he couldn't wait to get rid of me. Men are so vain! He just assumed I was still madly in love with him and I assumed he'd be jealous of Tyler but he wasn't at all. I could have warned him of what that wicked old doctor had in her syringe but I didn't see why I should.

37

How Miss Swanson Saved Tyler's Life...

...and before he was even born.

The trouble with these small Jobcentres was that everyone knew everyone. Not only was Tyler's personal life on computer, but Miss Swanson, another St Rumbold's inhabitant, knew him and his associates by sight and reputation.

As it happened, Miss Swanson had no intention of sanctioning Tyler. She did what she could to protect him from the ravages of the State; she had, if not exactly erotic feelings towards him, at least maternal ones. She knew well enough that Tyler was the She Devil's grandson. La Swanson had worked for twenty years at Radstock and Shears, property developers. She had started work on the same day as Tyler's mother Nicci Patchett, and stayed at the same salary level until eventually being made redundant two years ago. Nicci, on the contrary, already a mother of two, had become PA to the managing director within the week, and left within the year having not returned to work after maternity leave. Miss Swanson knew Tyler's mother well and did not like her. Nicci was smart, practical, wore almost transparent white blouses and tight black skirts, went clickety-clack with high heels about the office, talked about herself non-stop, had had a gastric band and an ongoing relationship with the married CEO.

Miss Swanson encountered her on ciggie breaks when Nicci would squeeze spots and pluck hairs in the office Ladies' Room, while Miss Swanson – more the party girl in those days than the career woman – shaved her legs or put in curlers. Nicci would talk obsessively and at length about what an evil mother she had, so evil indeed that Nicci's therapist had described her as 'a typical narcissistic, deserting mother', the worst kind of mother anyone could have. Nicci had long ago broken off all relations with her mother Ruth and prevented her little girl twins, then aged nine, Madison and Mason, from having anything to do with the monstrosity that had begot their mother. Evil by name and evil by nature: She Devil.

It was Elaine Swanson who had held Nicci's head over the wash-basin in the ladies' loo twenty-three years or so ago when Nicci was morning-sick with Tyler, her marriage to her third husband already breaking up. The third husband was the famous Gabriel Finch, the plumber-filmstar (or so Nicci described him, though Elaine Swanson had never heard of him); it seemed he had been plumbing a film producer's wife's house when a string of lucky coincidences had promoted him from Bronze God male stripper to action-hero actor. Nor was her conversation with Nicci that day the kind one forgot.

'If this bloody baby wasn't a girl,' Nicci had said, in between retches, 'I'd fucking abort. I couldn't stand a boy, greedy like his father, great clumsy oaf, hitting and bashing and chewing one's nipples.'
'But you can't be sure it's a girl. Isn't it too early to tell?' asked Elaine, tentatively. Nicci seemed so sure of herself.
'It's a girl all right. I saw it for myself on the scan. They won't

tell you, of course, until it's too late. And one only gets sick with a girl. And I've had two, I should know.'

Elaine Swanson, feeling sorry for the innocent unborn child, shocked by Nicci's apparent lack of maternal feeling, didn't say what she knew to be true, that at three months no gender diagnosis was certain.

Thus it was that through Miss Swanson's intervention, or lack of it, Nicci's baby was allowed to come to term, and emerged from the womb a boy. When Tyler Finch Patchett turned up in her life again, Miss Swanson, who had long since parted company with Nicci, felt Tyler owed her his life itself, and when he turned up at the Jobcentre Plus had resolved to do everything she could for him. He could, she thought, do with a little chiding, and so she chided. He really should get away from Hermione. What he needed, like so many young men, was a good girlfriend to turn his life around.

38

No Place Like Home…

…if only one could get out of it.

Sylvan Lodge was a misnomer for Tyler's home, a splendid but thin-walled four-bedroomed new-build on the Endor Grove estate to the west of St Rumbold's. Here he lived with his mother Nicci and his twin sisters Madison and Mason, with their gender-neutral names. They had moved in a month ago. It was shaming to live with a mother at his age. But Tyler could not afford to leave, and seeing no prospect of anything but a minimum wage job, supposed himself to be stranded there for life. It was a good thing he had been born a cheery fellow or he might have been quite depressed. The twins were in their thirties and could afford to go but seemed to feel no impulse to leave home, and looked blankly at the family therapist Matilda Eavens when she kept suggesting it. They were good at blank looks.

Endor Grove was a new estate. There were no trees to be seen. It had concrete and decking for a garden, a glimpse of sea in the far distance and a maze of roads and houses unbroken by shops, schools, clinics or parks in between. (Actually it did have one shop which could afford the ground rent and that was the new Co-op Funeral Parlour.) Sylvan Lodge had been bought with funds provided by the twins' property-developer father, Billy Didcot. Billy had made Nicci pregnant when she was fifteen, and he was forty-six. This was shortly after Nicci's stepmother, Mary Fisher, had died and her father Bobbo Patchett had been sent to prison for fraud.

Nicci was at boarding school at the time: Billy Didcot, a bigwig at the council, came to the school to explain to the girls the advantages of a career in local government. Nicci, no beauty but with her mother's evident gift for seduction, had been responsible for 'showing him round'. Nicci then insisted against all advice – except her stepmother's – on going ahead with the pregnancy.

Billy Didcot's life thereafter had been focused on not letting his wife, or the police for that matter, find out about the twins' existence. That Nicci had told him she was seventeen and on the pill could be no excuse. One might almost suspect it was intentional on her part and a very sensible career move in the circumstances; as indeed it was. Just as well that property dealing had made Billy very rich. Nicci, Madison and Mason had recently fancied a grand if eco-plywood new house in the Endor Grove estate, Billy Didcot's latest project, and had moved in. Billy Didcot's name was kept secret from the twins, and indeed Tyler, although they knew of his existence as the source of all riches. They referred to him as Mr Nobody.

Nicci at least kept her part of the bargain: he would provide, she would not tell. She was set up for life, but she was not happy; and the blame for this, with a little helpful encouragement from Matilda Eavens the therapist, she laid at the door of her real mother Ruth, the abandoning mother, the narcissistic She Devil.

Nicci took it for granted that her jailbird father Bobbo had abused her. He must have, or she wouldn't be so unhappy. The fact that she couldn't actually remember anything about it proved that the memory was repressed. And every day Tyler seemed to be growing more and more to look like his father, the wretched Bronze God – but also his grandfather Bobbo when young. It was intolerable. Tyler himself was intolerable. At least the girls took after her side of the family.

39
All You Need Is Hate

Bobbo has a burst of energy.

'Would I like to see my children "before I go"? *Go*, nurse? Go where? Bloody stupid you are. I'm not going anywhere. If I'm fucking dying, I'm just going to stay where I am, only dead. And no. Why would I want to see my children? What can you have in mind, little Miss Baneful? Some kind of deathbed reconciliation scene? You sound like Mary Fisher: *All You Need Is Love.* Well, I didn't and she didn't, and love is what she died from, though they called it cancer at the time. She died for love of man – me. Unrequited, I may say. Ha ha. And as good mistresses go, she went. But not far enough. I can sniff her in the air, an ozone smell. Metallic. Do you believe in ghosts, Miss Sanctimonious Cunt?'

'Please watch your language, Mr Patchett. Yes, I do. They say it's Mary Fisher still hanging about, and whose fault is that if not yours? It's her who goes moaning in the wind, practically shrieking in the storm.'

'I'll say that for the stupid cow, she was a noisy lover.' And Bobbo cackled, a horrible noise in a large echoey room, which once housed as great a light as human ingenuity could contrive. 'Too much information, Mr Patchett,' said Nurse Samantha, primly.

'*All You Need Is Love*,' sang old Bobbo. 'Swan song of a generation. Now love is out, and sex is in, and tell a good man by the
size of his tool – seen that show on the telly? Let me be your
sex object, darling.'

And the terrible thing was, she obliged, just as once Ruth
Patchett obliged old Mr Carver the park-keeper, long long ago
and far away. Fate has the oddest ways of balancing things
out; a single act of infidelity bouncing around like a deflating
balloon, uncontrolled and uncontrollable, is acted out again.

40

Portions And Parcels Of The Dreadful Past

Mary Fisher indulges in a little self-analysis.

Wooo-h, wooo-h, wooo-h! There is a certain, not exactly effeteness, a certain girliness about Tyler which I adore. I used to go for big strong men into whose tweedy lapels I could bury my little head – how seductive the masculine smell of pipe smoke used to be – but now I seem to look for more sophisticated, spiritual enticements. Well, they would appeal to me in my current form, wouldn't they? Let those who are without lust cast the first spell.

My poor Tyler! I am in love with him, exhilarated by him, transfigured by him, but my love being stripped perforce of physicality, I also pity him. I suffer with him, feel for him so. This bodiless love of mine, I notice, is threaded through with pity: the kind one feels for a mewing kitten, a fledgling fallen out of a tree. I never felt like this for Bobbo: I suffered too much; I feared the moment when he would stop loving me, start hating me. The fact that he was married, was stolen property, forbidden, increased rather than diminished the excitement and urgency when we made love. But the source of my pleasure was always masochistic: I loved to suffer, which drew others to me. Bobbo's love for me was sadistic, the pain he inflicted on his wife intensified the pleasures he had with me – oh, oh, I am such a disembodied miserable wretch!

Because I am so pitiable I must pity Tyler. Momus seems to demand it. For Tyler too is pitiable, caught up by forces he does not understand, born to a mother who did not want him and put him in a crèche when he was two months old, the government of the time assuring everyone that childcare was beneficial to the intellectual and social development of babies. I never had babies myself (I preferred to look after my figure, not some squawking brat), but why have a baby at all if all you're going to do is just hand it over to someone else to look after? It doesn't make sense.

And of course his mother Nicci was a devout feminist, and the last I heard of her she was running some anti-Pro-Life organisation – a Woman's Right to Choose, all that – which is no way to make money. Murder never is really, unless you professionalise it and end up as a soldier. So Nicci toiled long hours being true to herself, making sure other women got rid of their children while leaving her own to look after themselves.

I catch these horrible thoughts as they fly, and whether they come from Tyler, from me, or from the Great God Momus' determination to turn me into some sort of usefully villainous, if unwilling narrator, I have no idea. Perhaps to see him as the Great God has been my great folly. I can see clearly now. There is no 'Great' about him! He has no business up there on Olympus. He's nothing but a hack: a spewer of corny plots full of slapstick sight-gags or violent denouements, the writer of B-movies no one ever wants to see while they wait for the main attraction. Which is not to say I'm not going to make the High Tower come tumbling to the ground any minute. But that's different. Kill them all, that's what I say, starting with smarty-pants bitch Valerie. You see, I am not myself. I really have nothing against Valerie Valeria. Yet.

All that dry rot. I can smell the mushroomy stink getting stronger and stronger as I *wooo-h, wooo-h* round the High Tower, which is odd, since I am a person without nostrils.

Something is about to happen. Bobbo's going to die? But I don't want him to die, I don't want him turning up anywhere near me, filthy old man. I want to be with Tyler. Oh Tyler my love, love, love, love, stronger any day, any night, than the beastly Momus.

Almighty Momus, praise be thy name, hear my prayer, listen to my supplication. Let Bobbo go. Give me Tyler!

41

The Dream Of Steady Promotion

Or is it a nightmare?

Hermione dropped Tyler off and zoomed away into the dark to a part of her life he preferred, when it came to it, to leave undefined. Tyler was in no position to lay down terms of engagement – me in your bed and only me – and they both knew it. He was beautiful but he was entertainment, not serious business. He wondered what it took to be serious.

To earn regularly, he supposed, and not minimum wage, but money of a steadily increasing nature – the kind a person with a good degree got, which involved a salary not a wage, steady promotion and a path to the top, kicking others below you off the ladder as you climbed. So if you were ruthless enough you ended up as some kind of paunchy executive telling other people what to do. A line manager or something, whatever that was. But there'd always be another line manager on top of you unless you ended up as CEO of a mammoth company. More likely to be line-managed himself – like his sisters, on the other end of a call centre helpline while they were hoping against hope to find some 'serious' guy who'd be their meal ticket for life.

Or you went into the do-goodery world and hoped to end up running UNICEF. More likely end up like his mother fighting her anti-abortion-clinic crusade for pitiful wages. Though she had at least found her meal ticket for life early on. If ever he or his sisters enquired as to who, where, why or how this meal ticket was, the expression on the maternal face, though fleeting, was so savage and cruel all three quickly desisted.

Or there was self-employment. All right if you could end up inventing something like Uber, or a 'career' in IT, mending other people's computers, but you had to have the right kind of mind and he did not want to live a nerdish life.

The careers master at school had congratulated him on his 'soft skills'. He spoke without mumbling, looked people in the face, didn't seem shifty, washed and dressed up for special occasions and had his hair cut regularly. It would be better if he wore men's shorts when the weather was hot rather than borrowing his sisters'. And he should keep away from Hermione Slinger.

Miss Swanson at the Jobcentre Plus had upped the ante a little. While admitting he had 'soft skills', her definition of that seemed to be that he could communicate if he had to, seemed not likely to run off instantly with the takings, did not seem to be surly, evasive, or a mad axe murderer. He could tell the time from a pre-digital clock and at least present himself as though he were not on drugs. Camp wasn't too much of a drawback these days, but it did rather seem sometimes that he was putting it on as an act. And wasn't that Hermione Slinger she saw hanging about outside on that anti-social vehicle of hers?

The careers tutor at college, female, had told him he needed to 'bring some substantive expertise to the table', but when he asked her to translate, had just said 'Negativity will get you nowhere,' suggested golden curls did not seem sufficiently businesslike, and called the next student in. The trouble was, Tyler supposed, he had left college with no 'substantive expertise'.

His mother had said college would be a waste of time, and it was beginning to seem as if she might have been right. Back then it had seemed desperately necessary to Tyler to get to university. Nicci, though, had cut off relations with the missing Mr Romeo Bronze God Finch whom she at least acknowledged had fathered the boy – which left Tyler with no one to sign his student loan form. Nicci refused. Too expensive. Hermione Slinger had offered to forge Nicci's signature but fortunately Mr 'Anonymous Benefactor' had stepped in and paid up front, three whole years at £6,000. Now Tyler wondered if it had been all that fortunate.

42

The She Devil Doesn't Like To Make Mistakes

This time she thinks she might have made one.

Another afternoon is becoming too much for me. I tell Valerie Valeria that I am going to my room to take a power nap. I leave her to get on with the party preparations, and I remind her we are only inviting women. She must find a way to un-invite Tom Brightlingsea, he of De-Gender Now, awkward though it may be, or I'll have her guts for garters. Men are men and women are women and that's a fact of life. Once it was proved for women by the monthly pain in one's guts, but of course no more for me. I have to remember what it was like, and these days girls can get pills to bring on a false menopause so they can get on with their lives as men. I daresay Valerie has done just that.

The girl took a subsidiary module in Event Management alongside Feminism in Development during her time at Sydney, but now it turns out she has never organised a big party and doesn't understand what is required, or what can go wrong. However, it is too late now and partly my fault for being so inattentive. I have to acknowledge that it's thanks to Valerie that parity is no longer seen as a boring side issue in feminist discussion – and since our alliance with Mumsnet was agreed – narrowly, I may say, and I was against it – our overall agenda is changing.

If the IGP is now seen as the one crucial mover and shaker by all those involved with rights for women, then good. But the chorus of approval now seems to include male voices – baritones as well as tenors and counter tenors – and this is not so good. I'm beginning to have niggling doubts about my wisdom in bringing Valerie Valeria on board, and declaring myself her mentor. 'New blood,' I'd cried. 'New blood at all costs! We're all so old.' I'd forgotten quite how ignorant the young can be. At the next meeting of the Board it's perfectly possible that Valerie will be elected a member of the Advisory Committee and if that works out she might even end up one of the trustees.

The wind's blowing up. I can hear it even down here in 1HT/2. The light dims and then recovers. Another lightning strike? Black clouds will be massing. A storm is brewing. With any luck it will be like this on my birthday, only colder, and the procession will have to be cancelled. The party will just have to be indoors. Good.

43

A Strange Enchantment

Momus pulls the strings.

Yah-yah-de-yah-yah, w*ooo-h, wooo-h, wooo-h* over land and
sea. What a blow, in every sense of the word! My strength
is as the strength of ten because my heart is pure. Praise
be to Momus – I have fallen in love! It was destined. This
thing is stronger than the two of us. Our souls are as one.
One moment one is alone and sad – the next, love strikes
and the world changes. See, how love is eternal, outrunning
even death? Put that in your pipe and smoke it, Dame Ruth
Patchett, She Devil. I am in love with your grandson, Tyler
Fitch Patchett. And *cute*, is he *cute*! Forget your old Bobbo.
Wow!

There have been rumblings on Mount Olympus. Asclepius is
in decline and Momus, God of fabrication, has been throwing
his weight around; I reckon his eye has fallen on me and mine,
just as my eye has fallen on Tyler Fitch Patchett. Or I think
this must have been what happened. I go on circling round
the High Tower, but my mind, such as it is, this shy, fragile,
footling thing, keeps going back to the beautiful but troubled
Tyler Finch Patchett, perfection in mind as well as body, and
everything shifts and changes. I hear Nat King Cole singing

Nature Boy, telling me that wisdom lies in understanding that you must love before you can be loved. Is this my happy end, is my release from purgatory at last in sight? But the song ends unhappily! Is this love to be unrequited? Oh please no, Momus. Please not unrequited again. No, impossible. Only believe: '*Love is an ever fix'd mark that looks on tempests and is never shaken*'.

By 'troubled' I mean that Tyler takes more drink and drugs than friends and family think advisable, and by 'beautiful', that he looks rather like the young David Bowie, in his blonde hair, smoky-eyed phase – though alas without the latter's musical ability or gift for making money. But to be young and beautiful is a great advantage for either gender, however hopeless on the guitar, or with no apparent source of income. If you are familiar with the Tarot pack, see Tyler as the Fool, blithely stepping into the unknown as the sun shines on, blithely unaware of the precipice below.

It was in Momus' script that I should first encounter Tyler down at the shop in the village, where in poltergeist mode (I am allowed these few pleasures) I had been spilling lentils and squashing blowflies to annoy Mrs Easton who runs the place, and there was Tyler, sweeping up in the store, busy but unpaid in his obligatory 'voluntary' community work! Oh the darling, strange, enchanted boy!

44

What Valerie Doesn't Know

And the She Devil does. There are no safe spaces.

But the rate of acceptances had been excellent, thought Valerie. What was the She Devil complaining about? 60 per cent yes, 30 per cent no, 4 per cent will-if-I-can, and 6 per cent had presumably thrown the card and brochure in the bin, should they have one. Many of the institutions and individuals contacted ran paper-free offices so there were no bins. If she'd been able to get the invites out earlier, the take-up rate would have been better still. The She Devil had insisted on using snailmail instead of just pinging the things over electronically, but since she forgot everything anyway Valerie had gone ahead with email for most and left cards for those few who were not familiar with computers. More sensible, surely, to make a list of those few who did not use computers, and reserve the old letterbox method of communication for them. Postage was so expensive! It was extraordinary what the old chose to waste their money on to no apparent purpose. They'd use landlines instead of texting. She did not understand the reluctance of patrons to communicate by phone with some disagreeable person who might batter their eardrums. Texting was safer and somehow nicer. And the party bag offer had worked a treat, in spite of the She Devil's fury.

But it was a really good result: the new brochure had worked well; 15 per cent had actually upped their contributions and only 2 per cent had cancelled, possibly reacting to the imagery of the tempest-ridden High Tower now perhaps more obviously phallic than before. There was a fine line to be drawn between what was subliminally suggestive, and what was a turn-off – as some found the bursting spray of the popped champagne bottle held at crotch level by Grand Prix winners. If the new logo was on the right side of that line for all but 2 per cent, this was success indeed. The Women's Widdershins Walk at the High Tower had managed to slip into the text and was not just going viral online but being entered in a whole lot of diaries. Which was what counted.

Sometimes Valerie felt she had crossed the world only to find herself back with her complaining mother, or at least with a version of her, and that she was doomed.

45

If Only One Had Substance!

Wooo-h, wooo-h, wooo-h, and only the occasional wheee-h.

'*Somethingsomethingsomething, on thy cold grey rocks, oh sea.*' It's poetry now, not old songs I hear. Words I learned as a child flutter round my head, '*portions and parcels of a dreadful past*', as Tennyson would have it. Fluttering like the baby in the womb when its new soul enters in, not that I would know anything about that having chosen not to have a baby myself. Anyway, flutter, flutter. Like '*birdie, birdie, cheep cheep*', or is it '*baby, baby, cheep cheep*'? It's no longer clear to me.

How did the Tennyson go? Primary school, Standard 6. '*And I would that my tongue could utter*' – oh indeed, would that I had a tongue! – '*the thoughts that arise in me.*' How does it go on? I try and make the connections, but fail. I have what I can only describe in my present state as the floppiest kind of mind. I have to catch these thoughts as they fly. Never any peace. '*O why, why must life all labour be?*' No, that's from *The Lotos-Eaters*. Other people's thoughts keep interfering. Bet that was Ms Bradshap, always moaning. No, I remember now, it's '*And the stately ships go on, To their haven under the hill, But O for the thoughts of a vanished mind and the sound of a voice that is still.*' Or something.

That's a shift: an improvement, a flash of good cheer, a break in the clouds, sunlight. *Wooo-h, wooo-h, wheee-h, wooo-h* round the High Tower.

Back to work.

46

Nature Knows Best

Tyler's eye and Tyler's I look in both directions.

Tyler's wall eye had blighted his childhood, as had his mother's refusal to have it 'seen to'. She believed that surgical intervention only ever made matters worse, except when it came to terminating pregnancies or getting thin, when it was a different matter: a belief in which Matilda Eavens the therapist encouraged her.

'Interfere with a wall eye and you'll get an unsighted eye,' Matilda would say. 'Nature knows best.' She also saw fecundity as sacred, in which understanding she was very much at odds with her Nicci. Matilda was a vegetarian and wore long full skirts and also had two daughters – but of the serious academic kind. She had a large and welcoming bosom and would have made two of Nicci, who after her gastric band surgery had given up dungarees and Dr Martens boots and taken to white blouses and tight black skirts and kitten heels. But Matilda was a good feminist, if rather of the blood-and-soil kind, and the whole family, Nicci, Madison, Mason and little Tyler, went along to family therapy once a week, no matter how the youngsters complained.

Nicci liked to refer to her son as Cyclops and the childcare and school authorities took to using it too, not unkindly, thus identifying the child and his disability in one go. When Tyler got to sixteen he applied for NHS surgery off his own bat, a procedure for which permission was granted, but not before quite a time had to be spent on legal discussions about parental rights versus the rights of minors. After the procedure life took a turn for the better, if only because Tyler could look others in the eye at last. The girls took to calling him 'The Experiment' instead of Cyclops, which was something. Nicci, affronted, did not speak to Tyler for months, not that she was home much to do it anyway. The battle between Pro-Lifers and Right to Choosers was savage and ongoing. 'I can't see why Mum complains so about our grandmother,' said Mason to Matilda once. 'We hardly see Mum from one week to the other. Isn't she an abandoning narcissistic mother too?'

'That's quite different,' said Matilda, but didn't explain why.

When Tyler began to display male traits like smelly feet, clumsy elbows and knees, general knobbliness, a squawky voice, a love of football and making models he was banned from the therapy group for a while. His sisters began to look at him with disdain: they jeered at him on Facebook, laughed at him on Twitter, sexted his rapidly growing parts to their Friends (they had few real friends, he noticed, but did not remark upon the fact, being a kind and generous lad, brimming with empathy and loving them in spite of all). He endured all slights. He could understand why the twins had never wanted a brother, Nicci's maternal love being in such short supply. And they were not, frankly, very bright. He only wished his parts were more impressive: criticism of them seemed endemic.

Even though he was never bullied at school – too cheerful and well disposed towards others to present himself as any kind of victim, and, with his eye eventually 'seen to', quite impressively good-looking – Tyler suffered from fits of quite unreasonable anxiety. Currently it was because Hermione had suggested he lacked finesse in sexual matters, and he had rather assumed finesse was his compensating strength. He had always felt at a disadvantage amongst his randier, more brutish if better-hung friends. If during the drive home to Sylvan Lodge he seemed withdrawn and quiet – which Hermione took to be jealousy on account of her visiting friend but was not – it was because he did not feel one bit like chattering. He was anxious and offended.

47

Matilda Eavens Has An Explanation...

...about the Finch Patchett family.

So where was I? Oh yes, Tyler. Nicci didn't breastfeed, of course. The nursery fed him on formula in his early days, by means of plastic bottles warmed in the microwave, thus pouring into his little body a large dose of phthalates, the chemical in plastic which, imitating oestrogen, affects male reproductive development, sperm quality and male hormone levels. Phthalate absorption in youth doesn't make men gay but does make them a little finer-boned, a little less bearded; a little more emotionally sensitive, shall we say, more metrosexual, than they otherwise would be. The rural male is these days different from the city male – the wide open spaces breed men, 'real men' – but a plastic feeding bottle can turn the one into the other, from a boy who longs to run round bashing other boys and playing with guns, to one who likes trying on his mother's jewellery.

Not that Nicci had much jewellery, she being an old-fashioned feminist, and eschewing personal adornment or anything that could be taken as an attempt to please the male. A string of amber beads, an heirloom from Brenda, her paternal grandmother, was pretty much all she had. Brenda had preferred to live in a hotel than a regular home. Perhaps dislike of housework runs in families. Certainly little Tyler had used the beads as a transitional comfort object, his baby hands clinging to them in desperation night and day.

It had not helped Tyler in his quest for masculinity that he had twin sisters to contend with. Madison and Mason, nine years older than he, had resented the advent of a little brother from the beginning. Tyler's father – Gabriel Finch, the actor/plumber/Bronze God – had been the twins' stepfather for a couple of years, in which time they had been taught by their mother to despise him as a muscle-bound despot. The girls had little enough attention from their working mother as it was. She simply hadn't had the time to give it to them: her career – the State having declared a job should be thus described and be seen as the pinnacle of female achievement – absorbed all her energies. Breakfast standing up, a frozen TV dinner on the sofa and each other's company was the best her children, Madison, Mason and little Tyler, had of family life. Mason, aged seven, was to snarkily refer to her mother as 'our night-time babysitter'.

The twins had loved and hated Tyler all his life. Like their mother, they would have welcomed a baby girl, but a brother was a different kettle of fish. When he was a baby they played with his little willy, shrieking with pleasure when it reached into the air and sprayed its pee. Madison attempted to give him a blow job when he was five – a disappointing experience for everyone. The two of them admiring him dressed up in his mother's white shirts, black skirts and kitten heels; having him change into their cast-offs when he was home from school. Tyler did not object. He loved the feel of silks and satins against his skin, the sensation somehow warding off the pins and pricks of outrageous fortune – the way everyone called him Cyclops, when surely he had two eyes not one, even though they stared in different directions, and the liberties the girls took with his willy: why did it seem to them such an object of mirth?

His sisters, meanwhile, grew up to be lost to social media, earnest reality-telly fans, were great party-goers but no great shakes at school. They annoyed their mother by keeping their rooms in such a jumble of cosmetics, scents, discarded clothes and soft toys that she could hardly bear to go into them. The twins were strong-willed – so much so that, running to fat in their early years, both girls followed their mother in having gastric bands installed when they were sixteen, and after that moles removed and noses fixed, eyelids raised, lips plumped and so on.

Their own natural father, a property developer trying to hide their existence from his wife, paid up.

Like grandmother, one might suppose, like granddaughters. But the girls had been trained to hate and despise the She Devil as the one who had blighted their mother's life, and by extension theirs, the source of all ills – the abandoning narcissistic mother which I, Matilda Eavens, their family therapist, have so well described in my various books as the 'loathsome-she-devil archetype'.

48

Poor Nicci, Deprived Of A Mother's Love

So she takes comfort where she can.

Wooo-h, wooo-h, wooo-h! It's Mary again. Nicci has never had anyone important to her die – though she complained like mad to Matilda her therapist in the weekly sessions that her mother had murdered her guinea pig when she'd burned down the family home in suburban Nightbird Drive. Perhaps that's why she can so easily shrug off her She Devil mother. But how can you wipe a mother out of your life? How can she make someone not exist who does exist? It baffles me. And someone as real and powerful as her mother Ruth. I suppose Nicci can't risk meeting the real, living, suffering mother she has. Nicci is determined to be the only one who's suffering. She feels she has to wreak damage on those around her, jabbing with sharp elbows wherever she goes. She lacked a mother's love herself, so why should her son fare any better?

'O, well for the fisherman's boy, that he shouts with his sister at play! O, well for the sailor lad, that he sings in his boat on the bay' – all that. Tennyson cheers me up. If the 'O wells' of the past have morphed into 'O, well for the gastric band', so be it. If Nicci and her daughters Madison and Mason (names of non-specific gender, carefully chosen) can skip around instead of lumbering

around, good for them. All three have had gastric bands, of course they have. Like mother, like daughters. I would define them as selfie slim, not spiritually slim: it's not something that involves sacrifice. In my novels the slim girl always got the prize – that is to say, the man – nor was much attention paid to diets other than to get into the wedding dress. But that's romance for you. *'But O for the touch of a vanished hand, and the sound of a voice that is still.'* Such agreeable melancholy!

Both the girls have sharp elbows too, I fear. But then they too have no acquaintance with death, which might yet soften them. I hope so. Tyler is about to lose his grandfather, I think, pretty soon, if the cry of the seagulls is anything to go by. They have fallen rather silent. *Timor mortis conturbat* a whole lot of creatures, not just *'me'*. Asclepius will lose his power and then perhaps, Momus willing, I will be set free.

Poor Nicci always found Tyler too hot to handle. Too hopelessly beautiful from the beginning for her to compete with, and win. She made the most of the wall eye but it wasn't enough. She just didn't want him in her life, a constant reminder of every disappointment she'd ever had – more like her own mother than she cared to admit.

'The tender grace of a day that is dead, will never come back to me.' Oh the grief of it! If only I had eyes I would have tears in them. I'd weep for Nicci and the girls if only because no one else ever will.

Perhaps the twins will visit their natural father Billy Didcot in his nursing home? He hasn't long to go, either. He's the one who owns the house they live in, paid for their surgery, will leave them his fortune – what guilt will do for a man! He's had a stroke and his wife has died. But the twins don't know who he is and Nicci has never told them. She wanted them to be immaculately conceived births. She just didn't like men – though I think her quarrels have been more with women than with men. But it's so easy to get things wrong.

I remember now how that Tennyson line goes: '*Break, break, break on thy cold grey stones, O sea.*' So many broken hearts, let alone broken lives. If only one had substance, what a river one would cry, and even raise the sea level around the High Tower: not global warming doing it, but the tears of men and women lamenting lost love.

49

Valerie Valeria's Eye Falls On Tyler

He will be useful to her...

Ms Laura tottered into 2CC/12 where Valerie preferred to work these days – the second floor being less exposed to spray from breaking waves than the ground floor. When the tide was high rivulets of seawater would run down the window forming strange Rorschach inkblot shapes as they ran, leaving a salty crust behind. Was that her mother's face? The man who assaulted her when she was seven? Could that be her cat, Joey with head lowered, tail raised? She was probably imagining it all, and it was highly unlikely that ghosts could tap your memories so effectively, but the fact remained that offices on the second floor had a much better atmosphere than ones on the ground floor.

'And when I said that was because they kept sending us young men she told me to put my request in an email and put the phone down on me before I'd had an opportunity to say I didn't use email.' Ms Laura was lamenting to Valerie that it was already mid-December, and she had failed to get sufficient temporary catering staff for the event on the 21st. The Jobcentre Plus in Shapnett hadn't been in the least bit helpful, and were even rather rude, claiming the IGP had turned down too many of their applicants.

Valerie, who thought it wise to keep Ms Laura onside, merely suggested that she should try putting a card up in the St Rumbold's shop. It was sometimes sensible to side-step bureaucracy. Ms Laura said her legs didn't allow for traipsing down there.

Ms Laura was one of seven trustees on the IGP's Board of Governors. Well, eight, if you included Bobbo. Valerie already had Ms Bradshap onside, also Ellen the photographer and Ms Swithin the accountant; Ms Laura, she suspected, remained undecided in her loyalty. Before long, Valerie reckoned, the Board would realise – or with any luck the Charity Commissioners would point out – that they could do with an injection of youth and energy. A majority vote would be required. If the vote were to split, the She Devil would have the casting vote. Valerie, who saw running the IGP as a useful career step towards a high position at, say, Amnesty or even the WHO, very much needed Ms Laura on her side.

Valerie said she'd run down with a card to the village store herself. Ms Laura said she thought it was about to rain. Valerie, missing sun-soaked Australia, said, 'Whenever is it not?', and the two women laughed companionably as though half a century of difference in their ages was as nothing. They made out the card together. Valerie suggested saying 'minimum wage plus 10 per cent', Ms Laura said that was setting a dangerous precedent, and Valerie prudently conceded.

50

Opportunity Knocks

Valerie falls – if not in love, at least in lust.

The village of St Rumbold's wasn't far down the road and Valerie had been glad of the excuse to get out of the office and deliver Ms Laura's card to the little shop. The wind had dropped as soon as Valerie was out of the shadow of the High Tower; the wintry sun shone out of a clear blue sky, frosted branches sparkled and seagulls soared above. It was a beautiful day. Valerie realised she did not get out enough. The company of the old could be debilitating. She admired her hands as she walked. Small, firm, white, perfectly polished nails, colour-matched to her lipstick – Estée Lauder Defiant Coral – not a liver spot to be seen; such a relief after the old withered hands she had lately become accustomed to working alongside. She carried the appointments-vacant card carefully, as though it were a missive from the Gods.

Elated by a sudden happiness, she did a little skip and a jump of pleasure. The world was her oyster. Bad things were safely in the past. Her mother's suicide when Valerie was sixteen, the oh-so-painful split with her adored and apparently adoring Charlotte in Sydney (the split the reason why she had applied for this any-old job in the first place) were all fading into the past very satisfactorily. Another hop and a skip, and she was dancing along this deserted road and a song going through her mind. '*Chirpy Chirpy Cheep Cheep!*' Her mother's favourite song. The kind which once it landed in your head you couldn't get rid of for days.

Valerie Valeria was the little bird who'd lost her momma. That was what had happened. She had woken up one morning and her mother was gone, not a word of warning, *gone*, not just far, far away but further than anyone could ever reach. Roselle Valeria had hanged herself, on the spurious grounds that her husband, Valerie's father, had left her for a younger model. And here her daughter was, dancing to the vulgarest of tunes (an absurdly cheerful one if you considered the lyrics) and chirpy-cheeping in the road. But somehow Valerie couldn't help it. There was another song, the Beatles' '*Why Don't We Do It in the Road?*', very rude too, lurking around somewhere, interfering, but not nearly so good a tune.

Though at least the urge to dance faded, this quite unreasonable sense of elation remained when she reached the store. The old biddy stuck the card on her notice board with a smile. As she turned to go, Valerie caught sight of a young man working between the stacks: elation and good cheer took a quantum leap into something greater.

It wasn't so much love at first sight, as lust at first sight. Odd, because this normally happened for Valerie with girls, not boys. But this particular boy – early twenties, she reckoned, with the face and physique of Adonis – was something different, special. And he looked so perfectly alert and intelligent as well: most males discovered sweeping shop floors tended to look sullen and discontented. Intelligence did matter to Valerie, as wasn't the case with so many of her friends, who liked to virtue-signal non-élitism. Where had this paragon of delight been all her life? Valerie had been practising celibacy lately, and she had to acknowledge that her senses were probably sharpened as a result. Or did she recognise him from Facebook?

'Who is the young man?' she asked the old biddy.

'Pretty boy, isn't he?' she replied, and she told Valerie he was Tyler Finch Patchett slumming it, and was the unemployed grandson of the She Devil who had family in these parts, not that any of them spoke to one another, or perhaps Lady Patchett would see fit to find him a proper job – everyone should pull together in these hard times.

So this was Tyler in the flesh, and she was right! He would look so, so good heading a Widdershins Walk! Young and virile and full of hope. He was the future! She would not give up. And if she could get him up to the High Tower she could get to know him better, and who knew what would happen next.

A sudden gust of cold wind whipped round her ankles. Valerie was struck by so unaccountable, unexpected and unfamiliar an attack of shyness she fled from the shop, telling herself that at least now she had a real face to a real name it would be safer to go through Facebook.

51

At Last! A Close Encounter For Tyler And Valerie

Since Mary Fisher – dead or alive – just cannot leave well alone.

Mrs Easton is the widow who runs the village shop in St Rumbold's and runs it very well indeed, thank you. It is far from posh but it is serviceable if you have little money to spare, and few in the village do. Mrs Easton is pleasant, helpful and always good for a chat. But she is old, old; the kind who writes handwritten letters and makes out shopping lists, takes statins and has no idea what social media is, let alone a hashtag. Old, old. She is the kind the young most despise. She has a landline for a phone and has no computer. Algorithms do not apply. It is a marvel her kind survives at all.

But Tyler is not like most of the young: he likes the old and overlooked, being young and overlooked himself, and they like him. He does what he can to assist Mrs Easton, sweeping up lentils from the cracks between her floorboards because her back hurts when she bends.

Besides, needs must when the Devil drives, and Tyler does not want to be sanctioned by Miss Swanson at the Jobcentre Plus.

His undertaking of voluntary work in the community helps his status as an active jobseeker, not a scrounger.

How the lentils, little pinkey-orangey things, come to be on the floor so often is a mystery; rats, people suppose, gnawing away, little teeth biting through plastic, though they leave no other traces, and the packets seem to be still untouched upon the shelves. Mrs Easton has rung the council in Lewes, and they have sent in the rat catcher but no rats were caught.

Mrs Easton may be seventy-three, but she does her best to keep the store ship-shape and clean and ready for inspection, fighting an ongoing battle with the forces of entropy – demonstrated only too forcefully by the occasional plague of bluebottle flies, let alone the ongoing scouring effect of the sand and sea-spray mix which nightly beats upon her shopfront. She likes to be professional, feeling that the health and wellbeing of her clientele is her responsibility. Hers is the only shop left in the village – all the others have long closed. Mrs Easton is fond of Tyler and grateful for his help. Old she may be, but she is a practical and cheering sight, wearing her kitten heels ('Widefit' from Marks & Spencer), smart white blouses and black skirts from the charity shops in Lewes – as it happens, Nicci's cast-offs.

Today Tyler sees a card in Mrs Easton's window advertising a job. It is handwritten and has the IGP logo on it, a phallic-looking tower with waves crashing around its foot. It goes: *'Part time work at the High Tower to trained catering staff over weekend of Dec 21st–23rd, £7.85 per hour (minimum living wage), no Sunday overtime'*, then a phone number and email address.

Well, it's not much, but it's better than nothing, certainly better than the food bank in Brighton, though Mrs Easton can usually be relied upon for the odd frozen chicken pie or bag of sprouted potatoes.

'They're always desperate for extra catering staff up there,' Mrs Easton observes as Tyler puts his broom aside to enter the details in his phone. 'I can't think why they don't pay staff properly and be done with it. It's for some big do or other, "widershins walking", whatever that may be, lots of bigwigs staying. Anyone who's anyone is coming; though I doubt it myself, far too near Christmas, people will be wrapping presents.'

Mrs Easton warned Valerie about it being too near Christmas for take-up but Valerie had just laughed and said the people she was after had minions to do their Christmas shopping, they just did the partying.

'I despair,' says Mrs Easton. 'People today!' At which a stack of Jaffa Cakes slowly and graciously collapses like a tower being demolished and the packs lie scattered on the floor.

'Now how did that happen?' asks Mrs Easton. 'Did you catch it with your elbow?'

'Not that I noticed,' says Tyler.

'You must have,' says Mrs Easton firmly.

'That young Valerie brought the card in herself just now,' says Mrs Easton. 'Bright red lipstick and legs up to her armpits. I reckon she was glad to get out. Everyone so old and serious, and the electrics gone again, probably.'

'I didn't see her,' says Tyler, as he sets about re-erecting the display. He really likes the sound of Valerie with her bright red lips and legs up to her armpits and asks if she's likely to be calling in again. Perhaps he'd better go and see her – sometimes you get a good response from a potential employer if you turn up in person, as Miss Swanson at the Jobcentre Plus never tires of telling him. Mrs Easton says there is no point in Tyler applying since the High Tower only takes on girls – the IGP being some kind of feminist charity. Tyler literally stamps his foot in frustration and rage and the Persil display trembles and loses its crown.

'That is totally unfair and probably illegal because of the new equality laws,' says Tyler.

Mrs Easton says that since the card asks for catering staff without mentioning gender the High Tower is acting within the regulations. In practice it just so happens that they take on only females. She watches in dismay as Tyler's face grows hot, flushed and swollen; his lip quivers in an apparent fit of despair, hurt and bewilderment mixed. He wipes his knuckles across his eyes and they come away wet with tears. It's some kind of moment of truth. He is usually so cheerful and even-tempered. Mrs Easton is shocked. She takes him into her back room and gives him a bottle of Coca-Cola from stock. He calms down and apologises.

'I'm sorry,' he says. 'It's just every move I make, ever since I began, girls get there first. I'm a second-class citizen.'

'Well,' says Mrs Easton, briskly, 'Buggins' turn for men now, I daresay?'

There's a noise from the shop. When they go back in to investigate they find the whole tower of Persil boxes has fallen to the floor. A sudden gust of wind is rattling the shop windows so hard that the panes are threatening to crack and break.

52

Sudden Gusts! Sudden Gusts!

Practice makes perfect.

Wooo-h, wooo-h! Sudden gusts are easy to do, but I'm aiming for more subtlety: better temperature control and so on. It's rather like learning to whistle – I never knew quite how one did it – or learning to waggle one's little toe independently of the others.

I'm managing to control the muscles of my non-existent mouth better all the time: pursed, tiny and ladylike for the sudden icy gusts, medium wide for a steady blow and wide as wide for the angry shout of a good storm. I can think of obscene analogies but I won't go into them.

When that foolish girl does her Widdershins Walk (she's such a doll, that Valerie, suggestible as anything) I'll have to make sure she doesn't get much fun out of my Tyler. Premature ejaculation will serve them both right. I shall try stirring a mini whirlwind and sweep the whole lot of them out of the way and into the sky. Though I probably won't: they're all so sensible, well-intentioned and politically-correct it would seem a pity. On the other hand, groups of people sceptical about ghosts disconcert me and diminish my powers no end.

But Widdershins is just not a good idea. It has always been known to be baneful. Momus won't like it. Though he does like events, things that happen: such as old Bobbo dying. Bobbo hasn't got long, but is that nature or is it Dr Simmins? God knows what she puts in her syringes.

53

Can This Be True Love?

Or is it Mary Fisher meddling again?

Valerie had come down to the village with no other idea in her mind than to walk straight back to the High Tower once she'd delivered the card. But she was so overcome by emotion after seeing Tyler that she went instead into St Rumbold's church to recover. She lit a candle for her mother. The church grew suddenly cold and windy. Once she was outside the weather took such another turn for the worse that she was obliged to take shelter back in the village shop.

Perhaps she just wanted to take another look at Tyler to see if he was real? He was. He was behind the counter now. He smiled at her with his kind and understanding soft blue eyes. He was flushed and pink around the eyelids. He even gave a little sniff. He'd been crying. Resistance melted away. She had vowed never to have anything to do with men again, crude penetrative creatures, but perhaps this one was different. He was capable of tears: he was vulnerable, like a girl, full of feeling, had anima as well as animus. Was his left cheek swollen: did he perhaps have toothache, poor thing? It marred the perfect symmetry of his face.

Now where did that phrase come from? Of course. School. *'Tyler, Tyler, burning bright, in the forests of the night, what immortal hand or eye could frame thy fearful symmetry?'* Or something. Wasn't there something else about a lamb and the tiger lying down together? She could see the temptation.

'You again?' said Mrs Easton, out of nowhere.

'I was just going to say,' said Valerie, flustered, 'about the card. We're really desperate up at the High Tower. If a man applied I daresay we wouldn't say no. I've never agreed with their policy – it's just the others.'

'Ah yes, those others,' said Mrs Easton, who was not so dim as she appeared, and this flustered Valerie even more. She was not used to fluster. The world usually advanced in orderly footsteps instead of rushing at her with new experiences. She had become too accustomed to life in the High Tower. She must get out more. Look what happened when you did. Tyler.

Ambition was all very well and sacrifices must be made in pursuit of the new true feminism. The She Devil must be toppled from her perch and she, Valerie Valeria, was the one to do it. All that. And everyone knew that any girl who wanted to get to the top had to avoid babies at all cost – but surely, just occasionally? There was always the morning-after pill, though she'd have to go in to Lewes to get it.

'Do you hear that, Tyler?' asked Mrs Easton. 'Men allowed. Reason has at last prevailed. Hope for the world yet. Time and a half, too.'

'No thanks,' said Tyler, and apologetically to Valerie, 'Family reasons. And it's no fun being the odd man out amongst a whole lot of women.'

'Tyler doesn't think much of her Ladyship up in the High Tower,' said Mrs Easton. 'She being a Patchett and his estranged granny. But like a lot of families round here they don't get on too well.' 'That's putting it mildly,' said Tyler, who seemed almost as besotted by Valerie as she by him.

He stared at her as one entranced. His tongue was loosened. He explained the family relationship to Valerie, his mother's suffering at the hands of a narcissistic mother, the villainous She Devil. Valerie said she worked for Tyler's grandmother and understood only too well how Tyler's mother must have suffered by illogicality and unreason. The She Devil kept on changing her tune and double-binding about a simple thing like a Widdershins Day. Valerie's own mother had killed herself: apparently a suicidal impulse was strong in the narcissistic parent – 'Look at me, me, me,' they cried.

Chirpy Chirpy Cheep Cheep. Did Valerie think that, or did she sing it? Perhaps she too had a narcissistic mother? Perhaps that was why she and Tyler had this bond? Both seemed to feel it. The bond. The greater than you feeling. Tyler was six inches taller than she was. She could lay her head upon his manly chest. She did. She felt protected. He felt protective. She needed him. He needed her. It was oh, so all sorts of *lovely.*

Mrs Easton, thinking that they must be on some kind of drug, but glad that they seemed to get on (at least this one made a change from Hermione, was smart and clean and not a goth), retreated to her room to do the books.

A passing lorry (it must have been) shook the ground so a whole cascade of corned beef fell to the ground: two blonde curly heads touched as they bent together to pick them up, and a kind of electric shock of recognition ran through them both. Before they had time to consider the folly of their ways, both were rolling about on the floor in intimate congress – a plug, to put it bluntly, looking for a socket and finding it. But the fusion did not last long, and Tyler, whose problem this happened to be, felt he had betrayed himself. Had let himself and her down. For her part, Valerie remembered how little penetration had to do with satisfaction and was glad enough when they were both back on their feet and adjusting their clothing.

'I'm really sorry,' said Tyler. Valerie was not quite sure what he was apologising for, for being too quick or that it had happened at all, but it seemed an appropriate thing for Tyler to say.
'That's okay,' said Valerie, generously. But the incident was so out of expectation or character the memory of it seemed to have no lasting hold on her mind. No one likes their vision of themselves overturned and Valerie had assumed she was a rational and self-interested person.
'Remember the job's open,' she did say, as she strode out. She walked like a man, he thought, long, firm, steps. 'Contact Ms Laura up at the High Tower if you're interested.'

Tyler thought about it and decided he wasn't. It might get to be even worse a prospect than the Brighton Beaux Agency. And he'd better not tell Hermione. They had an open relationship so she could hardly complain. Even so...

Mrs Easton came out of her office and asked why there were

corned beef tins rolling about on the floor. Tyler explained that a passing tractor must have shaken the shelves.

'I didn't hear a tractor,' said Mrs Easton.

54

Be Afeared Of The Ghost Of Mary Fisher

Dread mistress of the unforeseen.

I did that! Tee-hee-hee!

Makes a change from all that *wooo-h, wooo-h, wooo-h*ing round
the High Tower, or even the very occasional *wheee-wheee*ing.

And a chirpy chirpy cheep cheep to all my readers!

55

Valerie Just So Happens To Run Into
Dr Simmins

Or is it Dr Simmins running into Valerie?

Dr Simmins happened to run into Valerie in 3HT/2 and they had a little chat. Dr Simmins warned Valerie that Bobbo did not have long to go. He might hang on a week, a month, no longer. He'd be lucky to see Christmas out.

'Shit,' said Valerie, 'but thanks for telling me. If he pegs out I might have to cancel Widdershins out of respect for the dead.'

3HT/2 was the room used for visiting MPs, sponsors, journalists and so on, with its really spectacular view out to the open sea on fine days; though recently these did seem in short supply. But everyone agreed there was such a thing as climate change. It was to be expected. There were no change deniers in the IGP except possibly the She Devil herself, who tended to blame the sun rather than people, should things be hotting up. The sun was rather large, people rather small. It was not a view that won her much sympathy on the Board or the Committees.

Valerie and Dr Simmins were treating themselves from the drinks cupboard. Each assumed the other was lesbian but neither cared to pursue the matter. Both needed to recover,

Dr Simmins from a recent visit to Bobbo, Valerie from a session with a particularly tetchy She Devil.

'Respect!' said Dr Simmins. 'What respect? The sooner he's dead and gone and I'm saved that walk upstairs the better.'

'Not that I'd mind all that much if I had to cancel,' said Valerie. The actual event was already a PR success, and was proving more trouble than she had anticipated. She had left it to Ms Laura, who'd been helping out Ms Bradshap, to organise catering staff for the 21st. Ms Laura, nearly eighty, was in the early stages of Alzheimer's, a sweet old thing if not at the best of times the sharpest knife in the box, and had only managed to raise ten agency staff. Valerie reckoned she needed at least twenty extra for a party of a hundred and fifty who expected drinks, canapés, hot sausages cooked on the spot under canvas and a buffet lunch indoors. Umbrellas, blankets and rugs would have to be hired – the She Devil had been right: the forecast was none too good – and awnings to cover the outside would have to be hired from a firm chosen by Ms Laura – an all-girl bakers called Luxuriette who were now doing events and parties and were bound to get it wrong, having diversified too fast for their own good.

Valerie had been outside to check that a circuit right round the High Tower was feasible and thank the Gods it was. Just a few steps down to sea level would need to be created (it wasn't only the She Devil, but so many of the guests who were elderly and not too steady on their feet) but out of solid rock and apparently there'd need to be a hand rail too. She was on a tight budget, and all-female firms who handled heavy machinery and were prepared to do anything at short notice and at a low cost were in short supply.

She seldom picked off more than she could chew, but she had a terrible feeling that this time she might have. She felt stressed. Perhaps she was suffering from bipolar syndrome, and not quite in control of herself? She felt afflicted by emotions, rather than just having them. And sometimes she felt elated for no reason. The strange business with Tyler down at the village shop; so out of character! He hadn't applied for the job. She'd rather thought he would.

Valerie confessed that things were getting her down rather and Dr Simmins said she could come by for tranquillisers if ever she wanted them.

'I daresay,' Dr Simmins said, 'it would suit you rather well if Mr Patchett shuffled off his mortal coil around the week before Christmas.'

'I suppose it would,' Valerie said, laughing merrily. 'I do so hate things going wrong. Better if they don't happen at all.'

'Wretched old man,' said Dr Simmins. 'One less useless soul on the earth. But one mustn't forget one's Hippocratic oath.'

'That old thing!' said Valerie. '*I swear by Apollo and by Asclepius* and so forth – rather outdated, don't you think?'

There was a sudden flash of lightning that almost blinded them. The ground even shook a little. They waited for the thunder but it didn't come.

'Femina Electrical,' said Valerie, 'seem to create lightning bolts out of thin air. I don't know why the Diabolissima puts such trust in that dreadful firm.'

'Diabolissima!' repeated Dr Simmins. 'Not Diavolessa. That's really good!'

56

Depression Is Just Postponed Anger

Mary Fisher faces her demons – better late than never.

No *wooo-h, wooo-h, wooo-h*s this time. I'm so angry I could scream, but I took charge of myself in time and brought the wind back under control. Sometimes I think I *am* the wind. I almost broke the windows of the village shop in my temper. One must be careful not to blame the wrong people. Mrs Easton is a fool of a woman, says stupid things and is very annoying but she is well-intentioned, and my anger needs to be reserved for the She Devil.

It is the She Devil's fault that generations of women feel free to so denigrate men. Women are ungrateful. Men are glorious creatures, designed by nature to look after women, support them and their children, guide and advise. Though I have to admit, in his time Bobbo rather failed in his advisory role. Women are so wishy-washy in their multi-tasking, they never get anything of importance done. I hate to see Tyler sweeping up: cleaning is for women and servants to make the place nice for men. That loud-mouthed sadistic bitch Elaine Swanson has reduced my love to this. She will be punished.

I must say that recently I have begun to feel stronger, more conscious of being 'myself'. My leeway for independent action is less limited than it was. While once I was confined to making *wooo-h-wooo-h*-ing noises round the High Tower, crashing the odd wave against a window and sending the occasional bird to its death, I can now venture abroad and make my presence felt.

I put it down to my love for Tyler, but then I would, wouldn't I? I do so *love* being in love. The eye brightens, the step quickens, the very skin glows; the God approaches: rationality is for the birds; ah, the languorous, drowsy succumbing. A whole life changes within the day. If only I had substance. Girls nowadays have no idea. For them a vibrator will do as well as the real thing. And it's safer. Just as a Facebook friend is safer than a real one. Their Gods have feet of clay. And for this, rightly or wrongly, I blame the She Devil, an angry, spiteful woman who turned my Bobbo against me. Now she has distressed my darling, my delight, my Tyler! She has brought tears to his precious eyes. The tides of battle swing to and fro. She will not win this one.

But these are not even 'my' thoughts. They hover in the air about me. It's the great plotter who sends them, Momus, the puppet-master in the sky, forever looking for his story, searching for event. I am in the wind about me. I am the wind. I vanish and return, sometimes soft and gentle, zephyr-like. I reckon if I got to hurricane strength I could blow the High Tower itself away. Its structures are riddled with dry rot. Even I can smell it and my senses are nothing to write home about, Momus knows.

57

Valerie Ups The Game

Things are going well – perhaps too well?

'Diavolissima,' said Valerie Valeria, 'less than a week to go before the Widdershins Walk. Shall we go down and inspect the site? We've put in railed walkways over the tricky part so no one's going to get their feet wet. Amethyst Builders have done a splendid job. And it's a lovely day: it will be really good for you to get out and get some Vitamin D.'

And it was true. The sun was actually shining. Everything was going well in the preparations for the day. Valerie had found an all-female construction team, Amethyst Builders (who apart from an annoying determination to communicate by email rather than telephone, so both Ms Bradshap and Ms Laura had been of less use to Valerie than usual), and they had come up trumps with good ideas. Why try and carve through solid rock when you can build up above with wood? You could now walk round the whole Tower complex in about ten minutes – if ageing limbs allowed – and there would be frequent stops for speeches, the Feminista Singers and the Trans & Co. Brass Bandsters had promised to put in an appearance.

Contract staff numbers were up to scratch. Ms Bradshap had

even agreed to get outside caterers in to provide a more robust kind of food than she felt comfortable supplying. Valerie had called in the Luxuriette cooks. There would be cream and sugar a-plenty; meringues and hot chocolate would be served after the Walk (a once a year treat would surely do no one any real harm), and Shepherdess Pie, followed by a Peach Melba for the sit-down supper in the Castle Complex before departure. The She Devil wanted women – she would get women. This way the Widdershins Walk would not only be celebrated as an annual Women's Feast Day but be looked forward to worldwide. Valerie meant to go far. The High Tower today, UNESCO tomorrow.

Valerie had managed to hire two hundred umbrellas from Harrods Wedding Boutique to be delivered on the 20th should the three day weather forecast suggest rain or snow, but the long term forecast still looked hopeful. The High Tower kept five hundred blankets in-house anyway, along with other emergency relief stores, on behalf of the Coastal Community Foundation.

Everything had been prepared, everything was looking good, and had been since the rather extraordinary encounter with the She Devil's beautiful grandson. It had meant nothing, of course, but it had been exhilarating for some reason and the sun had shone ever since. Bobbo could die whenever he liked, and no skin off Valerie's nose. Dr Simmins must make her own choice about the ethics of the timing.

Yes, things were going well. The She Devil had even given up lamenting the split with her children, now she knew that Tyler existed. Valerie might yet persuade her that it would be a really good idea to process with Tyler on this auspicious day of the 21st of December, so as to declare a new alliance with the former enemy, man. Valerie was already preparing a press release: *Hand in hand at last – Patriarchy meets Matriarchy.* Or should it be the other way round? Valerie would somehow contrive a prior meeting between grandmother and grandson, and she, Valerie, would have a reason to see Tyler again soon. Perhaps the heretics were right and female sexuality, lesbianism, was a more moveable feast than male gayness.

'I take pills for Vitamin D,' said the She Devil. 'I do really prefer not to go outside if I can help it, especially not in winter. But I will trust your good judgement. I have agreed to walk. So walk I will, and even head the procession. If you tell me that walking widdershins will end up with a photo of me that won't make me look like a witch rather than a sage, so be it. I will do it once, not more than once. If I go outside now I will only catch cold and be ill on the twenty-first. Is that what you want?' It was a long speech. Her voice cracked and hoarsened as she spoke. She was old, old, old.

Valerie sighed but conceded. She said she had so wanted the She Devil to see the sheltered platform Amethyst Builders had made where sausages could be barbecued for the Widdershins Walk trail-blazers.
'*Sausages?* Ms Bradshap has allowed bought-in sausages?' The She Devil was incredulous.
'I had a word with her. And Luxuriette are doing the catering. Their motto? "*A treat now and then – and do it again!*" And this is once in a year.'

The She Devil nodded serenely; but it seemed to her that Valerie was gaining altogether too much power and influence with the Board. She must be on her guard.

'Tell you what,' said Valerie. 'I know where your grandson is to be found. Supposing we took the new Mercedes – nice and warm, and a really comfy ride – and took a look. You don't have to talk to him, just look at him. You might change your mind.'

'No thanks,' said the She Devil.

58

But What Is This?

Matters come to a head...

It was 2.15 in the morning when Tyler, a little lame from another round of wild sex with Hermione at her cottage – so they can't have been all that finesse-free, no matter what she claimed – walked up Echo Close towards his front door: so different from Hermione's, no worn stone step and bedraggled foliage, but a smooth maintenance-free concrete patio. All the lights in the house were ablaze, all the windows were flung open (someone was in a real temper) and '*Full Moon Mass*' by The Cnuts was blaring out into the road: Danish death metal. That would be Mason's doing – Madison preferred Lady Gaga.

Fortunately the other four houses in Echo Close, though under offer, were still empty. They all had a clone-like family resemblance, the best new-builds Endor Grove estate had to offer, with 'traditional brick, grey slate roofs, picture windows on the ground floor, flexible floor space, ample storage, low heat-loss water cylinders'. The sounds of screaming and hysterical sobbing merged with the sounds of the song, and it all seemed of a piece to Tyler, whose taste was trance music.

He had hoped to go peacefully and quietly to bed in a sleeping household; he stood hesitantly at the door. Then it was kicked open from the inside and his twin sisters burst out, first Madison, then Mason, manhandling a collection of cases and bags into the outside world and lining them up on the kerb. Someone else slammed the door as soon as all the bags were out of the house. Someone upstairs turned off the thrashing music in mid-song. Someone downstairs closed the windows and drew the curtains. Apparent normality returned to Echo Close.

Tyler thought it prudent to hide himself in the shadows until their taxi should come – presumably the twins were waiting for Uber; who else at this time of night? – but they caught sight of him and pulled him out into the lamplight. They were dressed alike, except Madison's pussy pelmet length fake fur coat was mauve and Mason's was pink. They shared the same aesthetic sense (or lack of it, as Hermione observed) but liked to distinguish themselves by colour. Madison's fishnets were green and Mason's blue: both had the same black hair in retro beehives. Those gastric bands distorted everything. They should never have done it – but their mother had done it first and swore by it: two girls with long thin legs and short ribby torsos, lean and hungry faces and bad tempers, necks too short and heads too big.

'Trust you, Cyclops,' said Madison. 'Spying again!'
'Loser,' said Mason. 'Dirty stop-out.'
It was a familiar kind of greeting and Tyler took no offence. He asked where they were going.
'To a hotel,' they chorused. They were identical so often chorused. 'We're not spending another night in that shitty hole.'

'She's a lesbo,' said Madison. 'Nicci our mother is a fucking dyke. It's disgusting.'

Tyler had thought for years that this was a possibility, but it had never seemed sensible to raise the matter with either his mother or his sisters.

'We came back from evening shift expecting tea but that woman was moving in,' said Mason, 'and not just her but her two girls. Little sluts.'

'Not just staying over but shacking up with us, all bloody three of them,' said Madison. 'All their clothes, pots and pans, pictures on the wall. If you were any sort of man at all, Cyclops, you'd throw them out, but you won't. If Mum hadn't had you this wouldn't have happened.'

'And you keep your own room, and we have to share. Just because we're twins, and girls, and you're a boy. It's not fair.'

Well, they were upset and no worse than usual. Tyler smiled placidly and asked them who it was had moved in and the girls chorused, 'Matilda, her name is Matilda.'

'Mum's therapist?' The twins nodded in unison. They seemed really shocked and miserable, he thought, now the hysteria had died down.

'Everyone needs a personal life,' he said, comfortingly. 'And it's Mum's business, not ours.'

'Out of her fucking mind,' said Madison.

'Finally flipped,' said Mason.

It was Nicci's sleeping plans which seemed to have upset the twins more than her sexual orientation. Nicci's proposal had been that Tyler could keep his room – you could only just get a small single bed into it anyway. She would share the en suite with Matilda; Madison and Mason would move in together; Jane and Jilly (Matilda's girls, seventeen and fourteen) would have Mason's room. So they'd let her know what they thought of that.

Things had thus turned nasty. Nicci and Matilda were all loved-up and mooning in the kitchen instead of unpacking. It had started with Jane and Jilly opening a window because their room smelt of Matilda's joss sticks, so letting all the central heating out. Mason had emptied a whole bottle of scent onto her bed. Jane had asked Madison to turn The Cnuts down because of her homework so Madison had put it on a loop and turned it up to maximum. Jane had opened all the windows and Jilly had turned on all the lights. Madison had dropped Nicci's smartphone down the loo, she couldn't remember why but she had been provoked. Mason had tried to grab Matilda's phone, shouting that she was going to ring Child Protection and get Jane and Jilly taken into care by reporting them as being in a sexually non-safe environment; Matilda tried to use a thumb lock on Mason (specifically forbidden under the Mental Care Act, 2008). Nicci kicked Matilda in the crotch. She had kicked back. Jane and Jilly tried to pull Nicci's hair out. There had been so much noise and violence that Mason and Madison had no choice but to put essentials together and leave.

The twins locked arms, beehives all but tangling, a four-legged splodge of mauve and pink under the fake-Georgian streetlight, and wept.

'Our mother doesn't love us,' they cried in unison, then turned to Tyler and said viciously (Mason more so than Madison, there were some differences), 'Loser, what would you know.

Stop staring. Bloody man!'

The Uber car came and Tyler wondered whether he ought to go with them to make sure they were all right. But he was so tired he just waved them goodbye and went inside. They would have to look after themselves.

59

The She Devil Goes To Town

But Valerie makes a detour on the way home.

On the 16th of December the She Devil went up to London to speak at a symposium organised by the University of the Third Age on the necessity for gender-friendly medication for older citizens: IGP research had revealed that most drugs had been initially tested on males and calibrated for larger, younger bodies – an issue far too often overlooked by a male-dominated medical profession where, though there was parity in numbers, male doctors worked full time, while female doctors preferred part time.

Valerie accompanied the She Devil. They travelled in comfort in the back seat of the Mercedes, one old lady in her eighties, one young woman in her twenties. It was midnight, very late for the She Devil to be out. They were on their way home, travelling south. Valerie lowered the tinted window of the Mercedes to breathe in a little unconditioned and unscented air, but shut it again as a red security light in the carpeted ceiling flashed and a pleasant female voice warned '*Achtung, Achtung, Fenster, Fenster!*' and the chauffeur turned her head and said, 'If you open the window, darlings, I can't be responsible for temperature control.'

This was Leda, a serious and intent young woman in her thirties from the IGP's Security team, certificated to a high level in close protection and evasive driving. She wore her peaked uniform hat at a jaunty angle: Valerie rather fancied her, or had, though the idea of penetrative sex appealed perhaps more than it once had. Leda was a smooth and able driver.

'I find it shocking,' said the She Devil, 'that this machine costs so much and yet can only talk to us in German.'
'It is German, and second-hand: it would have cost so much more to have an English-speaking satnav put in, and we'd have had to wait for delivery.' She's amazing, thought the She Devil, the girl has an answer to everything! They were travelling in the Institute's own bullet-proof Mercedes S600 Guard, bought at great expense at Valerie's insistence. This was almost its first outing.

The need for a presidential limousine had come up at a Board meeting, following a suggestion from Valerie, whose stock had been high at the time – her fundraising efforts having proved so successful that the IGP for once had money in the bank. If Valerie said the appearance of prosperity bred prosperity, she was probably right. She had been asked to address the Board in person. Only the She Devil herself objected to her reasoning.
'But Valerie, who's going to fire a gun at me? I'm an old lady. We live in a peaceful land. We fight the gender war, but we must put our trust in voices, not weapons.'
'You never know,' said Valerie, sombrely, the amazing eyes flashing from under the thick black eyelashes as she looked up. 'History shows that sooner or later words must give way to actions if ends are to be achieved. It's inevitable. The Mercedes

I have in mind, an S600, is only armoured to stage one, which is bullet-proof. I could have suggested nine, which is bomb-proof. But that's only really necessary for Heads of State and gets rather heavy to steer. And the extra cost is atrocious.'
Ruth had been outvoted four to seven, which was troubling.

The used car had been bought in the face of the She Devil's wishes, an entirely unnecessary £200,000 had been spent, and nicknamed the Iron Maiden. Once upon a time such a defeat would have been unthinkable. The She Devil wondered if she had the will to resist the rise and rise of Valerie Valeria. The girl was bright and energetic, a force to be reckoned with, but she seemed incapable of realising that though gender might be on a sliding scale, men were still born bigger, stronger and less empathic than women: if women gave way to biological imperatives, the patriarchy would come surging back. The price of liberation was eternal vigilance. Too much accommodation of the male principle was dangerous; male/female apartheid was the only way ahead.

'Diavolessa,' said Valerie, out of the darkness, 'we're five miles from home. Shall we drop by St Rumbold's and take a look at the house where Tyler lives?' Valerie quite alarmed herself. This was the worst kind of crush behaviour. It was unrequited love which drove silly girls to stand mooning outside the loved one's house: just to look at the same sky, breathe the same air. Ridiculous! She was Valerie Valeria who was gay – and she felt this for a *boy*? How her friends would gloat.

'Supposing we didn't,' said the She Devil. 'An even better idea, it being the middle of the night.' But Valerie was already waving her hand over some contact pad and the window between her and Leda slid open. Valerie was already organising the detour. 'Do we have to?' asked Leda. 'Her Ladyship must be tired and the petrol light went on a mile back.'

'The Diavolessa is never tired,' said Valerie. 'And no one runs out of petrol in a car like this.'

'That's what I thought,' said Leda. 'So the sensors can't be working. I'm ever so sorry, Val. I should have checked with the diagnostics before we left. It's the first time I've driven this thing. I'll make it up to you.'

'I'll make sure you do,' said Valerie with meaning and the She Devil asked what all the giggling and whispering was about, but was ignored. Leda had to stop the car to read the instruction book, and Valerie got in front beside her to help.

Then there was trouble because the estate was so new that not all its streets came up on satnav. Valerie stayed in the front with Leda. The She Devil drowsed in the back, and eventually Echo Close was discovered after the Iron Maiden had nosed and nudged like some great black worm through a warren of quiet sleeping streets, tightly packed, all more or less identical.

Eventually they pulled up in a short row of rather larger houses. Most of them were unoccupied, but one was blazing with light from all its opened windows. Dreadfully loud and discordant music made the air quiver. Swearing and shouting came from inside.

'This is where my grandson lives?' asked the She Devil, wide awake. 'With his mother, my daughter?' Valerie admitted that it was.

'I see we have rather come down in the world,' was all the She

Devil said, and then – with such ferocity that Leda turned the car and left, fast – 'Home, Leda, at once. These people have nothing to do with me.'

Nor did the She Devil talk to Valerie all the way home.

60

I Always Meant Well

Wooo-h, wooo-h, wooo-h!

It wasn't my fault, I didn't mean to die. But I was all she had. A stepmother. Nicci's real mother had run out on her and her father was in prison. I should not have disappeared from her life when I did. I should not have let the little seed of cancer take root and destroy me. I should have stayed alive to take her out of that dreadful free-thinking school, and given her a little self-respect and a sense of proportion, taught her that '*love is not love which alters when it alteration finds*', and to tell a man you love him when you are fifteen and are on the pill is to put temptation before him he cannot resist, no matter how plain, spotty and fat you are.

Bobbo was not much use to her. He was a typical man of his generation, who saw children as the mother's concern, not the father's. He fed them and clothed them and had a sense of ownership but what they felt was no concern of his. He was simply there to provide. And after Bobbo was with me, of course, he did not even have to do the providing – and then the She Devil contrived to have him put in prison so he had even less obligation to his children, who were thus doubly abandoned. It may have even been a relief to him not to have the responsibility any more. So whom did little Nicci have to look up to then? Only me. And I died.

The school did not let her out to come to my funeral. The real mother was nowhere to be found, but I was only a stepmother.

After every successful revolution, as Father Ferguson, once my mentor and guide, told me, it's the next generation, the children, who pay the price. He was right. The feminists will have their revolution, he predicted, albeit a bloodless one, and change the social order, and little by little the new order will become the establishment, and that in its turn will be challenged and overthrown. So civilisations proceed, until they themselves collapse and die. Father Ferguson was a real downer to a girl like me. He had no faith in love.

I should have put Nicci on a diet the moment she stepped through the door moaning not that her mother had let the family home burn down but that she hadn't bothered to save the girl's guinea pig from a horrible death. I was too busy covering up my nakedness and my hair after the mussiness Bobbo had made of it – I was always happy to prove my love to Bobbo whenever and wherever he wanted it; a woman in love can do no less: Bobbo in his great love for me could be on the ardent and impatient side. I should have explained all this to Nicci. Should, should, should! So many shoulds... how they torment me!

One thing to have a man's baby because you love him so – quite another to fail to terminate an unintended pregnancy with twins, even though the father will pay, and he will have to support you and yours for ever and ever. But all my fault! I must take the blame for Nicci's perfectly horrible behaviour. Ugh, what a loathsome child!

How easily and fluently expressions of remorse flow from my lips. That's because they are untrue. I tell lies, as is my custom. I am a writer of romantic fiction. Lies flow from my lips as they do from my pen. Happy endings are rare. Love does not end with a kiss and a wedding, life goes on afterwards, all difficulty until it ends – if you're lucky, unlike me for whom it doesn't.

Oh wooo-h, wooo-h, wooo-h, woe is me, mea culpa! Is that what you want, Momus, Great Script Writer in the Sky? Will that satisfy you?

The smell of dry rot is bad today. I am growing to quite like it. I fan the fungus as I circle the High Tower. Perhaps it will collapse and crumble. *Wooo-h, wooo-h, wooo-h!*

61

Meet Your New Sisters

All change for Tyler.

By the time Tyler waved goodbye to his sisters it was all but half past two. He had had a long hard day. Another morning with Miss Swanson, and then Hermione, careering around on the back of her motorbike and in her bed. Then all this with the twins. And now his mother with her new lifestyle to be faced. And before that the remarkable if dreamlike encounter with the girl from Australia in Mrs Easton's shop. He marvelled at how boring life could be for years on end and then suddenly and alarmingly erupt into exciting event. But no way it wasn't exhausting.

All seemed serene when he went inside. The front door entered straight into the living room thanks to flexible spacing, so there was nowhere to hang his coat or put his woolly hat. There were half-unpacked boxes scattered all over the white nylon carpet. The boxes were of the smart kind that professional furniture movers deliver in advance of the move, so presumably the therapist's arrival had not been an impetuous move but a considered decision. His mother was the kind who did things in a hurry. Matilda had always struck Tyler as being rather the opposite – slow and deliberate. This was all Matilda's doing.

Matilda was lying back in an armchair facing Nicci in hers; a pleasant enough looking person, if rather square and dumpy, twice as broad as his mother but rather better looking, with flat short brown hair, in jeans and sweater. He didn't mind her as a person; she had been quite supportive of him in therapy sessions, though he did not like to envisage what she and his mother would actually do in their shared bedroom. At least they were not holding hands or anything, but slumped opposite each other looking quite exhausted.

Matilda raised a weary hand in greeting.
'He wanders in when the trouble's passed,' said his mother. 'Typical man. Meet your new sisters. That's Jilly, that's Jane.'
Jilly was stringing up Christmas decorations above the chaos of the floor. They were of the hand-made and rather vapid variety, but Tyler was pleased to see them. Nicci and the girls did not really do Christmas, though they had micro-wave M&S turkey dinners on the day itself. Jane was in the kitchen area patiently emptying a packing crate of bowls and dishes onto one of the normally bare kitchen shelves. The Finch Patchett family tended to graze rather than cook. Nicci claimed that feminists didn't cook, but if Tyler ever offered to give it a go, told him she didn't want him messing up her kitchen.

Both girls seemed of the quiet, studious, old-fashioned kind. They smiled at him as if in welcome – to his own home. They seemed to quite like the look of him. He thought perhaps this new life would not be so bad. Honestly, really, it couldn't be worse than what had gone before. With a sex life his mother might even be happier?

Jane and Jilly, up so late, were sent to bed. They went without arguing. Matilda got up and said she thought everyone deserved a nice cup of something. There was organic hot chocolate on the counter as well as tea and real coffee, milk in the fridge along with eggs and cheese, butter and marmalade, nut cutlets and jars of jam and peanut butter. Usually there was only tomato sauce. Tyler marvelled.

He excused himself and went up to bed. The twins had packed in a hurry and left items of strewn clothing along the corridor. He undressed and put on an orange polyester nightie of Mason's. He felt happy and relaxed and safe, and slept soundly.

He woke briefly to hear a thundering knock at the door. There were blue flashing lights outside. It was the police, summoned by a report of a disturbance. But they soon went away and Tyler went back to sleep.

62

A Matter Of Ethics

Dr Simmins is distraught.

It was the 18th of December. Three days until the Widdershins Walk. When Valerie, usually so conscientious, was late with her morning coffee, the She Devil imagined something had gone wrong with the preparations. So much could: Luxuriette might have been closed down by Health and Safety (a cockroach infestation?), Amethyst Builders might have used water-based paint on surf-splashed wood, computers might have crashed at Harrods Wedding Boutique – it was amazing in this modern world that anything worked at all.

But then Valerie had a magic touch: everything usually went smoothly when she was around. She was amiable, easy and optimistic and everything turned out well for her – she expected that it would, so it did. The She Devil wished she herself had that knack. Was it Napoleon who said the best quality a general could have was to be fortunate? Valerie had just been born lucky. So most likely nothing had gone wrong. Valerie was probably just having a nice lie-in with Leda and couldn't drag herself away from her bed.

The She Devil had a glorious view from her window if she sat up in bed on a good-weather morning. Today – a crisp clear morning, an early sun. An expanse of sea, green hills in the background, white foamy waves breaking on rocks below, for once almost no wind, and an arch of cloudless pale blue sky above. It seemed almost too good to be true, as though nature itself were waiting, laughing up its sleeve, plotting drama and disaster. On such a clear and peaceful day a bomb fell on Hiroshima, the Twin Towers came down, the tsunami rolled over Fukushima.

The tap on the door was almost a relief. The She Devil put on her splendid red velvet dressing gown to go and open it. This took her a little time. Her arms didn't stretch as easily as once they had. Valerie had wanted to turn it into a cloak for the She Devil to wear when she headed the procession, but the She Devil would have none of it. If procession there must be, so be it, but she drew the line at fancy dress.

'Coming in a minute,' she said, because opening a door was no longer easy and automatic, and when she was fresh out of bed it took time to draw breath and manage balance.

It was not Valerie, it was Dr Simmins, who wanted a word; she had been up, she said, since six o'clock. She had come up from the village early to do fasting blood tests for six residents who needed them. A pity, she said, that the canteen closed for breakfast at nine-fifteen sharp, Ms Bradshap thinking it was no hardship for anyone, no matter how old and feeble, diabetic or otherwise, to go without breakfast occasionally. But that could wait, Dr Simmins was in a hurry and had to get back for her morning surgery. But she had looked in on Bobbo and the She Devil should be aware that the old man did not have long to go. His pulse was fluttery; his breathing was Cheyne-Stokes; he was picking at the bed clothes.

'He's acting,' said the She Devil, flatly. 'For the last ten years the old bugger has been pretending to die, but he never does. He's strong as a horse.'

'Um,' said Dr Simmins, 'even horses die,' and asked if the She Devil was legally married to Bobbo.

'What do you mean?' asked the She Devil, affronted. 'Of course I am.'

Dr Simmins said it was a matter of the legality of the DNR notice should anyone ask questions.

'DNR?' asked the She Devil. All this, and before her coffee. 'And why should anyone ask questions?'

'Do Not Resuscitate,' said Dr Simmins, grimly. 'These are issued in consultation with family, which does not include exes, and I am checking that I can refer to you as Mr Patchett's wife.'

'I have no recollection of going through divorce proceedings,' said the She Devil, haughtily, 'so you can refer away. Do you have any idea exactly – when? It is rather an awkward time for everyone, with all these guests arriving for Valerie Valeria's Widdershins Walk shenanigans.'

'I am well aware of that,' said Dr Simmins, crossly. 'But dying is not an exact science.'

'If we had to cancel the whole hoo-ha, I would not be too unhappy. I must say I rather dread the occasion. The cold and the wet!'

'I see,' said Dr Simmins. 'Well, your husband, as you will have noticed, does not give up easily. And that idiot of a nurse doesn't help. She is very nubile and has no principles. If he deigned to actually swallow his sleeping pills things might go quicker.

They are quite strong. But I have my ethical position to consider.'

The She Devil said she appreciated that, and Dr Simmins was conscientiousness itself, getting up early so her patients wouldn't even miss their breakfast and the weekly visits to Mr Patchett and so on, and perhaps Dr Simmins would care to borrow the Iron Maiden Mercedes for her rounds? The She Devil hardly ever used it herself.

Dr Simmins said grudgingly that it might come in useful, but was it diesel or petrol? The She Devil said it was petrol, wasn't it? which seemed to be the right answer, because Dr Simmins said in that case she would take up the offer, but perhaps Lady Patchett would care to make a visit to the sick bed quite soon, if only for appearances' sake.

'Of course,' said the She Devil, pathetically. 'But it's so distressing. He doesn't even recognise me.'

'Um,' said Dr Simmins. 'For someone with advanced dementia your husband, as you've said, is a very good actor.' And she went away, duty done. But not before asking for the car keys, which the She Devil told her to pick up from Security.

Ruth found herself weeping, she was not sure why. Bobbo? Actually dying? Ceasing to be? She had spent so much of her life hating him, she thought; it was his existence that sustained her. Hating Bobbo, she could hate all men. He had become the prism through which she looked at the world. How would she occupy herself in this new strange leftover life? As herself at the age of twenty-two, before she met him, in an eighty-five-year-old body? Without Bobbo, She Devilry would melt away.

Without hate to sustain her, hate to energise her, to give her reason for living, she was all too likely to wither away. And how would the generations that followed after her manage if she collapsed now?

When Valerie finally arrived the She Devil was red-eyed but composed, any necessary grieving for Bobbo done and dusted and before the event. It had not even happened yet. She must concentrate on the future. Dr Simmins would no doubt use her ethical discretion. And with any luck the good weather might keep up.

Such a lovely morning! Valerie said she was sorry to be so late with the coffee. Femina Electrical had reported that a mouse had got into the wiring for the platform lights and they needed to know what her views were on humane killing.
'What are your views?' asked the She Devil.
'Australian,' replied Valerie. 'Just get rid of it,' and they both laughed.

63

Nurse Samantha Gets In Touch With Tyler

She needs company.

At around eleven the next morning Tyler was sitting down to breakfast with his new family. His mother and Matilda were to get married; the banns had been called the previous Sunday. It was to be a church wedding in Brighton. Matilda was buzzing around cooking eggs and tomatoes; Jane and Jilly were making toast. Cutlery had been unpacked, and the table laid with matching knives and forks. The salt was in a cellar, not in a carton, the butter was in a dish, not its wrapper. There was even a butter knife. It was unprecedented. Things were looking up.

'Don't just sit there, Cyclops, and expect to be waited upon,' said Nicci.

'Oh don't go on at him, Nicci,' said Matilda. 'Give the boy a break. His name is Tyler.'

'But I was told I'd have a Tayla,' said Nicci, 'I still can't get used to it. I'd have aborted him if only I'd known.'

'Do try not to be such a bitch, Nicci,' said Matilda. 'Tyler deserves better.'

Tyler wished he'd had Matilda for a mother. His phone rang: the *Mission: Impossible* theme. He didn't recognise the number.

'That's right, boy,' said his mother. 'Disturb the peace. Face nothing. Avoid the chores. That's my Cyclops.' Why would anyone want to marry his mother of their own free will, Tyler wondered? Have her in their bed on a permanent basis? Was an empty bed such a terrible option? Women were a mystery to him, but it was his fate to live amongst them. He took the phone outside to answer it.

It was an old school friend, Samantha Travers, out of the blue. Did he remember her? They'd exchanged rude selfies and had their phones taken away? Yes. He remembered very well. She'd been trying to contact him again for ages but failed. Did he never look at his Facebook? Tyler said since he had nothing good to report he seldom did. She said she was sorry about that but thought he ought to know that his grandfather was dying up in the High Tower and if he didn't come soon it would be too late.

Tyler said he knew he had a grandmother but he didn't know about a grandfather. Samantha said yes he had one, but only just. Security might not let him in since they were very fussy about men in the High Tower, but if he dressed up she'd smuggle him in and risk it. She had a black wig he could wear. It had belonged to Samantha's mother when she was having radiation treatment. Tyler's grandfather was difficult but at a time of letting go he needed loved ones around. There had to be reconciliation and peace. A well-managed passing away could and should be a blessed time. Old Mr Patchett was already seeing people who weren't there. And there was a daughter, wasn't there? Perhaps his daughter could come with Tyler. 'You mean my mother?' asked Tyler, and said he didn't think so, she wasn't the kind to do deathbeds. But he said he'd come up with Samantha next morning.

Tyler went back to his breakfast eggs, satisfied. His mother's ire was focussed on her mother, not on her father who had hardly ever got a mention. She could not stop him going, and it was time he took back some of the moral high ground. He rather fancied the image of a black wig. He could surely dress up as a girl without feeling his sexuality was threatened? He was so obviously and securely a man, it didn't matter what he wore. And once in the High Tower he might catch a glimpse of Valerie.

64

Oh Death Where Is Thy Sting-A-Ling-Ling?

Tyler and his grandfather find each other at last.

Tyler followed Samantha into the Lantern Room.
'It's your grandson, Mr Patchett. Nicci's boy Tyler come to visit you.'
'What is this, you stupid cunt, a deathbed scene? You want me dead?'
'Take no notice of the language, Tyler. It's a slippage in his brain, not the real him. It happens in old people sometimes. A subset of Tourette's. It's all in my Grade 3 notes.'
'I believe you, thousands wouldn't,' said Tyler. He was accustomed to bad language but from the young, not the old. He found it quite shocking. But then the whole scene was not at all as he had expected. The vast shadowy room, the great windows, the small high bed in the corner, a withered old man upon it like some garden gnome; not the source of dignity and wisdom he had supposed.
'He's so much livelier this morning,' said Samantha. 'I hope I haven't brought you out all this way for nothing.'
'God you're a stupid cunt sometimes,' said Bobbo.
'You see,' said Samantha, 'I don't care what they say. It isn't dementia. Bobbo has all his wits about him!'

Dressing up as a woman had been the easy part, a pleasant night or two in Mason's nightie had acclimatised Tyler to the idea. The wig had made him look too like his sisters so he had rejected that and was wearing a spare white, crisp uniform of Samantha's. He'd belted it tightly – he liked the sense of containment, of being unusually compressed in some parts, and unusually freer in others. He'd combed back his golden hair and run his fingers through it, so instead of curling round his ears it stood up like shafts of young wheat. He couldn't manage Samantha's heels so was wearing some nice shoes of his own instead. He'd put on her blue cloak to disguise his flat figure and they'd passed through Security easily enough; they'd chosen a time when most of the team were at breakfast. It was fun, he thought, being a girl, and could be perfectly well endured in a good cause. It was sort of like being reborn, starting afresh. If Samantha could deal with this disagreeable old man, he decided, so could he.

'Come nearer, dear boy, if that's what you really are. A genuine Patchett whelp, a Tyler out of Nicci out of Ruth, I'm told. Dreadful bloody names.' Tyler had to bend down to hear the old man. His breath didn't smell good, but it wasn't intolerable.
'Nicci is my mother, yes.'
'And who else are you out of, might one ask? Or does the birth certificate just read father: sperm bank?'
'My father's name is Gabriel Finch,' said Tyler, haughtily. 'You might have heard of him. He's a Bronze God.'
'What's that? Something like a brass monkey? Nothing surprises me.'
'A kind of social entertainer,' said Tyler, patiently. The old man could hardly be expected to keep up with the times.

Bobbo had featured very little in his mother's liturgy of family woes other than as a weak old jailbird of low intelligence. But the last hardly seemed to be the case. His mother was evidently an unreliable narrator. And if so about a grandfather, perhaps about a grandmother too?

'But my father doesn't count. He walked out on my mother as soon as I was born.'

'Good man! Must've decided he was well out of it.'

'Oh no. I was born with an unsightly vision impairment and he wasn't man enough to face it – according to my mother, that is.'

'Nicci? She always was a spiteful little thing, forever trying to break me and Mary up. Not that it was that difficult. Nicci's your mother… Once a cunt always a cunt. You poor lad, if lad you are.'

'My mother is a good woman and has done everything for me,' said Tyler, automatically springing to her defence.

But even as he spoke Tyler began to feel sorry for himself. 'Poor lad' just rang so true. How had he ended up a graduate and unemployed, still living at home, here, dressed as a woman, if it had not been for a mother who'd insulted him, undermined him, every step of his life? Perhaps she'd been bent on destroying him from the beginning? Thwarted in doing so while he was in the womb, she had done what she could during his young life to achieve the same result. Poor him.

'You're sure you're a boy, not a girl?'

'Yes, I am, sir.'

'My eyesight isn't as good as it was. I'm ninety-four, you know.'

'You are doing very well for your age,' said Tyler, politely. There are certain circumstances in which lies are excusable, even necessary. At least his mother had taught him manners.

'So help a poor old man, prove it. Show it to me,' said Mr Patchett. His voice was becoming hoarse and ragged.

Tyler looked bewildered.

'Do it,' said Samantha. 'Show it to him. It's simpler in the end. Otherwise he'll get upset, poor old thing.'

Tyler hitched up his skirt, pulled down his knickers, thought how simpler this was than taking off belts and undoing buttons, and showed his private parts. From this angle they seemed purposeful enough.

'Yes, you're a man,' said the old man. 'Not bad at all. Much as I was in my day.'

Tyler, accustomed to his mother's and sisters' derision, felt relieved and hid his parts again. He marvelled that it was so simply done.

'Fucking cunts of mothers are the source of all evil,' croaked the old man. 'It was because of my mother that I married your grandmother.'

'Don't take too much notice of him, Tyler,' said Nurse Samantha. She had brought Tyler here and wanted the reunion to be a pleasurable experience for everyone. 'He talks nonsense most of the time. He's on his way out but no one comes and visits him if they can help it.'

'I can understand that,' said Tyler. 'I'm surprised you put up with it.'

'A job's a job,' said Samantha. It was a litany in these parts, Tyler had heard it often enough. On the coast, out of season. *A job's a job.*

'Idle lying bitch of a woman, your great-grandmother. I was ill, low with hepatitis. She said one wife was much like another.

I believed her.' Bobbo was wheezing badly. He could hear it himself. So the old Labrador of his childhood days had wheezed when it was dying. The very fleas were fleeing from his skin. Brenda his mother had stood over the poor old fellow with the Hoover to catch them as they fled. Perhaps old Dr Lezzer was right and he was indeed dying?

'I can hardly be held responsible for my great-grandmother's sins,' said Tyler, piously.

'I don't see why not,' said the old man, and began to cough and splutter. He'd held the last of the doctor's pills (to hurry him on, he was sure) tucked between tongue and tooth. In trying to make sure they were still there he had swallowed them by mistake. Bobbo hawked and hawked but they were gone. Well, that was that. Dr Simmins had the last word. Outside the wind got up. If he were dead he wouldn't have to listen to the howling any more. God, women were awful. He fell asleep.

65

The She Devil Calls A Meeting

When in doubt, discuss.

The She Devil had called a Board meeting, to discuss-last minute preparations for the Widdershins Walk. Only two days to go.

There were eight members present; four had opted out, for reasons of health, boredom or general weariness. Dr Simmins had been asked to attend. It was quite a formal affair, beginning with a call to order and an official adjournment. The She Devil was Chair, Ms Bradshap Executive Officer, Ms Sidcup was Treasurer, these days using Valerie as her right-hand woman. The agenda covered Health and Safety, a field mouse infestation, changes in Security, canteen catering, general policy changes, accommodation, and at the last moment Ms Bradshap had added an extra item: the election of Ms Valeria as one of the trustees. The She Devil was in no position to object: someone would have to replace Ms Laura when she retired, which thankfully would not be too long in the future, and Valerie apparently had the necessary skills, having qualifications in financial administration. Or so she said. The She Devil had thought about asking Human Resources to check, but decided it wiser not to. Better have Valerie in the tent pissing out, than Ms Laura outside the tent pissing in.

The meeting was held in the penthouse of the Castle Complex, 3CC/1. Its large triangular window looked out to sea, and it was at its best on a day like this when the wind was quiet and the waves benign. Santa Barbara Ltd, architects and Feng Shui specialists, had decided to model the whole complex on the basis of the millennial trend for supermarket design: *'when bicycle shed meets consumer palace, low culture and high culture meet'* was the mantra of the Santa Barbaras, and why they'd got the job. The new building had its advantages and disadvantages. At least, being steel, glass and concrete, dry rot was not a hazard – as it was the other side of the walkway to the High Tower – though many came to understand why coastal cottages had small windows and thick walls: *it's the weather, stupid!* Central heating roared and knocked throughout the winter and hummed and hissed all summer. Coffee was served, rather against Ms Bradshap's wishes – caffeine ingestion blurred cognitive capacity in elders – but also her favoured green tea.

The mouse infestation was declared over, thanks to a new eco-friendly poison for the traps. The extra expense of real cream instead of synthetic cream, vegetable fat and intense sweeteners for the meringues was approved. Lighting for the new walkways had been put in. Valerie was able to explain, quite poetically and to the satisfaction of most of the Board, why it was appropriate to invite men to a celebration of forty years' pursuit of gender parity. The She Devil and Ellen the photographer abstained from voting on this, the She Devil still muttering that it was the thin end of the wedge… parity was initially about pay: no one had anticipated such a change in gender attitudes that men would demand parity with women. But again the effort of arguing defeated her. She was tired.

The sky had darkened again. Someone turned on the lights, though it was midday. The matter of the Lantern Room came up again; to dedicate such a large and valuable space in the High Tower itself to a single invalid was hardly reasonable. Ruby Simmins said she thought the problem would soon enough resolve itself. Valerie said she'd had an idea. The Lantern Room could eventually be used as a feminist library, a safe place open to the public, and its original purpose as a lighthouse – to shine a helpful light into the hearts and minds of all genders everywhere, shining out over sea and land. Valerie was inspiring, heart-lifting, a palpable role model for women everywhere.

The wind got up. Black clouds swirled outside the window. The clouds turned to rain, concentrated tiny drops that pattered so hard against each pane and seemed to explode into a yet tinier spray as they landed. There was a rumble of thunder. Ms Bradshap started to scream and point and jabber. She was on her feet.

'Do you see it? The face, the face at the window. Enormous! Staring in! See there, the running nose all squashed up? The two eyes. It's her, it's her, the ghost of Mary Fisher!'

Dr Simmins was the first to rise to her feet and try to calm the shuddering, screeching Flora Bradshap. She accomplished this with a hard sudden slap to her left cheek. Ms Bradshap quietened a bit and sat down, but kept pointing and gibbering. 'Wish fulfilment, Ms Bradshap,' Dr Simmins said. 'You saw what you wanted to see. The amount of sheer female hysteria in this place is beyond belief!' But some observers did think they saw what Ms Bradshap said she saw, a giant misty female face pressed against the window. Then there was a sudden flash of lightning and a bang, and with that the rain stopped and the window pane was clear, other than for a few quite innocent leftover drops.

'Will someone close the curtains?' said Dr Simmins, and Ms Laura hobbled to do it.

'Take Ms Bradshap to her room and give her a nice cup of herbal tea,' said the good doctor to Valerie, and Valerie rose and obliged. She was nippier on her feet than the others. The She Devil left the room to discover the source of the bang – she was right to be prudent – lightning had avoided the conductors as ever and struck the walkway, where it had started a small fire. She then had to call Security to make sure it was properly extinguished. By the time she got back to 3CC/1 a vote had been taken and Valerie had been appointed as a trustee, unanimously.

Well, so be it. Her more immediate worry was the weather. Valerie had said the low front was passing and a warmer front moving in, but 'warmer' could still drop below freezing, and the equinox tide was to be at a record height. The She Devil could see that one way or another the Widdershins Walk might be the death of her. Valerie's promise of a steady helping hand over wet and slippery rocks could not be taken at face value; the helping hand could so easily turn murderous. Just a little push and over she'd topple.

If only Bobbo would die, she could be overcome with grief and stay in her room to mourn.

66

O Grave, Where Is Thy Victory?

Still he won't die.

Tyler would have very much liked to leave while the old man slept, but had to wait until Samantha finished her shift, and he could slip out with her unnoticed. She'd brought a couple of tuna sandwiches up from the village shop and they ate them while they waited for Bobbo to wake, if he ever did. They weren't very nice sandwiches but at least the bread was white. The canteen only served brown, with, as Samantha put it, wood chips in it. The Lantern Room was vast and gloomy, and though lined with great windows pointing north, south, east and west, sunlight seemed reluctant to enter. Tyler, texting away to Hermione, waiting for Bobbo to wake, had to ask Samantha to turn on the light.

'It's already on,' she said, and so it was. The great room was sulking, she told him. Once the whole countryside had been flooded with light from its lantern; now, deprived of its purpose, it was in a permanent bad mood. Even at midday in bright weather it stayed dark. And the sky was beginning to cloud over.

'You are weird, Sam,' said Tyler, admiringly.

'So would you be,' said Samantha, 'stuck away all day like this with him and Mary Fisher. She's the ghost. I've never seen her but she's all around. I used to be frightened but I feel quite safe now, and she's glad I look after Bobbo. When Bobbo goes I expect she'll go with him, though he is quite difficult. I hope she does. She loved him. It's ever such a romantic story.'

They whispered. Their voices echoed. There was very little furniture in the cavernous room. There was the high narrow hospital bed in the corner where Bobbo spent his life, the armchair in which he sat, the chair for an occasional visitor, the table where Dr Simmins put out her medications, syringes, pills, an autoclave, a cupboard or two, the little kitchen with its microwave and kettle. In a far corner, incongruously, was a wide white velvet antique sofa.

'That's the sofa where they were in the act of love when your grandmother burst in on them. I don't know why someone doesn't throw it out. I reckon it's why Mary Fisher hangs around, like a moth to a flame, keeps trying to get in. I do tend to stay this side of the room.'

Tyler shuddered and the old man woke. They went together to the bed.

'You still here, then? Got one last coffin-stick for a dying man?'

'I don't smoke.'

'That figures.'

Nurse Samantha brought him water and took his blood pressure.

'Completely normal,' she said. 'You are a one, Mr Patchett. You quite frightened us all.' She put her cool young finger against his neck. He grabbed for it, but she snatched it away in time.

'Cunt, cunt, cunt,' Bobbo said, at the rejection, and began to

feel better. He turned his attention back to the young man. He'd
soon get rid of him.

'You a vegan?'

'I was for a time, sir. Not any more.'

'Don't "sir" me. I've got no money to leave you, if that's what
you're here for. Your Grandma stole it from me, malicious
bitch. It's in a bank in Switzerland.'

'She did?' People didn't tell lies when they were dying, surely.
Then his mother was right: the She Devil was truly evil. If dying
was what the old man was doing. He seemed to have woken up
with a new lease of life. His eyes glittered; he was even enjoy-
ing himself. Samantha tenderly dabbed his lips with a damp
cloth. Bobbo, instead of grabbing, pushed her away so that the
bowl spilled.

'Clumsy cow. See what I have to put up with? But once your
legs go, what's a man to do? Not that she isn't a hot little cunt.'

'Don't try and offend me, old man,' said Nurse Samantha,
briskly. 'It won't work.'

Bobbo ignored her. He had a new audience.

'Bare-faced robbery, wrongful imprisonment, that's your
Grandma, slimy piece of shit. Turd in the water supply. Always
was. All over a bit of nooky. What about you? Not a vegan? Not
a poofter, you say, not dropping anchor down Pooh Corner?
Just a transvestite.'

Tyler raised helpless eyes to heaven. The man should be locked
up. Age was no excuse.

'Not that I was averse to a bit of skirt swishing myself sometimes. Saves time. *Au naturel*. Ask any Scotsman in his kilt. But
take my advice, boy, cut off the curls. That's what I did. Chip
off the old block. Come closer.'

Tyler leaned nearer, though reluctantly. Supposing old age

was catching? Bobbo's eyes glittered through rheumy slots of useless skin.

'Careful,' said Nurse Samantha. 'He's going to fart.'

He did, long and horribly.

'Did he do that on purpose?' Tyler asked. This was just more terrible than anything he had imagined.

Samantha moved across to the wide east window and undid the ratchet which kept it locked. She opened it, as she was under instruction not to do in case the old man plunged to his death. So strong and chilly a wind blew in that she closed it again almost at once, but it was enough to clear the air of noxious vapours. 'Of course it was on purpose,' said Samantha. 'It's one of his best defence mechanisms. What else would you do if you were him? *"Inappropriate sexual and excretory behaviour and speech is a function of generalised geriatric psychiatric disorder and a symptom of increasing dementia"* is what my Grade 3 notes say. But I think it's just to remind others that you're alive.'

Another sudden fit of energy possessed the old man; he lifted his head from the pillow. He sat up, took Tyler's wrist and clung to it. Though Tyler did what he could to remove the claw fingers, they were too strong and he was nervous of snapping them. The wind had become noisy and sporadic rain spattered on the windows. Was the white sofa sliding gently across the floor or was the whole High Tower slipping to one side? No, an optical illusion. His own head was to one side; that was what happened when you nearly fainted. Tyler wanted just to get home before something really bad happened. But what home? Nicci and Matilda? Hermione? It was bad, bad here and there was nowhere to go. Perhaps Mrs Easton would take him in? He should never have come. And still he couldn't take away his hand from the dreadful grip.

'And you get away from us, bitch,' Bobbo cried. 'Cunt, cunt, cunt!' He was staring at the great east window, where a con-figuration of clouds had formed that looked for all the world like an enormous face.

'It's her,' Samantha cried out. 'It's her, Mary Fisher.'

Tyler thought: 'No, I'm imagining this,' and even as he thought it the clouds re-formed and the vision was lost. The claws on his wrist tightened.

'Well, at least she's gone,' said Samantha, calmly, 'and I'm glad I actually saw her. But I don't like the look of him at all. He's too lively. It's like my mother when she was about to pop. I'm the eldest of six, you know. We were Catholics. She'd run round like a mad thing cleaning the house. Perhaps he really is pegging out, poor soul. The last dregs of energy, firing up just before they go out for good. Death like birth is a wonderful thing. Shall I video his last breath, Tyler? It might go viral.'

Tyler said he really thought no, it would be disrespectful. This was his grandfather, after all. But shouldn't she fetch somebody? Samantha said no, they'd only find Tyler there and she'd be in trouble. Tyler realised she was taking a selfie with Bobbo and trying to fit in his own captive wrist as well. He remembered Samantha had been the first in the class to go on Facebook back in 2009. She had always assumed virtue lay in sharing.

Outside the window storm clouds collided, thunder rolled. The tempest had finally broken. Samantha counted aloud for the lightning, 'One, two, three,' and there it was. The sky lit up for a split second and sudden wind drove heavy rain across the window. All the wrinkles and harshness seemed to drain from Bobbo's face. He looked translucent, young again. Tyler suddenly saw a resemblance to himself. The lips smiled briefly, in some inward communion. The bony fingers on Tyler's wrist relaxed their grip. Old Bobbo's head fell back onto its pillow. His eyes had stopped seeing, though they remained open.

His breath had stopped coming.

67

We Are The Ghosts Of Mary Fisher

And here we are pattering on the window pane, virtue-signalling.

We are not one, we are legion. We are the thousand, thousand souls in every drop of rain: we are the dead who cannot die, for here we still are, common elements, two parts hydrogen, one part oxygen. Stardust. We are the suddenly dead: the soldier dying on the battlefield, the starving mother with her child, the family that the un-manned drone destroyed. All, all on the wrong side of history. But all, all, the rich, the poor, the good, the bad, here today, gone tomorrow.

From stardust we came, to dust we will return, with our hates and rages, loves, longings and disappointments. There goes our Bobbo in the rain: no virtue-signalling for him! At least he never pretended to be good. Soon the She Devil will join him. What can we say of her? Well, it makes no difference now. History marches on, good side, bad side. Love, love, love, even the She Devil moans (if it wasn't for life how good I would be!) me too, all I ever needed was love. And now all this.

We are the ghosts of Mary Fisher. We are without physical form but show ourselves in the single enormous face pressed against the dripping window pane, spying, a flattened nose, a weepy eye, horrid, dimly discerned through salt spray and mist, sea from the ocean, rain from the sky. Hydrogen and oxygen, multi-faceted. Me, me, she moans, what about me? Where is the beauty now, she wails? Where the love? One day perhaps she too can be quiet, when the great red giant sun of the future implodes.

In the meantime we are the ghosts of Mary Fisher. We drench you with rain, batter you about the head as hail, muffle you with snow. You take no notice – you have to live.

'Particularly nasty weather,' you say, putting up your bright umbrellas. 'Tickle your arse with a feather!' Raining cats and dogs, *comme une vache qui pisse.* Is that a flood I see before me? Good God, the railway track has been washed away; the nuclear power station has exploded. Water got into the works. The cooling ponds were not enough, the tsunami barriers imperfect.

We are the ghosts. Do shut up, Mary Fisher, pressing your stubby nose against the window pane; you have no right to your love, love, love is all you need. You never did. It never worked for you.

68

The End Of Bobbo

But no such luck?

Tyler felt a great desire to giggle. He had to remind himself he was in the presence of death. Was this all it was, just someone stopping? It was an anti-climax, not the bang, not even the whimper. Yet he found himself looking round the room to see where the old man had gone, for gone he certainly had. But the soul, if that was how you could describe it, was nowhere in the room to be seen. The body in the bed, deprived of its living malevolence, was there all right, but now just a shoddy pile of scrap flesh.

'Christ!' said Samantha. 'Shit, he's gone. I was switching to video. I missed the last breath. And it could have gone viral.' Death seemed to make her angry. She had changed. Tyler felt as though something of her had gone with Bobbo. She put away her iPhone. She stepped forward with purpose, as though about to assault the body in frustration and rage, but all she did was close the rheumy eyes.

'Are you meant to do that?' Tyler asked.

'Oh yes,' she said. 'We're meant to close the eyes as quickly as possible.'

'Why is that?' asked Tyler.

'It's a vacant house,' she said. 'And you don't want anything nasty getting in.'

Tyler removed the bony fingers from his wrist and stood up and shook himself.

'Mind you, he was a dirty old man,' said Samantha. 'I can say that now he's gone. I'm not likely to get anything worse. I can probably do my Grade 4 now and move over to admin.'

'He had a hard time from the women in his life,' said Tyler. It seemed right and fitting that at this moment something should be said in his grandfather's favour.

'You can say that again,' said his grandfather. Tyler could swear he saw the dead lips moving. He heard his grandfather say, louder and clearer in death than life: 'The money's yours. Shit, fuck, dog's droppings.'

Tyler was not sure which was worse, the lips of a corpse speaking or what they were saying. Samantha did not seem to notice or hear. She was pulling the sheet up over Bobbo's head.

'I saw the lips move,' Tyler said.

'Really?' she said. 'It must be like with chickens. They can run round after their heads have been chopped off.'

'And he was talking,' said Tyler.

'It's a funny room,' she said, 'echoey. You were hearing yourself. There is no pulse, there is no breath. Dead as a doornail.' It was clearly what she intended to believe.

Tyler thought he heard a chuckling sound coming from beneath the sheet and saw the chest heaving, but now lightning was pattering the sky and it was hard to tell what was what he really saw and heard and what he imagined. Like when he thought he saw the sofa sliding across the room.

'I'll have to call people,' said Samantha. 'Stay in the shadows or something. Try not to be noticed. Not that it matters. I'm out of a job anyway.'

PART TWO

Altogether Now!

Chapter 1
Nurse Hopkins

I ran the Vesta Rose Agency for the She Devil back in the seventies: a small agency which catered for working women, doing their shopping, collecting their children, opening the door for the meter readers, waiting in for deliveries, that sort of thing. It's now grown into an internet giant, providing domestic services for career women worldwide. I ran it until I died, or part died like Mary, two days before the first World Women's Widdershins Walk. I had grown very wealthy. You'll just have to put up with me now that Mary Fisher has gone from the script. You will find me to be a more down to earth and less fanciful figure haunting the High Tower. And now Bobbo has gone new rules apply.

I imagine it was Bobbo's departing spirit that swept Mary's tremulous ghost up and away, or possibly down and away, and carried it with him – which he won't much like, I daresay, and as for her, she'll need to do a lot more self-examination before she can settle. It is a great mistake to think that things ever, ever end. They don't. The next life is just more of what went before, but on some different dimension, one step forward, two steps back or vice versa perhaps, according to the weather on Mount Olympus. I think Bobbo swept up some part of his bimbo nurse with him as he went – old habits die hard. Tyler certainly found her changed, but I daresay she'll recover.

I was emailing the She Devil with condolences on hearing of Bobbo's death (one has to go through the motions though I knew the old thing would be happy enough to see the back of him and rumour had it that she only kept him alive to sign necessary documents) when I was afflicted with a sudden and rather terrible pain in my chest and I seemed to die. But no such luck; it now seems I only part died, like Mary Fisher before me.

So here I am, left in this rather irritating limbo, circling the High Tower and keeping watch in Mary Fisher's place. Being bodiless is actually a great relief to me: it was never a body to be proud of any more than the She Devil's was before she had all that work done on it, silly woman. I have never had cosmetic surgery myself, I disapprove of it. I earned my title 'La Jolie Laide' in the A-list celebrity stakes, through exercise and healthy diet, not spending money.

I find it strange – I have almost nothing in common with Mary (and certainly not a belief in 'love'), except that I too am now perforce a conscripted functionary of The Great Fictional Religion and a devotee of Momus. He has work for me to do. But I'm fucked if I'm going to do all that *wooo-h, wooo-h, wooo-h*ing business. Most people just ignored it. You have to ignore the paranormal, the intrusion of alternative universes – eleven of them, apparently, our Cambridge cosmologists are currently claiming – if you're going to get on with things, otherwise you would live a life of constant terror. Mary suckered

Valerie and Samantha and even Ms Bradshap, but most people took her with a pinch of salt.

Anyway, that's me. The formerly corporeal Nurse Hopkins and I'm going to tell you what happened...

Chapter 2
Tyler

Tyler, at Samantha's suggestion, hid away in a shadowy corner of the room. Dr Simmins signed the death certificate: *cardiopulmonary event due to aspiration failure.* The She Devil deigned to come down and weep a tear. Ellen took photos. Valerie took notes and Samantha laid out the body as she had been trained to do.

When the room finally emptied Tyler slipped away unnoticed. Or would have had he not been stopped by Security. He had forgotten about his shoes, Balenciaga's sneakers, bright blue nappa leather with grey laces, barely worn, a whole £10 in the Help the Aged charity shop in Steynswick. It was true, they were rather startling when worn with his nurses' cloak: well, worn with anything, come to that. But who wouldn't need cheering up when visiting the dying, he asked himself? Tyler was to have a gruelling time of it, for such a sunny, innocent lad.

'Nice shoes,' said the Security girls. 'Just rather large for a girl.' They made a pleasant cluster, Tyler thought, most of them under thirty, in smart blue and black braided uniforms, but shrewd-eyed and well-exercised, with long legs and well-developed shoulders. They made him strip down to t-shirt and jeans and looked him up and down, but asked for no further proof of his maleness, though he would not have minded if they had. Death was so strange that the normal assumptions that went with everyday life were jolted out of true. It all seemed rather dreamlike. Anyway, he had nothing to be ashamed of. He had time to spare.

Asked if he was going home he said yes; but it seemed no kind of sanctuary, just another nest of females – Nicci, Matilda, Jane and Jilly, and for all he knew Madison and Mason would return. He was the odd one out. He wondered where all the men had gone. In India they aborted girl babies, and the rest of the world thought it a scandal. In middle-class England they aborted boys, because girls were so much more desirable than boys, fun to dress, went to college, got jobs. Would he, who'd only escaped abortion because of a mistaken gender diagnosis, become the rule, not the exception?

Well, he still had friends, they still had sofas, he would resign himself to sofa surfing and a diet of pizza and chips, and call on Hermione from time to time. She might even ask him to help with the business. He could not stand the humiliation of the Jobcentre Plus any more. Miss Swanson would have to look after herself.

Asked how he had effected entry in the first place he told them the truth, that Samantha had smuggled him in so he could be at his grandfather's deathbed. Truth, in his experience, took up less time and caused less trouble than lies.
'Oh, soppy Samantha,' said the one called Leda. 'That figures. So the old man's finally gone, has he? That'll please Valerie.'

Could they mean his Valerie? The one with legs up to her armpits? The one he'd had a passing 'thing' with in the village shop when he'd been so upset? Apparently so. Tyler had assumed Valerie to be some kind of low-ranking secretary but apparently she was a power in the High Tower. Everyone seemed to like to talk about Valerie, under whose aegis Security now fell. He listened. Valerie was now on the Board, as they had all hoped. Young blood at last. Perhaps now the food in the canteen would get less flower-powery and more suitable for young appetites. Perhaps Valerie would give them new uniforms designed in the modern era and eschew flared jeans. Valerie wanted the Lantern Room for use as a Parity Library, open to the public, which meant more staff and higher wages but was problematic because men would have to be allowed in and some twat was bound to demand a men's loo which would be disgusting because they always missed.

But now the old man was no more the Lantern Room was free, and at least Security wouldn't have to be running up and down the stone stairs at night when Samantha was off shift, putting up with his antiquated rages and general imbecility. He used to throw his false teeth at them. The stairs were so steep they were dangerous and not really suitable for public access. Valerie would have to check it out with Health and Safety.

The aptly-named Leda, who seemed to be the leader of the group, a tall, dark and sultry girl with a strong jaw and heavily fringed almond eyes, said she was sorry the old man had gone but it was a blessed relief for everyone. And what would happen about Saturday's Widdershins Walk? Would it have to be cancelled? They were all looking forward to it. Didn't Tyler know anything? Tyler said no he didn't.

He thought of how different the attitude of a group of male Security guards would be. He said as much and they laughed, stuck out their stomachs, slouched their shoulders and grunted and snorted at each other in what seemed to be a practised routine and said theirs was not a hierarchical dog-eat-dog organisation but a team of friendly bitches working together and Tyler should be careful of what, being male, he might grow into. Tyler felt uneasy.

And then Valerie herself came tripping down the steps. The weather had cleared. It was a bright, bright beautiful day. Tyler realised how alike he and Valerie were, a pigeon pair the way they normally dressed, he male, she female, jeans and black sweaters – hers expensive, his Tesco's – blue-eyed and with cropped fair hair. She stopped stock still when she realised who it was. She ran her fingers through her hair, and seemed embarrassed to meet his eye.

'Good God,' she said. 'It's you!' It occurred to him that their brief encounter had meant more to her than it had to him. And that couldn't be bad. He liked a powerful woman. He was accustomed to them. If another chance came he would certainly take it. She could be very helpful. He might even finally meet and mollify his mysterious grandmother; he might even get a decent job. If the Lantern Room was to be a public access space, and a Gender Parity Library open to men, and he was on good terms with both Valerie and the She Devil, and one fancied him and the other was family, why could he not be the librarian or something? Stranger things had happened. How quickly ignoble possibilities arranged and rearranged themselves in one's head, while one was staring into someone's eyes. Valerie's blue eyes. Deep pools, all that. They seemed a great deal more pool-like than they had in the village store. Could he be turning into his grandfather – all lubricious thought, self-interest and power play mixed? He realised he was holding her hand.

Security was apologising to Valerie for the security breach: Tyler had been let through in the first place, without so much as a signed pass. Valerie said it was all right, she was cool about it, Tyler was a relative and could come and go as he wished: a far worse breach in protocol was their handing over the car keys of the Mercedes to Dr Simmins, who had apparently lost no time in driving it away. Really, they must check any instruction from Lady Patchett with her, Valerie. The She Devil was old, upset by her husband's illness and death, and did not know what she was doing. Valerie needed to go to Lewes at once to register the death at Births, Deaths and Marriages before it closed. They should bring out the Lexus since the Mercedes was unavailable. Tyler had better come with her since, though she had the necessary documents, it was as well to take a family member with her.

'Is this him?' Leda, the one with the fringed eyes and jutting jaw, asked Valerie. She seemed upset.
'Yes,' Valerie said, 'it's him. Isn't he pretty? I'm sorry, dear, I told you I was bi. Get used to it.' Leda looked flushed and upset.
'Hasbian!' said Leda under her breath. Tyler was beyond making sense of anything. This morning his long-lost grandfather had been alive, now he was not. All anyone seemed interested in was practicalities. He'd never seen anyone die before, if that indeed was what had happened. But they wouldn't say anyone was dead when they weren't quite, would they?

When the car came round, a serviceable Lexus with an old number plate, he got in beside Valerie and they drove off. She pulled in at a lay-by outside St Rumbold's and said he looked as if he needed a joint. Tyler said he did and she rolled one expertly, using one hand, which he thought admirable. Their cheeks touched and the same familiar shock of electricity he'd felt down at the shop seemed to run from her to him, him to her. Of course she wasn't a lesbian. This thing would run and run.

Chapter 3
A Board Meeting

Minutes of Emergency Board Meeting, Friday, 10.30 a.m., 20th December.

In attendance: Ways and Means and Ethics Committees.

Venue: 3CC/1

Apologies for absence: Dr Ruby Simmins.

The Minutes of the meeting on 18th December were read and approved.

Matters arising: Urgent steps were under way to remove alleged dead rat from beneath the Archive Room floorboards. One objection was noted; an acceptably quick and humane death for a field mouse did not equate with a slow and lingering death for a single rat, who had crawled away to die. The Ethics Committee had this under discussion.

Agenda:

1. Staffing concerns:

Miriam from Human Resources informed the Board that Samantha had laid the body out sympathetically and had received her P45, plus a week's money in lieu of notice. Ms Sidcup reported in her rather tremulous voice – she was eighty-four and one of the founder members of the IGP – that dear Ms Octavia had kindly donated her unbleached bamboo linen shroud, cost £175, for which she would be compensated in due course. Leda from Security explained that the body was now housed in the walk-in chiller in the staff canteen until further deliberations as to its disposal were concluded: the body had a shelf to itself and perishable items were kept well away, though contrary to common belief, cadavers were not in themselves a biohazard. Internal bacteria kept themselves to themselves and flourished inside the corpse initially, not outside. Dr Simmins had signed the FFI form in case of questions (Freedom From Infection, required for burials at sea). That left:

2. Matters relating to funeral.
3. Matters relating to tomorrow's celebrations.
4. Vote of thanks to Valerie Valeria, for 10 per cent membership rise over two years.
5. Policy direction.
6. Any other business.

The She Devil was Chair but she was tired. She would like a holiday. It must have been ten years since she took one. But where would she go? With whom? You got to a certain age and people started dying and friends had never been her forte. She supposed she could count Nurse Hopkins as one – the She Devil had set her up in business years back, and she had ended up a multi-millionairess of the start-up age, luxury yacht and all – but now even she was gone. The She Devil had this very morning received a black-edged email with a mourning emoticon which told her that Nurse Hopkins had died the previous day – had collapsed at her desk. She'd found that more distressing than Bobbo's death. Old friends were worth more than old husbands. The She Devil had been comforted through many vicissitudes by knowing that Nurse Hopkins was simply *there*. Their worlds did not mix, of course.

Nurse Hopkins too, no doubt egged on by the She Devil's urge to self-improvement, had become fashion-conscious and become known in celebrity circles as 'La Jolie Laide'. She had invited the She Devil onto her yacht for a luxury Mediterranean cruise, but it had not seemed suitable. If you were running a charity, these days you had to be so careful.

There'd probably be more people at Nurse Hopkins' funeral than there would be at the She Devil's own when her turn came. More would be grateful for washing machines mended, food deliveries taken in, children collected from school or walked round to nursery than they would be for anything the She Devil had done – driving them out to work in the first place, putting uncomfortable thoughts of independence in their heads – when in the end dependence was all you really had. Look at her and Valerie Valeria. If you so much as wanted to take a walk or address a meeting you had to have someone to help you. And she would not carry a stick – it was demeaning.

The She Devil had been on her way to visit Bobbo, Ellen helping her up the stairs, only to arrive just as his fool of a nurse was closing the old man's eyes. The eyes had started open of their own accord, which had freaked Nurse Samantha and her assistant out until Samantha had used her common sense and taped them down. Fortunately Dr Simmins was there and had written out the death certificate without question. Dr Simmins had made a rather unfortunate joke, however: 'Cause of death? What shall I say? By common consent or boring old infarction?' It would not do. Now Dr Simmins had the Mercedes, which she seemed to see as a gift rather than a loan, and there would be no stopping her ribaldry. The saying

'No good deed but goes unpunished' was in this case only too true.

And Dr Simmins couldn't even be bothered to come to this meeting – to which, come to think of it, the She Devil realised she had better pay attention, having called it in the first place. Perhaps the Widdershins Walk would be cancelled. The weather was great today, positively balmy, but tomorrow's forecast suggested storm, snow, sleet, lightning and gusts as a new low came rushing in from the west... Where had they got up to? Ah, still on:

2. Matters relating to the funeral.
It was decided, there being no legal requirement for a funeral and many options open as to the disposal of the body, that no actual funeral was necessary. So long as the person was decently, publicly and permanently disposed of and there was no biohazard, you could do as you saw fit. The normal route via the undertaker was unnecessarily complicated and expensive. Ms Valerie (apologising for her late arrival) argued strongly that parity must extend to the dead and that the *Walk the Other Way* slogan was strengthened not weakened by this break with burial tradition, and that on no account should the Walk be cancelled out of any hypocritical respect for the dead. So much depended on the dead and the life they had lived.

As for the weather forecast, she said, feminists had always struggled against adversity and should be seen to put their money where their mouth was, and venture out with spirit and courage to process, crying 'Widdershins! Walk the Other Way! Out with the old, in with the new!'

Nevertheless, a death had occurred and could not be ignored. Ms Laura had suggested, wisely, that guests should be informed of the death on arrival or, if possible in the short time allowed, notified by email. What amounted to a wake could then be incorporated into the victory celebrations.

('Victory now, is it?' the Chairperson Lady Patchett was heard to murmur. 'I thought it was meant to be a birthday party!' but no one heard.)

Leda from Security broke in at a sensitive moment to explain that to alleviate people's anxieties the body could easily be moved to the cold store, otherwise empty, and not remain in the walk-in chiller, and so long as the temperature was between 4 and 5 degrees Celsius there was no problem with that.

'Will that keep you happy, Valerie?' demanded Leda, fringed eyes flashing.
'It does,' said Valerie cheerfully. 'No worries. I've nothing more to say anyway. You always did hate me making speeches.'
'Hasbian! Burn in Mordor!'
'Is something going on here I should worry about?' asked the She Devil, coming to life. Was that a love bite on Valerie Valeria's neck? In which case why didn't the girl wear a polo neck? Oh, such a typical exhibitionist!
'No worries,' said Valerie, apparently blithely, the girl who had once been the She Devil's assistant but now seemed to be running the show. But Leda walked out in dudgeon, so that was that sorted.

The no formal funeral matter having been decided (there

were no all-female burial firms in the area, anyway, the excuse apparently given was coffin bearers in the age of obesity had to be extra strong, which meant male), the disposal of the body was the next cause for discussion. Ms Octavia had changed her mind and thought the freezer was preferable to the cold store, but was over-ruled. Time was of the essence. It was normal to bury bodies in the earth (ecologically sound) or have them cremated (ecologically unsound). But there was a new form of cremation called alkaline hydrolysis, which turned the body liquid and was thus an improvement on both. But Lady Patchett said, 'Enough is enough. I will not have him poured down a drain,' and the debate took a different turn.

Some said even to suggest it was tactless, the She Devil's bereavement being less than a day old, while others argued that attending to ecological issues must always be a priority. The She Devil was known to be something of a climate change denier, blaming it on changes in the sun rather than human activity; someone who refused to join in the waste sorting exercise at the High Tower, upsetting Ms Bradshap by seeing it as appeasement of the Almighty – 'Dear God, if I get mucky fingers sorting the food waste bucket, will you promise not to burn the Earth to a cinder?' – was such a person fit to comment on cremation? Everyone knew that mercury tooth fillings of cremated oldtimers dangerously polluted the air and belching crematorium chimneys broke all CO_2 regulations. Alternative methods had to be found and the IGP had to lead the way. There was quite a heated debate until someone suggested it might be easier for her if Ms Valerie took over as acting Chair. Lady Patchett, surprisingly, stood down. She was obviously getting old.

Ms Serena of the Ethics Committee, who loved cats, rather to the distress of Housekeeping, suggested that taxidermy was the way ahead. Jeremy Bentham himself, founder of Utilitarianism, a philosophy much favoured by the IGP, sat mummified in pride of place at University College London as an inspiration to others. Housekeeping said to suggest embalming was ethnically and religiously insensitive; she was surprised Ms Serena had said that. Ms Serena apologised. Housekeeping said she wondered if Ms Serena would see her way to having her cat seen to: Tibbles had already had four batches of kittens, and finding homes was not easy. Ms Serena said she would do so and Housekeeping accepted her apology.

Burial at sea was mooted: though it meant hiring a boat and an exceptional sea depth was required. There was an authorised centre for sea burials at Newhaven, a mere six miles down the coast where deep water was near the shore, but it was closed at weekends.

Ms Valerie's interjection – 'We could hire a boat, No one would know' – was met by a rather shocked silence. But she added, 'Sorry, everyone, just a cadaver, not a person. But delete, delete!' and she was forgiven. She was young, and the young, though at home in the computer age, could be disrespectful of custom and convention. It was eventually decided that Mr Patchett would be buried in the small patch of sandy earth between the High Tower and the road, where ornamental sea grass was grown, very prettily. Lady Patchett did not 'do' funerals, even for a husband – and at her age she would hardly be expected to. Ms Valerie had arranged for a close relative to be present, so etiquette would be honoured and convention observed.

3. Matters relating to tomorrow's celebrations.
This was quickly dealt with. Security had dug up and dealt
with the dead rat – everything was under control. The weather
forecast was not too good but the BBC often got things wrong.
Luxuriette had agreed to serve hot chocolate as well as sausages at the scheduled stops. The umbrellas from Harrods had
arrived and would look very jolly and festive.

4. Vote of thanks to Valerie Valeria, for 10 per cent membership
   rise over two years.
This was passed and unanimously agreed.

5. Policy direction.
It was agreed that now was not the time for this particular
discussion, but that it would be No. 1 on next month's agenda.

6. Any other business.
None other being raised the meeting was closed and lunch was
served in the canteen.

*'Spice-crusted aubergines & peppers with pilaf or crisp kidney
bean curry with wild rice'* was served for lunch, followed by
*'Sticky stem ginger pudding (gluten free) or clementine & prosecco
jelly with oat biscuit'*. No one could say that Ms Bradshap didn't
try. Valerie Valeria kept a stack of Mars Bars, a variety of potato
crisps and pork crackling bites in her stationery cupboard to
which all were welcome. But after lunch today her office was
closed and Ms Valeric was nowhere to be seen.

Chapter 4
Valerie

Let's follow Valerie Valeria back from the meeting. She leaves
it with the little hop, skip and jump in the corridor that marks
her elation. Things had gone exceptionally well. The path
ahead lay clear. She would replace the She Devil as head of
IGP, which would go from strength to strength, she would be
head hunted by other charities, move once or twice – then the
national NGOs would take an interest, after that the worldwide
organisations. She could be the woman from the WHO telling
the nations of the world how to act in the face of epidemics,
the one from the IMF warning them of financial meltdown
ahead. Now the power of women had been released there was
no stopping them. She could be Mrs Gandhi, Mrs Thatcher,
Catherine the Great, hop, skip and jump! She was beautiful,
she was lean, she was smart, she was childless and now she was
in love. In love with an angel, the beautiful, the spiritual Tyler
Finch Patchett. Hop, skip, jump!

But what she must not do was have children. Everywhere she
looked, it was motherhood that held women back, that and
the monthly debilitating curse of menstruation, which sapped
energy, will and competence, caused girls to fail exams and
productivity to fall by 20 per cent every twenty-eight days.
The moon was full today: tomorrow it would be the equinox;

the moon would follow the sun; the tides would rise in obedience – her own sexuality rose and fell as the moon waxed and waned. It was high today. Forget Leda. 'Burn in Mordor' indeed! Hop, skip and jump!

Four years now since she'd been fitted with an intrauterine device which fed the hormone progestin into her system. That had been in Sydney. She no longer had periods, she could not have babies. A perfect solution – well, more or less perfect, it had been known to fail, just as lesbianism itself could fail. And the device, trade mark Femmefree, needed replacing. Its lifetime, according to the literature, was five years. Valerie Valeria – how she loved her name: it could take her anywhere! – was well within the limit; but even so. How she had loved and trusted the mother who had blessed her with that name. The only thing that had gone wrong in her whole enchanted life had been the sudden death, by suicide, of her mother. Valerie had been sixteen, in the throes of a first wondrous love affair with Amy, the head girl at school, both of them in the netball team, and her mother's death had spoiled all that. The reason for the tragedy stayed a mystery; the sight of it still appeared in dreams. Hanging. Oh forget it. Move on! Hop, skip and jump!

Valerie Valeria had a friend and fan in Dr Simmins, who had offered her help during a rare attack of self-doubt and weakness: she could no doubt see to the Femmefree concerns. Valerie would approach her as soon as the Widdershins Walk was over and done. Everything was under control: nothing could go wrong; she had seen to everything, overcome doubt and weakness; the world was her oyster. The Walk today, tomorrow the top tables of the world. Hop, skip, jump!

And now she was to be reunited with Tyler in 2CC/16, her bedroom on the second floor of the Castle Complex: one of the premium corner rooms, one side facing the bay, the other the noble iconic structure of the High Tower. She had dragged herself from her bed that morning to get to the meeting, resisting the temptation, as she was surely entitled, to claim preparation for the next day's work, but now at last she was free to get back to the embrace of her angelic boy's golden, muscly arms.

It couldn't be for too long, though. She would have to introduce him to his grandmother before the old lady took to her bed for her nap, and sort out all that family feud nonsense. That should be easy enough: if Tyler had turned out for his grandpa's death, with a little persuasion he would turn out for his burial and his grandma's eighty-fifth. The She Devil had walked out of the meeting early because of an apparent surfeit of grief at the thought of Bobbo being poured down the drain, but Valerie thought it was more likely to be future shock: face to face at last with her own mortality, and she needed a rest.

Come hell or high water, Valerie Valeria was determined: Tyler the beautiful would process on Widdershins Day. Fate had delivered him to her. The universe was on her side. Look at how lovely the weather was today, how clear the sky. The pathetic fallacy perhaps, but never mind. The High Tower had its own micro-climate, she was aware of that. Indeed, she'd always thought old Bobbo, with his so very male and disagreeable moods, tempers and flare ups, had something to do with this idiosyncrasy. Perhaps now he was dead the High Tower would find itself conforming to the national weather forecast. Though with any luck not as soon as tomorrow for which the forecast was, frankly, really rather bad. But these old ladies, however nutty, were brave and buoyant in the face of adversity with a courage that could put the young to shame. All except the She Devil, who seemed so neurotic about hot and cold. She had become quite fond of the old lady, in spite of her follies and fancies. But she needed to face facts: her day was done, her brand of gender politics stale and over.

And now for Tyler. He was two years younger than she was. You could tell it by the resilience of his flesh. Leda had been at least thirty-five. Hop, skip and little leap!

Chapter 5
Ms Bradshap

Ms Bradshap was in good time for the Board meeting at two, which was when the She Devil had told her it was – only to find it had already taken place that morning, and that Valerie had had the nerve to accept the office of acting Chair; that there was to be no funeral for Bobbo, but the Victory March was to go ahead with Bobbo's dead body paraded as though in a victor's triumph. Lady Patchett had walked out of the meeting in disgust. This she was told by a tall girl with dark hollow eyes from Security who was stacking chairs but happy to talk.

Ms Bradshap had had to sit down on one of them to take it all in. Valerie was far too young and inexperienced to be on the Board, whose median age was seventy, and had grown up, so to say, in the business of committees. Valerie had tapped in to a lot of new money with her tasteless logo and brochure – which had gone viral, whatever that was, but it certainly appealed to the lowest common denominator. She was young and bright, pleasant to look at and even interesting to talk to, but everything hung on her being young, and with youth came folly. Ms Bradshap said as much to the Security woman, whose name she remembered was Leda.

Leda absolutely agreed, and added that Valerie thought she

was Lady Marwen, but scratch her and she was just a bitchy, treacherous Orc like any other, good for heartbreak but nothing else, and a disgrace to Mordor. In any battle the troops would come out on the side of the She Devil, of Sauron.

'Is that *The Lord of the Rings*?' said Ms Bradshap, who at least recognised the name Sauron. She politely excused herself, her point made, and walked back to her hated dark and dreary office in the depths of the High Tower, 3HT/12. On her way she passed Valerie coming in the other direction, noticed the little hops, skips and jumps and they irritated her.

She'd been feeling quite poorly after her embarrassing fit of terror at seeing Mary Fisher's face at the window the previous day, though Dr Simmins had given her a jab of something which had calmed her and made her sleep in late the next day. She probably wouldn't have made the morning meeting anyway. Once back in the office she found the atmosphere quite changed; her pencils were still in the proper order in their box and she had no sense that they might move of their own volition. The musty smell had gone. She gave her great-niece Irene a call.

'Things are so much better here,' she said. 'The old man's gone. Such a disruptive presence. A male of the dinosaur school.' She suggested that Irene came along to the big party the next day. It was the birthday Widdershins Walk round the High Tower. Quite an event. Everyone would be very busy. Irene could slip in unnoticed, even bring the boys. A few men had even been invited, so gender purity wasn't an issue. The Lantern Room would be empty and Irene could sight-see to her heart's content.

'Did you say widdershins?' shrieked Irene. 'You're joking! That's so, so unlucky! Something terrible will happen. Witches go widdershins round the church at the beginning of the black mass. And if anyone looks like a witch it's the She Devil.'

'We aren't a church, we're a phallic symbol,' said Ms Bradshap. 'And that too is sinister. It's all a disgrace. And I don't think that Valerie is any better than she should be.'

'Yup,' said Irene.

'Wear some grey agate for protection and something amethyst to calm things.'

Chapter 6
Valerie Again

When Valerie Valeria returned to her room the blinds were still down: Tyler was still asleep. If he'd been a girl he'd have been up by now, bathed and fresh, blinds up and window opened, bed re-made, little lipsticked love-notes on the bathroom mirror. But Tyler still slept like a lovely log, arms flung out like a baby's above his head, open and unafraid, man not woman, seeking his own satisfaction, free of guilt. Valerie had found sexual satisfaction enough with women, affection, trust and more than enough emotional turmoil to satisfy anyone. But with Tyler the sense of the opposite was strong. More desire and involuntary excitement, if less turmoil. She must not forget to go to Dr Simmins. She could see she was more at the mercy of more primitive instincts than she had ever imagined she could be.

Leda's 'Burn in Mordor' left Valerie unafraid yet gratified, relishing the freedom of being what she chose to be: the more Leda suffered the greater her response to Tyler's male charms. The sense of being powerless, impaled, thrilled. Love was in the head and the heart, sex was in the clitoris. Compared with love, sex was trivial. It was exhilarating; no longer the thrill of conquest, the thrill of being conquered: more the joys of emotional masochism than the superficial thrills of tribbing.

There'd be no explaining it to Leda, whose eyes would only fill with baffled tears. Valerie was in love: she was happy. Love, love, love! She was Mary Fisher's child and heir! The She Devil with all her bitterness was the one to burn in Mordor.

Tyler had woken, drawn her fully dressed into the hot, steamy bed, smelling of man. Organ met orifice, limb melted into limb; she was suspended there it seemed for hours, impaled as a butterfly upon a pin. But what was easy enough with women seemed not to be with men: orgasm eluded her. She didn't make a fuss. He didn't apologise. Perhaps he didn't even notice. He was a man, after all.

Valerie Valeria, she of the blessed existence, could see it might become a problem – but they were new together. Custom and practice might make a difference. It better had.

Valerie made him shower and shave – oh those dear little black sprouts! His beard, like his eyelashes, was black; comb his hair – oh those blonde, shiny, bouncy curls! She'd never liked Leda's hair, greasy and flat; and then dress, lending him her baggy midnight blue Jason Lu sweater. It went beautifully with his trainers. Tyler did not mind instruction, thank God – girls often did, full of objections, insisting on garments which simply did not suit them.

And then she and Tyler were ready, all happy and handsome, to go and beard his grandmother, her boss the She Devil, in her den.

Chapter 7

The She Devil Meets Her Grandson

Valerie was the last person the She Devil wanted coming into her bedroom when she was taking a nap, and without bothering to check that she was up and dressed. Which fortunately the She Devil was, and sitting in a winter sun so warm she didn't even need the heating. She was a little minx, Valerie, with her purloined acting Chair, her airs and graces and her impulsive decisions! Valerie had an iron fist in her velvet glove. Of course the meeting had ended quickly, everyone always wanted to get away to their tea, or in this case their lunch. Though everyone reported that when they did the aubergine was overcooked and slimy, and the curry too crisp to taste. Who'd ever heard of a crisp curry anyway?

Valerie had deliberately placed 'Policy direction' as the second to last item on the agenda, before 'Any other business': the dustbin end, when nobody had inclination or energy left to argue but simply postponing the item until the next meeting was unthinkable.

And here was Valerie in person, bright and glowing with youth and energy even more than usual. She must be delegating well, or she'd be in a state of hysteria about her big day tomorrow. As ever, the She Devil's heart began to soften. But then, in shock and horror, she saw Valerie had been followed in by an emissary of the enemy, a man: a young and pretty man. Was it perhaps her brother? The two were not unlike each other.

'A long time since I've had a man in my bedroom,' said the She Devil, reproachfully but not too savagely, 'I'm happy to say. The last one now lives in the freezer downstairs. So who is this?'
Valerie explained that it was the She Devil's grandson, the one she had been talking about, Tyler Finch Patchett. He had been there at his grandfather's death.
'Ah, it was you,' interjected the She Devil, and smiled at Tyler as if she actually liked him. 'I thought you were some kind of hospice assistant. Well, you make a good girl, for a boy!'
And now he needed to be at the funeral, said Valerie. It was only legal to bury a dead body in the garden in a decent, obvious and permanent way. In the She Devil's absence, to have another family member there would obviate invidious talk.
'Um,' said the She Devil. The sun was feeling a little less warm. There were a few clouds beginning to form on the horizon. The sea was looking a steel grey rather than an innocent blue.
'But I am still expected to head the Parity Procession round the High Tower?' she enquired.
'Oh indeed!' said Valerie. 'But Diavolessa, we must keep up with the times. We prefer to call it the Widdershins Walk. Have you forgotten?'
'I haven't forgotten there is a walk, whatever you've decided to call it today. I was rather wondering where my red velvet dressing gown had gone, by the way,' murmured the She Devil. Tyler thought that something quite deep and intense was going on, but he couldn't be sure what. Well, these powerful women would just have to fight it out. His mother and Mason would

sometimes have fights like this. Men thought with fists, women with words. He was beginning to feel very hungry. He wished they'd just get on with it. There had been a lot of sex lately and not much food. A good dinner and back to bed with Valerie would suit him very well.

'I gave it to Housekeeping, to be altered,' laughed Valerie. 'To give it a hood to keep you nice and warm. But it should be back this evening.'

'Delegate, delegate, Valerie, that's the way,' said the She Devil amiably, but with a hint of sarcasm. Tyler thought she was probably rather angry. She was not unlike his mother, which he supposed was to be expected. His mother's voice went quiet before she exploded with rage. 'You're so good at it!'

'Thank you. I am, actually!' said Valerie, laughing again. 'As for the burial, one does hope that the soil is not too sandy. There needs to be three metres of good soil on top and three below the body to be safe. I could ask my legal girls to check.'

'Perhaps not,' said the She Devil, coolly. 'Let's not bother them now.'

'All the same one certainly would not want Bobbo bobbing to the surface,' said Valerie. 'A stray hand beckoning from the grave, the better to pinch a bottom.'

There was a silence. Valerie wondered if she'd taken the wrong tack.

'No indeed,' agreed the She Devil. 'What a joke that would be! And I suppose you'd like our little Prince here to process with me, King and Queen of the fancy dress ball?'

Valerie thought about this for a moment, and then began to declaim rather than speak.

'Diavolessa, we must be seen to honour youth, beauty and

innocence as well as the wisdom of old age. Let the young bury the old! Let the old rejoice with the young!'

'Valerie,' said the She Devil, 'calm down. Save it for the brochure.'

Valerie was quite pink from excitement. Tyler felt awed. This glorious impassioned creature in his bed, or at any rate he in hers. And what had she said? 'This thing can run and run.' How life could change in the space of a day. Years with the Jobcentre Plus and now this.

The She Devil turned to Tyler. 'You'd better be careful, young man. Next thing you know you'll be the Corn King, sacrificed to make the crops grow.' And to Valerie: 'I'll think about it, my dear. What choice do I have, faced with so much enthusiasm? But I must have a private word with my grandson. I think we both deserve it. It has been a long time coming. But perhaps we should go to my office, I don't know.'

Valerie said she thought there was no need.

After leaving them together, Valerie would have been seen to give a hop, skip and little leap once she was out of the room, had there been anyone around to see. As it was, Valerie found she had to turn on the electric lights once she was on the stairs. Ms Bradshap always maintained it was a wicked waste to keep corridor lights on permanently and all were on time switches. But the sky had suddenly darkened, a habit it seemed to have got into lately; the wind had turned to the east and grey clouds were tumbling into black.

Chapter 8
Family Bonding

Tyler considered the She Devil and wondered what all the fuss had been about. She sat upright in her chair, as if there was a cord running from the top of her head to the ceiling. She was wearing a wig, a kind of fuzzy bird nest cloud round her head of a neutral colour, a style the twins occasionally favoured and described as retro. The rest of her quite large bulk was draped in dark purple velvet with an occasional glitter of diamonds, diamanté, or glass – how did one even tell which?

But the eyes, if one dared to raise them, seemed hurt rather than cruel, glittered with what Tyler could only describe as a terrible wounded intelligence. At any rate that was something he shared with her. If he inherited from Bobbo, he also inherited from the She Devil. It was why he sometimes made bad jokes which seemed normal to him, but others found horrible and shrank away. Valerie seemed able to cope with it, even appreciate it, which was no doubt why she enjoyed sparring with the She Devil as she did.

Between Valerie and himself the sparring took a sexual form: it worked itself out through limbs, holes, rubbing and squeezing, coaxing, gaping or prodding flesh, ending inexorably in an explosion which started everything over again, as in the Big

Bang, with the possibility of new life. His mother referred to it, with disdain, as 'animal instinct'. He relished that. Orgasm was what made the world go round, each thrust an encouragement to the infinite. Valerie obviously liked him, loved him, or said she did. He was more cautious, less certain of a lasting commitment. Hermione's hurtful 'lacks finesse' still rang in his ears. Had Valerie been faking her own recreation of the universe? Had he done his best and failed? In which case he was getting renewed and she wasn't.

In some ways men had it easier than women, they pretty much usually had orgasms: perhaps that was the main thing women so resented. What the ithyphallic High Tower beamed out to the world was not so much encouragement to others but a cry for help. Valerie might claim to be bi, but she was probably basically and permanently and forever gay, a born lesbian. And in the meantime he was so hungry! How long since he'd eaten?

The She Devil seemed able to read his mind; she rose from her armchair, not without difficulty – Tyler tried to help but she'd have none of it – went over to the kitchen alcove, took a frozen M&S fish pie from the little fridge, put it in the microwave and brought it over cooked, with fork and spoon. In the meantime there was silence, just the sound of waves breaking at the foot of the High Tower, which Tyler took to be companionable. He wolfed the food down. It was still rather cold and raw in the middle but Tyler didn't mind.

'Better?' she said.

'That was a very grandmotherly thing to do,' he said. What on earth had Nicci been going on about, and Matilda? The destroying, narcissistic mother? Unless of course, this friendliness was as much a fake as Valerie's orgasm. All women were a bit mad, and the She Devil, though long past the menopause, still seemed to have a lingering femaleness about her, if you forgot the face.

Better always to look at her eyes than the face, which would put anyone off. If Tyler had had such looks, he would not have ventured out at all. His own wall eye had been bad enough: it had cramped his style no end. He had preferred to go about amongst familiars than strangers; people who were accustomed to what he looked like. Only when the eye had been fixed had he begun to live any kind of normal life. If he was young for his age, and people said he was, this was why. He was a mixture of too much understanding and too little.

The She Devil asked after his mother Nicci. Tyler tried to explain her without being too unkind. The sudden rages which had plagued his childhood, the way he'd learned to soothe and placate, anxious to prevent the moment when the maternal face would turn from an angel's to a devil's, devouring and smothering. How his sisters defied her instead of co-operating, as he, Tyler did, but they didn't seem able to leave home either. The rows, the noise, were addictive for them.

The She Devil observed that evidently his mother had chosen to join the ranks of the working classes rather than stay in the middle, who were far less noisy. Here at the High Tower everyone was middle class – they defended themselves with acid tongues. It did not mean they were happier, just more reserved in expressing their objections to life, times and other people. So more work got done. And she'd heard that Nicci was a good feminist. That was a cheering thing to hear, and she hoped that Tyler would ask his mother and sisters to come to the burial tomorrow, and join in the celebrations. They would be very welcome if they did.

Tyler said that one way or another it was unlikely. His mother thought all men were the enemy, the High Tower was the source of all evil, and if she knew he was even talking to the She Devil she would have kittens.

The She Devil seemed a little surprised, then said she could see Tyler might have had a hard time of it as a child. Self-pity overwhelmed Tyler, unaccustomed as he was to sympathy and understanding. He wept, he spoke, he searched for words, and searching, found them, all too many of them.

It had been his great misfortune to have been born as a boy. Even his mother had wanted to abort him because he was the wrong sex. All along the way girls had it so much better than boys. It had begun in nursery school: if you ran round and shouted and rolled on the floor they said why couldn't you be more like a girl and offered you Ritalin to keep you quiet. After that there'd been women teachers all the time. Men couldn't get teaching jobs, or didn't apply for them. They meant trouble. Parents of little children feared paedophilia; get to fifteen and girl pupils fell in love and claimed rape. Male teachers were constantly on gardening leave. Girls learned by copying, boys by understanding principles and applying them. Girls were bound to do better than boys, since teaching was done by women. He'd have liked to learn Latin but there was no Latin teacher. Too male a subject. Of course his mother favoured girls, girls didn't get ill, have autism, or get acne: they passed exams, got to college, got jobs, wore nice dresses, went shopping with their mums, chewed men up and spat them out. He worried about his sisters: they confused 'nasty' with 'strong'. They'd never find anyone to commit, because who'd ever want to? Women ruled the world. Men were second-class citizens and he was fed up with it.

'Just like your grandfather,' said Lady Patchett, when Tyler had finished his rant, sniffled a bit and seemed calm again. 'Moan, moan, moan! And look where it got him. Downstairs in my freezer, or perhaps in the cold room, whichever the girls decided.'

'That's what I mean,' said Tyler, bitterly. 'Men die, and women shove you in a freezer and bury you outside the back door.'

'Exactly,' said his grandmother. 'But feeling the way you do, you could always choose to become a woman? It's easily done.'

'Chop off my willy? No thanks,' said Tyler.

'No one gets it cut off any more, dear child, accept a few nutters determined to make a perverse point. It gets reassigned, peeled like a banana, turned inside out. Bits fitted in here and there, no sensation lost. Add a few hormones and Bob's your uncle – or indeed your Auntie.'

He couldn't tell if she was joking or if she was being serious.

'Think about the advantages, no more humiliations, no more remorse. No more fear of failure to get it up, premature ejaculation once you do, no more accusations of rape to worry about. No more abortions to pay for.'

Whatever it was she was being very indelicate and pressing buttons he would rather not have pressed – he could see again where his mother and the girls got it from. It was hereditary.

She was summing up his life in clichés and throwing it away, as if it meant nothing.

'Then you can be my heir,' she said. 'Solves everything for me. Another fish pie? I can tell you're a hungry boy.'

'Yes. Thanks, please.'

He spoke without thinking. It was true. He was still hungry. She warmed another fish pie and he ate.

'The money's in a bank account in Switzerland. I'm certainly not going to leave it to a man, and I don't like the sound of your sisters, let alone your mother. It has to go somewhere. There's quite a lot of it. All the money Bobbo did ten years in jug for. But at least I looked after him in his old age. No one can say I didn't. "*The Moving Finger writes and, having writ, moves on*" and all that. I don't suppose you did poetry at school?'

'They made us learn *The Schoolboy*. William Blake. The girls all liked it. I didn't know what he was talking about.'

'Really? "*How can a child, when fears annoy, but droop his tender wing?*" How much better to have been one of the girls. If you can't beat us, join us,' said the She Devil.

Perhaps she was mad. She couldn't mean all that about the money. But what she was saying wasn't totally mad, Tyler found himself thinking, as he scraped away the last of the browny crust round the edge of the dish. A girl! No more worrying about 'finesse', size and buoyancy. Rather, the feel of a dress, the freedom of the thighs, a bosom to push it up, a waist to belt it, the moving silkiness on the skin – but all that stuff about money – the old lady was out of her mind. Or just bullshitting. There was a knock on the door. It was Valerie, warning him that the canteen was about to close and if Tyler wanted to eat he'd better come now.

'I've seen to all that, Valerie,' said the She Devil 'You don't need to interfere. Come here. Be my witness.'

Valerie found the She Devil's notebook, the She Devil scrawled, Valerie witnessed, the She Devil tore out the page, which Valerie then folded and stuck it in her bra. Tyler was surprised she wore one, so self-uplifting did her small neat bosom seem to be.

'Just go away now, the pair of you,' the She Devil said. 'Trouble with you, Valerie, is you're all hot air. I make real things happen. Now just go away.'

When they were out in the corridor Tyler asked what it was that Valerie had had to witness.

'Just another of her wills,' Valerie said, airily. 'She makes them all the time. This one leaves everything to you, her granddaughter, Tyler of the IGP. But with an "a" instead of the "y", then the "e" and "r" struck out and replaced with an "a": "Tayla". Oh, she thinks she's so smart! But it does suit you. Oh, my darling Tayla! Shame she has nothing to leave – she's already given it all to the IGP.'

Chapter 9
Valerie And Tyler

Valerie had felt uneasy about leaving Tyler alone with the She Devil, and rightly so. Gaia alone knew what she was playing at. It seemed that the wicked old woman was actually trying to bribe Tyler to have a sex change. He would make a very pretty girl, it was true, but hardly the point. It was a no-brainer: she, Valerie, was as fit to run a big charity as Tyler was not.

The She Devil was not actually in the habit of making wills, and it might just possibly be valid, so Valerie would keep it by her just in case. It need never be found, but in case of need might have to be. And who knew what the need might be when the time came for the old lady to die.

'Tell me about the money,' said Tyler. 'I did think it was kind of, just old-lady talk. She really hasn't got any then?'

Valerie replied, truthfully enough, that mad old Bobbo was always claiming she had millions in a Swiss bank that were rightfully his, but that came through Samantha who was scarcely a reliable narrator, being a few cards short of the full deck. 'That girl talked to ghosts. Like a lot of dipsticks round here.'
'I don't like to think of the old man just shoved in the freezer,' said Tyler. 'Supposing he's not properly dead and wakes up?'

'Too fucking late,' said Valerie, rather callously, he thought.
'And I can't believe it's legal to keep a dead body at home.'
'It's not in Oz, but it is here. And I don't suppose it makes much difference to the dirty old bugger now.'

It was difficult to talk because her phone kept ringing. Luxuriette were agitating about having to change éclairs from artificial to real cream because Ms Bradshap said otherwise she'd take money off the bill. Amethyst were on the phone all the time about this building problem or that, and she told them to sort it out themselves, similarly Femina Electrical, fussing about lighting and wet wires should it rain – everyone worried about the weather. The She Devil was right about one thing: left to themselves women were more than able to get things done; it was just that through the ages opportunity had been snatched from them. Valerie herself was gifted at delegating. The She Devil acknowledged that. Valerie turned her phone to silent. Tyler needed her attention.

Now they were heading for the canteen, 2CC/4, as Tyler was still a bit hungry. Valerie had survived quite happily all day on decaff and pumpkin seeds (available 24/7 from the canteen), plus surreptitious caffeine pills and the occasional serious uppers which a rather fanciable girl on a motorbike turned up monthly to provide, and was surprised that even after a fish pie Tyler still had an appetite for the crispy curry, by now almost curry brittle, but he didn't seem to notice. He bit into it with his perfect, astonishingly white teeth. Valerie shivered to watch the hardness break through the crust and find the softness, and the flicker of the pink tongue as it licked the lips. She was seized by desire; she must get him back to her bed as soon as possible.

Lillian behind the counter seemed rather alarmed to find a male in the canteen – they were a rare sight, though sometimes the exigencies of good manners and/or Equalities Law made their presence inevitable – but Tyler did not look like someone from Health and Safety or HMRC. Valerie explained on impulse that Tyler was crossing over and Lillian beamed, said 'Go girl!', and went off to find some mayonnaise to help Tyler's curry brittle go down.

'Don't go so fast, Val,' Tyler said, 'I haven't decided yet. This is rather major. We don't know for sure about the money,' which shocked Valerie as being rather a venal sentiment in the circumstances.

She thanked Gaia that she'd got him away in time from the evil old cow. On the other hand, judging by Lillian's reaction if she, Valerie, could present Tyler as trans she could have him live with her here in the High Tower. How else were they to be together? And the old bat could hardly object, it having been her mad idea in the first place. And the She Devil would at last stop her stupid arguing about heading the Widdershins Walk with Tyler by her side. The She Devil would throw on her red velvet cloak, put on her crown, and off they'd go together. Ellen would get her pics, social media would buzz, add a funeral and Tyler as trans – oh wow! Next thing, Widdershins would go so totally global, and it was all the doing of Valerie Valeria: her mother would be so proud of her! Everything was going her way. And look at the weather, not a cloud in sight except a few gathering round the edges. Tyler was such a darling; now he was worrying about her turning her phone off – wouldn't she miss important calls? – and nagging about her taking wake-up pills (and trying to get her to eat a dolphin-free tuna sandwich – yuk).

And then they were in the bedroom and it was heaven, every nerve in her body alive; she didn't at all mind the sudden invasion of her body space. 'Every thrust a welcome thrust!' The words formed in her head, creating their own reality, driving her deeper and deeper into a submission so joyous she could hardly believe it, only rejoice in it. Mindless, mindless...

For some reason the cover of one of the old Mary Fisher novels came to her – lovely tender girl and glorious man, eyes and lips meeting, and love, love, love. All you need. Except it wasn't all she needed. Everything built up to climax but then the climax just didn't happen. Tyler the love object was also the hero in the porn films, the attacker, the invader of unwilling flesh, battering, damaging, frightening. It was all too personal, too intimate, too alive, not safely filtered through a screen. What with one thing and another she hadn't plugged her phone in. It might be out of juice. Out of juice was out of touch. Valerie had better bring this to an end, quickly. She uttered a few obligatory squeals and moans and Tyler came, rather noisily: more like a long shout of triumph than a female squeal of pleasure. But you could always have the vocal cords tightened to deliver a feminine murmur of satisfaction. If that was what you wanted. 'If you would really rather be a girl, Tyler,' she said, 'we could be so happy together.'
Tyler said nothing but he was beginning to think she could be right.

When Valerie looked at her phone she found the battery was shockingly low and there were twenty-five missed calls.

Chapter 10
No Walk

The World Women's Widdershins Walk was cancelled, defeated by the weather.

What had happened to an otherwise perfectly planned event was a lightning strike to the High Tower. Security had been up top with Femina Electrical – some kind of bird strike having pushed a few aerials out of true, affecting both reception and transmission at this crucial time. Leda (for it was she) had had the bright if rather suicidal idea of flying a kite – in honour of Deborah Franklin, Benjamin's common-law wife, the real power behind the throne – in order to protect the girls. But the lightning had struck the High Tower, not the kite, and all were lucky to be alive. Leda had to be hospitalised with nasty burns on the arm. 'Suicidal or stupid,' the paramedic (male and unfeeling) had observed. Valerie had to agree. Leda had already caused so much trouble.

Cell phones were mysteriously not working. The electric garage doors wouldn't open, so Tyler, fleet of foot and with Last of the Mohicans staying power, had run down to the Auto Solo Garage outside the village to contact the outside world by sending out a hundred and fifty emails, each with its regrets emoji. Not all arrived, out after all that, some getting blocked by spam filters as mass postings, some, it being so near Christmas, were simply not opened. Fifty-two of those invited turned up. One for every week of the year – Valerie noted, even in her distress that she could somehow use that in the next brochure. But no time now. She was too busy.

Worse, the top of the High Tower where it faced the sea, just above the aerial platform, was the epicentre of the strike and a great chunk of masonry knocked off had fallen straight onto the new wooden walkway and its scaffolding and smashed the lot. Thank Gaia Amethyst were still on their supper break so there were no injuries amongst them. But walking the Walk was out of the question, widdershins or even clockwise. A flood tide was rising and the wind was up, whipping the waves into frothy orgasms, and it looked almost like the High Tower logo.

Valerie's battery had gone dead when the electricity went, and there'd been nothing she could do but creep back into bed with Tyler.
'Just as well,' Tyler had said. 'Better cancelled than a disaster.' Which was annoying of him but Valerie had to admit Tyler was right. His lips were so lovely and tender, his skin so soft and moist… Leda's mouth tended to be dry and flakey but Valerie had never liked to say so.

Valerie could acknowledge a falling off in her usual efficiency. After all she was in love and therefore justified. There was such a thing as a life work balance. The sex had been cheering and good but not perfect. It obviously had been for Tyler, but she craved perfection, and would not rest until she had it. She sighed at the wilfulness of the universe, and returned to the work side of the balance: a useless smartphone was going to mean a hell of a lot of exhausting running around.

She thought of what Tyler had just said: perhaps, all in all, the necessity for a cancellation could actually be seen as a blessing? It would not do to have a disaster at this stage in her career; inexperience had led her into trying to cram too much into too small a space of time. With Amethyst still putting up the scaffolding at this late date, she had been cutting things very fine indeed. Too fine. But she, Valerie Valeria, was the kind to acknowledge her own shortcomings. How else did one learn? Meanwhile she was in love.

Chapter 11
Bobbo's Funeral

Bobbo's burial ceremony was brought forward to 10 a.m. the next day, and kept simple. To make death a matter of parity, of inclusivity, some sort of solemn rite was needed to support Valerie's initial concept: without the Widdershins Walk the interment might disappoint, be too like burying a dead tom cat in the back garden. A private family burial here and now was appropriate and should forestall gossip about the manner of death or silly jokes about the freezer. If anyone heard spades clanking on rock as Security dug into muddy sand in pouring rain, no one would have reason to gossip. If the body had to be re-interred as time went on, so be it. This was now and that would be then.

At least Tyler and Valerie were in attendance. Samantha was invited, and came. Dr Simmins was invited, and did not. The weather was far too atrocious, the She Devil claimed, for her to venture out; apart from that she had told Ms Laura that if Valerie was going she would not – Lady Patchett was at her most petulant, Ms Laura complained.

Security turned up in force – Tyler feared they were only too glad to see the back of his grandfather and came to celebrate rather than to mourn. Leda, of course, was still in hospital.

It was very much *pompes funèbres au naturel*, the coffin-less body, shroud-wrapped and pathetically small, placed on the sandy soil of the grave, soil so thin it seemed already to be caving in.

The service was taken by Ms Fawkes, one of the younger IGP members at sixty-four, who found a site called *Church Services for Unbelievers* on Google and downloaded something from that. But there was precious little said in affectionate remembrance, large lumps of hail soon replaced raindrops and the little cluster of mourners had to retreat to the lee of the tower for shelter. Everyone returned once the hail stopped bouncing to try *Amazing Grace*, but the wind and rain whisked their squeaks away and drove the words back down their throats, so they soon gave up.

Ellen had her camera under her umbrella and took a few useful shots, and Valerie's phone was back in action battery-wise so she could tweet and instagram away: '*Braving the storm – the family mourns; male and female mingle in pursuit of parity.*' Alliteration was always good.

The grave was filled in, or more or less fell in. Ms Octavia watched her woven bamboo linen shroud disappear under shovelfuls of sand – £175 down the drain; she could get a replacement but it was a lovely off-white tawny colour and she had been rather keeping it for herself when she died. But giving Bobbo a shroud rather than a bed sheet was the right thing to do. Good karma went to the giver, not the taker. Samantha threw in a rather pretty wreath of garlic – leaves and stalks intertwined and cloves as pendants. The rain and wind stopped, clouds parted, a ray of sun came down and hit the grave. All were taken aback. It seemed a rebuke from on high. If no one would take proper notice of Bobbo, heaven would. There was a moment of silence. Tyler felt justified, though he was not sure what for. Clouds parted further and he too was now in direct sunlight, though others were left in the dark. They were all staring at him.

Then the clouds joined up together, and the sun was hidden. The source of Tyler's epiphany, or whatever it was, had moved on; the funeral was over, an unknown number of guests would be coming in an hour's time, expecting a Widdershins Walk which wouldn't happen and a funeral which already had.

Valerie hoped to find the time for one more tryst with Tyler before the guests arrived. Dressed as he was in a white belted raincoat borrowed from Ms Octavia, he had looked so beautiful in the ray of sunlight, like the statue of Christ in the Catholic church in Kangaroo Valley when she was a child. She took it as a sure sign that they were meant for each other. But Tyler hadn't had breakfast and was hungry. She left him in the canteen telling him if anyone expressed surprise at his gender he was to emphasise that he was transiting. She gave him her cardigan because he was shivering with cold. She, Valerie Valeria, hardly ever felt the cold. Perhaps the motorbike girl's wake-up pills had something to do with it.

She went off to compose a quick poster explaining to those who turned up that they were at a cancelled event, but that everything would be done to make this birthday party a success. That they should admire the fervour of the storm:

pray for themselves as mariners in their own lives, that the She Devil was in mourning for her husband who lay shipwrecked at peace in the place he loved so much – but somehow her very talent for words exhausted her: it was all too difficult: there would be no poster: let the guests find out for themselves what was going on. Really she could not take responsibility for absolutely everything all the time any more.

Chapter 12
The Party

Valerie decided to help the Luxuriettes fill the éclairs with cream. They could never have got it done if a full complement of guests was expected. If she'd known about the lightning strike, she'd have stopped Leda flying her kite – well, possibly. The sausages had not turned up. She'd not checked when she should have checked. Twenty-five unanswered calls! This was what no orgasm could do for a girl. Tyler simply had to become Tayla. Same lovely person but without all that primitive thrusting in the wrong place.

The Lantern Room had been hastily given a coat of white paint by the light of oil lamps, the better to set off the antique sofa, hung with Christmas bunting – old sparkling strings of it found at the village shop, a job-lot from Woolworths, now defunct – and looked really pretty; though perhaps rather less so once the power was back on. But the guests were appreciative, genial and generous in their condolences – ten of the fifty-two were males, a good straw in the wind. The wine was good and plentiful, the chicken pie and the vegetarian option – courgette lasagne – really something. The side dishes all had calorie labels on them. The éclairs were in great demand, being in short supply and the icing chocolate not carob.

The first guest came promptly at one, the last drunken guest drifted away at midnight. Arguments about gain and loss, cost and catering and who paid what for what would have to come later. Ms Laura, or someone – but this was no time for recriminations – had forgotten to send off the cheque for the insurance.

Outside the great windows rain, hail and sleet still blustered at three o'clock. It was decided to pull the blinds down and turn up the lighting, now the High Tower actually had its power back. It was the shortest day, after all. Meaningful! Forget New Year. This was the start of the real, new future of parity. Valerie tweeted and instagrammed: '*And ten of us were men! The more the weather blustered, the more optimism blossomed!*'

That was on the Saturday. Sunday was spent clearing up. The She Devil stayed closeted in her room finishing an article for *Academica Feminica* and did not turn up for Monday's Board meeting. A vote of thanks went to Valerie for her enterprise in weathering the storm. Due to an Act of God only some fifty guests had been able to attend, but all had bonded, mixed and networked, which was, after all, what the point was. Tom Brightlingsea of De-Gender Now had created a working partnership with Mandy Masters from Anti-Trafficking Concern.

There were some issues yet to be faced and overcome. Ms Sidcup the Treasurer estimated a loss of £230,000 in the budget – Amethyst were having to bring in heavy machinery and possibly male labour to deal with the masonry fall, Femina Electrical had asked to be released from their contract – and so forth, but she was sure a rise in the membership fee from

£8 to £10 would compensate. Ms Sidcup said she was finding the duties of Treasurer in such a rapidly expanding organisation to be too onerous considering her age, and if everyone agreed she would like formally to share the job with Valerie who had a head for figures. Everyone agreed, and Ms Sidcup's longtime dedication to and hard work for the IGP was recognised, Ms Sidcup thanked and Valerie welcomed.

Valerie invited everyone to welcome the She Devil's grandchild Tyler, soon to become Tayla, who would be taking up residence in the Lantern Room during his transition. The new library would be in the Castle Complex. There was to be a World Women's Widdershins Walk a year from now, by which time true international recognition could be achieved. There were some murmurings from the floor but Valerie, as acting Chairperson, brought the meeting quickly to an end.

PART THREE

Tyler In Transition

Nurse Hopkins

There, you see! There was no need at all for all that *wooo-h,*
wooo-h, wooo-h-ing round the High Tower. The same plot development could be achieved without grotesque faces pressed
against windows in a rainstorm, spooky winds or spilled lentils.
All one needed, apart from a dead rat, was a timely lightning
strike to spoil the phallic perfection of the High Tower by
knocking off its seaward side (rather as an earthquake spoiled
the picture-perfection of Mount Ruapehu in New Zealand),
get Leda out of the way – and thus serve Momus' purposes
well enough. No need for the whole Tower to come tumbling
down or anything like that: Mary Fisher's dry-rot threat was
not required.

The connection between Leda and Valerie was stronger than
Valerie was prepared to admit. Momus' view was that any
sexual contact between two people has a lasting effect: the
reverberation of the least-considered one-night stand links you
to all sorts of other life paths. Casual sex may not create babies
any more, but that is a mere failure of intent, Momus argues, a
thwarting of the great basic urge to propagate the species; and
what should have happened but didn't is still there on the files,
as it were.

The union of Valerie and Leda, short-lived as it might be,

meaning so little to Valerie and so much to Leda, weighed heavier on the cosmic scales than did the union of Valerie and Tyler. Painful events may lie buried, but are not forgotten. Leda suffers; the pain in her poor burned arm is nothing compared to the hurt in her heart. Momus remembers the least of his children, bit-part players as well as leads.

Unlike Mary Fisher with her moaning and pity-me-ing, I don't resent my present state one little bit. I am happy where I am, thank you very much. I have always had rather a dread of heaven – all that flapping round with wings and worshipping, nothing to do but glorify, glorify, glorify and no events. The ultimate in boring. I don't think I am being punished so much as rewarded.

Look, I earned my salvation in my early days, all that nursing and caring for the deformed and wretched with the She Devil, and then looking after hard-working women the way we did at Vesta Rose. True, I did pretty well out of Vesta Rose, turning it in time into *VestaRoseagency.com*, a global organisation, as big as Uber, saving working women from the domestic chores that once ruled their lives. I was always one for praxis, not principle. True, I became very rich, which is seldom approved of by heaven, though Momus sees it rather differently, something at least plotworthy. Praise be to Momus, who has put me here to hurry on events in the service of plot rather than literature, spokesperson for my old friend the admirable She Devil who did so much to raise women out of servitude to their present state of grace.

But even She Devils have to die, and faced with the prospect of her successor Valerie Valeria employing the same cosmetic technology she herself once used – but this time to turn man into woman – the She Devil finds herself anxious and disturbed: what has she instigated? Male science has stealthily moved ahead, surreptitiously effecting a secret but potentially winning move in the battle between the sexes. The She Devil has not noticed. She has allowed herself to fall behind the times, and the times now move so fast that is hardly surprising. Man now controls the best weapon woman ever had, the body he so envied, its very moods and subtleties. He can become her, suck her up, subsume her. What will happen to the She Devil and her heritage? The old dream comes true all right, man will be as woman was. But what comes next?

The She Devil sulks, she takes sleeping pills, she eats too much, she regresses, she takes her own pulse to check it's still there, she is frightened of losing her step, of falling badly, of dying. Her little fridge bulges with squirrelled food, she stuffs her mouth with cream cakes, she steals Valerie's Mars Bars, she eats unhealthily and too much; then, bulimic, vomits her past up again. Ruth is in a bad way. I would help her if I could. She is my friend.

I stare in her window and am almost inclined to start *wooo-h, wooo-h, wooo-h*-ing like that idiot Mary, to startle my old friend into the awareness that suicide is no answer, but I know Momus wouldn't like it.

Tyler

Valerie rose from the bed and stood naked and beautiful at
the window, her arms raised to heaven. She had been faking it
again, Tyler was sure, but her thwarted passion seemed to have
an alternative route on standby: religion. She was a wonderful
sight, slim yet curvaceous, the pale almost translucent skin
alight with energy, tender yet immensely powerful – a High
Priestess summoning powers. She was completely nuts. 'Mother
Gaia, send your bounty down upon us, bless us on this day, for
we the young have done your bidding. Let the old wither and
perish like leaves on the tree, for they have closed their eyes
to you.' The prayer ended, the invocation was over. Valerie
slipped back into bed with Tyler. He had the most enormous
erection.

'That's all very well,' Tyler had said to Valerie when they'd got
back to bed after the Widdershins Walk post-mortem, and
things had calmed down just a little. 'But you're moving rather
faster than I'd anticipated. That was the first I've heard about
me moving in with you.'
'It was on the spur of the moment,' said Valerie. 'I needed to
nail in your status as a TS woman: IGP women aren't accustomed to having a man turn up at a meeting, let alone one who
looks like you. It would soften the blow if one of their number,
Tyler, both feminist man and feminist woman, were to occupy

the valuable and beautiful space of the Lantern Room here to be nursed through the pain and bewilderment of transition. It would be so symbolic, especially after Bobbo living there. Victory indeed! And the plan for the Lantern Room to be used as an open-access library has been dashed anyway, not by gender issues, but by two communications – one from Health and Safety saying that the stairs must be widened for public access, and the other one from the Planning Department saying that because the building is Grade One listed the stairs must not be altered.' Tyler ignored the last bit.

'Pain and bewilderment?' he asked, aghast. 'Nursed?'

'Of course not really, darling,' said Valerie. 'Only in the mind of the Board, so they pass the motion. The end justifies the means. We must seize the day. Thank heaven the She Devil has kept away.'

'And I'm not sure about the Lantern Room. It's where I watched my Grandpa die. Supposing he comes back to haunt it?'

'I shall be there to keep you company,' she laughed. She had a wonderful way of talking and laughing at the same time. It seemed to wipe away all doubts and fears.

The Lantern Room, she promised, would be made into a delightful apartment by Amethyst.

'Such a wonderful space. Three rooms, kitchen, bathroom, or possibly even two bathrooms, one for him and one for her, later of course one for her, and one for *her*. Bathrooms can make or break a relationship when there are two girls together.'

'So actually, it's you moving in with me,' he said.

'Of course. We love each other. We can't live without each other.'

True, Valerie had repeatedly said how much she loved him, and Tyler had even said it once to her, in the heat of the moment, and there were certainly much worse things than to be loved by someone like Valerie. There was also an indignity about it. A man did like to be asked. Men did not 'love' their sex slaves, they told them what to do and got pleasure at their expense, though that in itself could end up being a burden. One required a certain autonomy on the girl's part or there was just too much responsibility.

'And you could work for IGP as a librarian,' she promised, 'setting up the new library in the Castle Complex. You'd have a decent non-minimum wage job at last.'

His heart leapt. Now this was different. A job! A nirvana so desired. At last. But a wariness born of Jobcentre Plus experience cut in.

'Not minimum wage and zero-hours – for real? I haven't the right qualifications. There was a Librarianship module at uni but only girls ever took it.'

'Darling,' said Valerie, 'you have a natural intelligence and an aesthetic awareness and that is really all that is required. It'll be a proper salaried job with promotion opportunities.'

Tyler, still cautious, but pushing his advantage home, murmured that he'd require a formal written two-year contract with a six-month get-out clause, four weeks' annual holiday, medical insurance specified to cover the cost of what Valerie now referred to as his epiphany from M to F; and Valerie said no problem, she'd just speak to Miriam in HR, it could all be arranged. The IGP looked after its workers well.

She'd already conferred with Dr Simmins, who happened to be an expert in hormonal matters – a consultant to the North London Gender Reassignment Clinic for a number of years – and was happy enough to provide the counselling and medications required, though for the actual vaginoplasty they'd need a very good private clinic. Dr Simmins knew such a one in Harley Street, not too far away. The whole thing could be done in about a year if you knew what was what. Transiting men were no longer required to live for years as the kind of woman who wore fishnet tights and high heels before being accepted for reassignment. A few months in a skirt was now perfectly long enough, if you were dealing with the right doctors. Yes, said Valerie, of course, medical insurance would be included in the contract.

Tyler considered. A year out of his life. It was nothing. *Scrunched Zombies*, a single shooter game, would soon pass the time. He could play it undisturbed by mother and sisters, who switched it off at home whenever he switched it on. He was the She Devil's grandson, soon to be granddaughter: he must look at the moon, not mistrust the pointing finger. He was out of the doldrums, into the sunlight. He had trusted, believed, and everything had simply fallen into his lap. The old lady couldn't live forever. She was on her last legs. She'd promised to leave him her money: if she had any, and surely she must, he would then be free to do as he pleased. If it worked out with Valerie, he'd stay with her: they could even have a baby – her intact womb and his pre-op sperm frozen.

If not, they could go their separate ways. He was too young to settle, to be bounced into commitment now. Valerie would have lost interest by the time they broke up; too busy clawing her way up the career ladder to care. He was already beginning to think of Hermione a bit nostalgically. Pity how girls either loved too little or loved too much – both kind of threatened your virility. Hermione's indifference and Valerie's commitment were equally challenging. It would suit Valerie to have him female – he didn't suppose Hermione would be much bothered either way. His mother and his sisters would prefer him with a vagina rather than the oppressing penis. There would probably soon be a procedure which could reverse the whole thing anyway – medical progress moved so fast.

'This time next year,' cried Valerie in another fit of exultation, 'you, a young and beautiful maiden, will head the Widdershins Walk, all hardship behind you. What more could your grand-mother ask?'

It had never been in Tyler's nature to look before he leapt. He saw himself more as a hold your nose and jump kind of person. 'Oh fuck,' Tyler said. 'I'll do it!'

PART FOUR

As The Year Rolls On

January

Dr Ruby Simmins wound up her practice in St Rumbold's and moved in to 4HT/3, the better to supervise Tyler's transition to Tayla. She would have preferred to be in the Castle Complex but there was no room available. The fourth floor was bearable, however: there was at least elevator access at this level, so there were no steep stone stairs to worry about: it was light and bright and there was a glass walkway just outside her door which took her over rocks and (when the tide was in) waves, to the comfort and modernity of the Castle Complex and its canteen. The food served seemed perfectly acceptable, being plentiful and nourishing, but Dr Simmins was the first to acknowledge she was no sort of foodie.

She was kept busy enough but not too busy with the IGP residents, who on the whole were an uncomplaining lot, most of them still intellectually active – tough old birds, in other words. They had converted 3CC/5 for use as a clinic, and had it equipped properly and to modern standards by Maria Medical Outfitters, who also made available (only twenty-four hours' notice required) their travelling range of imaging modalities – MRI, CT, PET CT, X-Ray, Ultrasound, and even Nuclear (though those latter units were really heavy: even the High Tower seemed to tremble on their approach), but that might have been Dr Simmins' fancy, she was so flattered and impressed. Expense seemed to be no object for the IGP. Dr Simmins could almost describe herself as happy.

Even the storms seemed to have blown themselves out after their wild excesses over the Christmas season. Perhaps Femina Electrical had finally got their aerials and lightning conductors in tune with one another, so the High Tower basked in the best winter could offer in the way of cold, bright, clean, sunny weather with blue skies, little wind and glassy seas. The only problem was that noise from the Lantern Room on the ninth floor did travel – its vast windows, no doubt, and no double-glazing, thanks to Heritage UK.

When not ensconced and entwined with Valerie, Dr Simmins' single patient Tyler – soon to be Tayla – spent a great deal of time playing not just music but computer games at full blast, which meant that the hard techno music he now favoured, mixed with the electronic sound of gunfire, explosions, the roars of imaginary beasts and the shrieks of the slaughtered, rent the quiet of peaceful nights and made it hard to sleep. Tyler had lately switched from *Scrunched Zombies* to *Slash of War*, even noisier and gorier. Fortunately Dr Simmins could always self-prescribe Valium and Temazepam, and did so. Yet actual noise had still seemed preferable to the quiet hate that used to drift down the stairs in old Bobbo's lifetime and had made her fear things that went bump in the night.

No one else complained about the noise. All at IGP seemed stirred, excited and restored by this venture into the new feminism, the great experiment, the turning of Tyler into Tayla. '*Degenerate man into regenerate woman*' – as Valerie put it. These days elderly and serious IGP-ers smiled and chattered, swore and flung their hands about and embraced one another. It did occur to Dr Simmins that she might be handing out rather a lot of SSRIs (selective serotonin reuptake inhibitors), even perhaps too many. But these new medications were only risky when you stopped taking them. After the bliss of the serotonin world the real one did sometimes seem intolerable and suicide a solution. The FDA had issued a warning to this effect. Better keep things as they were. There was more risk in stopping, than continuing them.

If sometimes when working in the clinic Dr Simmins felt a breath upon her arm, and at night felt the need to pull the curtains in case someone was looking in, when outside was all black night and sea and stars, it was easy enough to ignore.

February

Dr Simmins remarked to Valerie after the monthly Board meeting that the She Devil was keeping a very low profile: she had not been seen in the canteen or library for some time.

'The Diabolissima?' asked Valerie. 'Oh, she's fine, just skulking in her tent, like Achilles. I take her wake-up coffee every morning. She's bright enough, just going through a mourning patch for Bobbo. They had been married such a long time!'

Almost overnight, it seemed, Diavolessa had turned into Diabolissima. Valerie had been acting Chair in the She Devil's absence, though as the good doctor noted, that had seemed something of a presumption on her part. But these days anyone who was anyone seemed to turn up to meetings, and 'anyone' was usually a friend and ally of Valerie's. The official reason for the She Devil's absences was that she was 'working hard, finishing a book', but it seemed to Dr Simmins to be half the story. And 'mourning for Bobbo' didn't quite wash.

So Dr Simmins ignored the 'Do not disturb' sign on the She Devil's door and had to knock a few times before she was reluctantly let in, and found Ruth, as she feared, to be in a bad way. The She Devil was unkempt and seemed anxious and depressed. She was still in her nightie, and the area around her computer was littered with sweet wrappers and doughnuts from which it seemed the jam and cream had been sucked and the sugar licked, the rest having been ignored and left to go mouldy. The bed was unmade and there were discarded clothes on the floor. The cleaners had not been in for a long time. Ruth seemed bloated and puffy, and complained of aches, pains and muscle weakness. Yes, she said, she was trying to work but somehow the words did not come. Her brain felt paralysed.

'You're in a bad mood,' said Dr Simmins, diagnosing severe depression and offering a prescription for 30 mg Seroxat once daily. The She Devil refused.

'Pointless to change my mood to suit the world,' she said, with a flash of her old spirit. 'Nothing would ever get done. Better to change the world to suit my mood.'

Dr Simmins enquired what had triggered the low mood and the She Devil just said, 'Finding I had a family when I hadn't expected it. And all that grandson to granddaughter business. I was only joking. I never thought the lad would take me seriously. Parity is about women deserving better and getting less because of male oppression. Nothing whatsoever to do with male and female genitalia.'

She complained that the IGP was being hijacked. Her baby was being snatched. She was not suffering from depression but a proper reaction to events. She was unhappy, and with good reason. And there was Valerie.

'Valerie has got above herself,' she said. 'HR says if I try to fire her it's too late, she'll only sue IGP for unfair dismissal and win.'

Yes, Valerie still brought in her coffee and breakfast every morning and was sweet as pie but she didn't trust her. Dr Simmins suggested that she leave out the morning coffee.

'Why?' demanded the She Devil. 'Do you think it's poisoned?' The doctor said of course not – the She Devil must be mindful of her age and not give in to paranoiac thought – but caffeine could be a double-edged sword. Slowed you down as well as picked you up. Kept you in perpetual flight or fight mode, your adrenals in a yo-yo state, irritating your digestive tract and exhausting you with anxiety. Decaf from the canteen was one thing, but Valerie was known to brew her own No. 6.

'Perhaps just avoid it,' said Dr Simmins, mildly. 'No point in upsetting our Valerie. Accept the coffee but don't drink it. Pour it down the loo.'

'Very well,' said the She Devil, meekly. She really was in very low spirits. But she did agree to take 15 mg Seroxat a day.

March

Dr Ruby Simmins faced the walk up the stone stairs to call on Tyler in the Lantern Room on the ninth floor, the sound of *Metal Gear Solid V: The Phantom Pain* growing louder and louder as she approached. Still very male: rage plus pathos – lovely Mike Oldfield singing *Nuclear* like a forlorn child – but rather less gunfire, fewer explosions. And Tyler, ever courteous, ever charming, actually turned the sound down when Ruby came into the room. He seemed to reflect sunlight, like one of the glorious heroes in a trashy Mary Fisher novel she'd read as a child. So few patients one warmed to. She hoped it would be the same when he'd been made Tayla.

She needed to give him his jabs, and check he was taking his 1.2 mg estradiol, 4.5 mg estriol and 5.4 mg progesterone daily while cutting down his carbohydrate intake. Valerie would not be pleased if Tyler ended up a fatso. Eight weeks in and he was already beginning to lay down fat, but not just in the breast and hip area, but under the chin as well. As Tyler's desire for exercise decreased so his appetite for chocolate increased. The over-eating would have to stop.

Back in January Dr Simmins had taken the S-Class into Brighton to the IVF clinic for Tyler to have his sperm frozen for future use, should he ever wish to become a father. Tyler had been reluctant – '*Who, me, a father when I'm a girl? That's pervy*' – while Valerie had seemed enthusiastic. Which Dr Simmins thought strange. Would Valerie risk even motherhood to nail Tyler into transiting? Everyone knew once a woman has a baby her hope of a meaningful future is lost. Relationships, career, family, will all suffer in the desperate quest for motherhood: the attempt to satisfy a meaningless primal urge is always better ignored. But these young people so seldom thought things through.

Dr Simmins worried that she was perhaps taking Tyler through his transition a little fast, but since it seemed everyone was happy and the good doctor hoped to go on using the Iron Maiden as her own – the She Devil had in effect given it to her – all was for the best. 5.4 mg might seem a little high to some, but was within tolerable limits. Juggling with hormones was an art as much as a science. There were always risks – Tyler's blood pressure might rise, mood changes were inevitable and suicidal impulses might occur – but the good doctor would keep an eye on things until the lad was well and truly one of the girls, and all in good time for the New Year's international World Widdershins Walk, hosted by the IGP in the High Tower! All was going well. The Iron Maiden had been a gift from the She Devil and not a loan, whatever Valerie Valeria chose to believe. But Valerie being such a power in the land these days it was as well not to offend her.

Emotionally, Tyler seemed in great shape. He scarcely needed counselling. His desire to use the gym was dwindling, which was just as well. The six-pack look was not a good look for one who should be aiming for Maureen O'Sullivan as Jane rather than Johnny Weissmuller as Tarzan. After ten weeks or so of fairly constant game playing and sitting about Tyler's breasts were budding nicely. At least the sound of rapine, slaughter, screams of agony and cries for mercy no longer disturbed Dr Simmins' sleep. Or perhaps the wind had just turned.

The golden boy-to-girl, MTF, had become everyone's favourite: after lunch in the canteen he'd bring out his guitar – bought from Amazon – and when the dishes had been cleared (girl-like, he'd even help) would give a small concert to the assembled company – *Bridge over Troubled Water* and *Chirpy Chirpy Cheep Cheep* were favourites with the older crowd – in a light, but still baritone voice. He was not proud and would give a hand with the washing up while still doing physical handyman work outside – Amethyst Builders were still having trouble with handholds for the Widdershins Circuit, as the exterior path was now called, and their digging machines couldn't get round the Widdershins path where it narrowed to single file. Even though many of the Amethysts were FTMs some murmured that a few good strong cismale muscles might help when it came to heaving rocks about. But wiser counsels prevailed.

Sometimes Tyler cycled down to the village with Valerie to see Mrs Easton at the Spar store. These were early days, and in retrospect very pleasant, tranquil days. The weather held.

Valerie, on the other hand, seemed extremely excitable and was losing weight. She chewed gum and brewed and drank real coffee but was never seen eating. Dr Simmins thought Valerie was probably an unacknowledged anorexic with a touch, or more than a touch, of bipolar, and could do with a dose or two of lithium. But unless Dr Simmins was consulted it was none of her business.

April

Bipolar or not, Valerie ran the monthly Board meeting with brisk efficiency. It was held in 2HT/3. Archives were kept in 1HT, meetings held in 2HT. Basement floors 1 and 2, though perfectly well heated and air conditioned, were underground and so without windows. This very lack seemed, or so Dr Simmins thought, to make everyone feel safe, secure and relaxed. Perhaps it was that living on the edge of sea and sky and too conscious of the approach of the infinite, the sense of blank vastness all around could be disconcerting: who ever knew what might not be lurking out there unseen, but looking in? Windowless was good.

This morning items were discussed and despatched at speed. Membership was up by 5 per cent. Interim statutory accounts had gone in good time to HMRC and the Charity Commissioners. Various interested movements – Feminist Man for Feminist Woman, Men Everywhere Speak Up for Women, De-Gender Now – had been invited as IGP associates at a reduced fee. There was some 'no better than dating sites' murmuring, and Ms Octavia walked out, but everyone was used to that, and ignored her. She had Parkinson's, was on 15 mg ropinirole, and showing signs of impulsiveness, shopping 'til she dropped on Amazon, even starting to internet gamble. The ongoing problem of Bobbo's shroud – for problem it seemed still to be for at least poor Ms Octavia – seemed to have triggered hallucinations. She now claimed to have seen Bobbo's right arm rising from the sand and shaking his fist.

Dr Simmins thought she might switch Ms Octavia to 8 mg estradiol, another dopamine agonist, not yet approved for Parkinson's but a rational alternative for an elderly woman with little remaining oestrogen protection against inevitable neural entropy. Nothing ventured, nothing gained.

Dr Simmins was sorting out these possibilities in her head and may have missed something but probably not. The Co-Treasurers were thanked and the meeting brought to an end.

Dr Simmins called on Tyler and was pleased to find his choice of computer games had changed again. Now it was *Assassin's Creed* and not nearly so noisy, a more female kind of murder. Poison. The slaughter still happened, but tended to be silent and secret. Oestrogen was fighting back. Tyler still had to shave, if only weekly. In the perpetual war between testosterone and oestrogen in the human body, oestrogen was edging ahead. Ruby Simmins felt prepared to cut down her own sleep medication and step up Tyler's estriol to 5 mg daily.

Dr Simmins called by the She Devil's rooms and found her in excellent shape, neatly dressed and at her desk, hair washed and combed, bravely wearing bright lipstick on her somewhat misshapen lips, cheerful, briskly competent in manner and finishing the book she had developed out of the paper for *Academica Feminica* with which she had been having trouble back in December.

The book was called *The Campus-Outrage/Outrage Cycle* – and concerned the artificial outrage fomented by a self-described 'dangerous faggot', a young man who toured universities provoking young fourth-wave students of both genders into outrage and absurdity, to the delight of a prejudiced media.

'I'm sure that's very interesting,' said Dr Simmins, politely. 'Whose side are we on?' These old ladies did so go on about their obscure political theories: they might as well be theologians for all the difference they made in the real world.

The She Devil laughed and said the purpose of these papers was to explore both sides and then sit on the fence, duty done. But by and large she had come to the conclusion that lamentation was never the answer. She understood Valerie better; the new world was so complicated it was not surprising that the young needed safe spaces where they could focus on just one train of thought at a time; it was not weakness but strength that led them to avoid trigger words. One must move with the times, and not lapse into easy condemnation. She understood better now that M to F, far from involving castration and the creation of a eunuch, was a mere reassignment of pleasure zones: that as medical science progressed sex change would be reversible. All at will could drift from one sex to the other, vigorous young Tiresias-es all, exploring the many sensual pleasures that the new world had to offer. She now understood that gender, like the State, would wither away and universal parity be reached, at least for the young.

'In other words,' said Dr Simmins, 'if you can't beat them, join them.'

'Quite so,' said the She Devil. 'One must conserve one's strength.'

And then, brightly, 'I'm so glad you warned me about the caffeine.'

She'd been accepting her morning coffee from Valerie out of simple politeness, she said, but had been pouring it down the loo instead of drinking it, as Dr Simmins had suggested. She felt so much better, so much younger, and no longer kept needing naps. Dr Simmins noted that her eyes were glittery and sharp, though red rimmed. The She Devil did seem to have taken Valerie's arguments on board rather wholeheartedly, but on balance 15 mg Seroxat daily seemed to be working.

Dr Ruby Simmins had always seen Valerie Valeria as a rather dangerous young person, rather similar to Lucy her flatmate years back, the girl who had stolen the love of Ruby's life from under her nose, the one who had destroyed Ruby's faith in mankind and with it her future. Valerie and Lucy shared the same manic ruthlessness. It was a welcome relief for Dr Simmins to realise, if only now, that it was not stupidity that had kept her young self from realising what was developing between Stephen and Lucy, but the sleeping pills that Lucy ground up for Ruby's coffee.

So whatever changed, Dr Simmins thought, except perhaps, these days, genders? There were nice people and nasty people and some of them were M and some of them were F: and a whole lot in between. So be it.

May

The She Devil chaired the monthly Board meeting in window-less 2HT/3 with a degree of formality Valerie had not aspired to. Dr Simmins attended at the She Devil's invitation. Minutes were taken by Ms Belinda Makepeace, once a very highly paid Company Secretary. She took them down in shorthand but her eyes had a rather fluctuating efficiency. Minutes of the last meeting were read and approved – no one having the heart not to. Dr Simmins paid proper attention. She had been right to cut down on the Prozac.

The first item on the agenda was 'Policy change'. The She Devil, standing straight and smart in crisp white blouse and red jacket, no longer the grieving widow but the bold executive, made a stirring speech about the necessity of a new interpretation of the word 'parity'. The feminist movement must move forward into a world where men should be seen as brothers in arms against the forces of prejudice and illiberalism, and no longer the source of these ills. Women of the world, unite, she said, you have nothing to lose but the chains of stale group-think. She declared this to a standing ovation. When she moved the appointment of a nominated Steering Committee of eight plus Chair, there were a few grumbles that an odd number would be preferable – as it was, the Chair would be left with a casting vote – but the movement was carried.

In 'Matters arising' Valerie said that plans for the Widdershins Walk next New Year's Day were proceeding nicely: the covered walkway was all but completed, Lady Patchett had agreed to head the procession with her grandchild, and the new age of parity was under way. There was a round of applause when Valerie was able to announce that UNESCO was considering the inauguration of New Year's Day as an annual Widdershins Day, a New Thought Day, suitable for worldwide celebration. And the IGP had been there first! Valerie quoted from the *I Ching*: '*Difficulty in the beginning works supreme success.*' Tyler would be playing the guitar and singing next Friday in the canteen at five o'clock and could everyone let their appropriate cohorts know. Everyone was welcome to come along. The applause for Valerie was almost as long as the applause for the She Devil, but not quite.

In 'Any other business' Ms Serena from Ethics asked if extra soil should not be brought in for the burial area; a recent high tide had washed completely round the High Tower and made her nervous: or failing that could not some kind of stone sarcophagus be erected? The first suggestion was carried: Amethyst Builders would be employed. The Co-Treasurer, Ms Amelia Sidcup, explained that the cost of a sarcophagus could reach tens of thousands and was unnecessary. Ms Bradshap intervened to say she was sorry about Ms Serena's nerves and perhaps Dr Simmins could be asked to prescribe something? Dr Ruby Simmins had done wonders lately, said Ms Bradshap, to make the High Tower feel less like a convent and more like a normal charity. The She Devil endorsed Ms Bradshap's remarks and ruled in favour of Ms Sidcup.

It was noted in the minutes that Ms Serena had then walked out of the meeting saying they had all gone mad, 'probably due to Dr Simmins' happy pills, and if anyone thought for a minute they'd realise Widdershins was pure Satanism, and did they really want old Bobbo to rise from the dead?' Ms Octavia followed her out.

Tyler, present by comment consent, sat at the back and played cat's cradle with a length of ribbon throughout.

The meeting resumed after apologies had been made to Dr Simmins. Ms Bradshap remarked that it was most important that the IGP should stick to its positive-discrimination policy. Parity of employment was still a priority. It was almost impossible to find female stonecutters for a sarcophagus locally; enquiries having shown that the national average within the trade was 94 per cent male and 4 per cent female, so it was pretty hopeless trying. She was sure extra soil would do the trick, and Amethyst had acquired a new JCB mini excavator suitable for rock and sand, second-hand but at considerable cost. Expenses had been split with the IGP.

The minutes recorded no other business and the closure of a most satisfactory meeting.

June

Tyler's choice of computer game was now that girls' favourite, *Dulcie and the Dark Mountain*. The sound track was quite
bearable. Dr Simmins feared she might indeed be taking him
a little too fast into femininity and added a little testosterone
to the mix. Tyler was now uncomfortable with the girth of
his Adam's apple, which somehow interfered with the otherwise smooth and gentle flow of his profile. The only crag left.
He had been massaging it night and day, rather hoping to avoid
the tracheal shave, or chondrolaryngoplasty, the surgical procedure in which the thyroid cartilage would be shaved through
an incision in the throat. An Adam's apple without the shave
was a certain giveaway of a cisman. But it was a nervy business.
Things could go wrong. The surgeon's hand could slip, the
larynx be damaged beyond repair. Tyler refused.

Nor did Tyler want glottoplasty to feminise the pitch of his
voice. The whole voice box would have to be removed in order
for the vocal cords to be tightened and shortened rather like
guitar strings, but with added blood. It was a reasonable fear
but Dr Simmins reduced the testosterone. It could make you
grumpy, and in grumpiness make the wrong decision.

The human body was a wonderful thing: it could be carved
and tucked and seamed into something entirely other and

still survive, thought Dr Simmins. The human brain was even more wonderful, add a chemical or a hormone and it would oblige by altering personality: the nice become nasty, the nasty, nice.

Tyler was not alone at baulking at glottoplasty, Ruby Simmins suspected – the final MTF frontier, the deep male voice of command and power was the most difficult thing to give up when transiting. To speak with the little plaintive enquiring trill of the female of the species was an irritation to those accustomed to telling others what to do. Men were happy to take on all parts of the female anatomy other than the voice: FTMs could rely on testosterone to thicken the cords willy-nilly and didn't have to bother with surgical intervention – MTF was more complicated: what was thick must become thin, and blood would flow. It was more of a sacrifice than altering genitalia.

And if a misnamed Tyler – surely he ought to be 'Tayla' by now – could keep an audience of elderly women rapt and enthralled over lunch in the canteen his vocal cords might as well stay as they were. In his new role Tyler might even end up on the world stage. He was considering buttock enhancement: then he would be even more desirable. Valerie was rather keen on that. There was nothing to be done to feminise hands or feet but fortunately these were on the small side to begin with, which was just as well.

Valerie wound her light limbs round Tyler and gazed into his eyes and said how happy she would be when he was Tayla and Tyler thought how easy to make this beautiful creature happy and no skin off his nose if he did; other parts could look after themselves and these days, especially if you went private, they were lavish with the morphine.

One way or another, Dr Simmins thought, Tyler was well placed to change gender. Sheer amiability would see him through.

July

Leda Blumer, head of Security, called by Dr Ruby Simmins'
clinic to have her skin grafts checked. She had suffered third
degree burns to arms and side on the Widdershins Day lightning strike seven months back – at least thus vindicating Ruby's
rather irrational (she was the first to admit it) fear of thunder-
storms. Fortunately there hadn't been a bad electrical storm
since, the weather having been so singularly benign.

Leda was doing nicely: the split-thickness skin graft had taken
well, with no sign of infection, and the face at least had not been
affected. Vitals were normal. But she lingered in the surgery for
no apparent reason and when Dr Simmins showed signs of
sympathetic enquiry she dissolved into tears. She was a tall,
rather slow-moving girl with good strong shoulders and jaw,
tree trunk legs, not much waist, cropped dark hair and beautiful sad eyes. It occurred to the doctor that she might be a trans,
an FTM, but Leda said no, she was a cislesbian, just awkward
looking and unhappily in love. She needed something to get
her through the night, pills, antidepressants, anything.

When Valerie had first turned up at the High Tower, Leda
said, she had been so happy; after years of loneliness and rejection she'd found a soul mate, the sex had been transfigurative
(Leda's word); they'd even agreed to get married and had an

engagement party but Valerie had suddenly changed, begun to avoid her and seemed to despise her. She'd taken up with the She Devil's grandson, a young MTF. Valerie hadn't even told Leda; she'd let her find out for herself. It was cruel and out of character. Did Dr Simmins think it could be something to do with Tyler inheriting money when he became Tayla? Valerie must know by now that cismen never really turned into women. They could tweak this and tweak that but at heart they stayed the same control freaks and bullies they were born.

Dr Simmins wrote out a prescription for Prozac. She had fellow feeling with all those betrayed and double-dealt. Back in the sixties she'd self-prescribed Librium and switched to Prozac when it became available. She had stuck to that: modern medications had their point, but the old ones often worked the best.

Leda dabbed her tears, saying that she was trying hard to wean herself off Valerie but if only Valerie wouldn't sneak round from time to time for a shag and break Leda's heart time and time again it would be so much easier. Valerie had told Leda she was an unlucky person – look at the way lightning had struck her and disfigured her and nobody else – and nothing would ever go right for her. Valerie was probably right and the best Leda could hope for now was the occasional mercy fuck. 'And for God's sake try not to look so *needy* all the time, or you won't even have that,' Valerie had said.

Dr Simmins tried not to affect surprise and doubled the daily dose of fluoxetine, Prozac, from 20 mg a day to 40 mg. Leda was able to go away happy with the prescription if not with life.

Dr Simmins wondered if she should bring the matter of Valerie's wandering eye to Tyler's attention and decided not. Tyler, so soon to be Tayla, was doing so well it would be a pity to upset the apple cart. There was also the issue of confidentiality to consider and of course the Iron Maiden and what the mind didn't know the heart couldn't care about. Or was it the other way round?

July Again

Board meetings were suspended for the summer and the Steering Committee met in their place. Lady Patchett, once again Chairperson, sent apologies – busy as she was dealing with the media storm stirred up by her Outrage Cycle article, but coping valiantly. So did Leda, the head of Security – she had a hospital appointment: her split-thickness skin graft was bubbling and buckling. Miriam from HR had an urgent meeting with Amethyst Builders, and Ms Serena from Ethics was 'taking my dog to the vet'. Odd, because she did not have a dog. Ms Octavia did not turn up, and was assumed to have forgotten. But that left the quorum of three which the rules demanded: Valerie, Tyler (replacing Bobbo as the obligatory male – T. Patchett not B. Patchett. No one would notice and he'd keep his signature wobbly) and Ms Bradshap. The meeting proceeded.

Dr Simmins was in attendance but found herself falling asleep from time to time during the meeting – Valerie's coffee? Ms Bradshap drank only green tea and Tyler was off stimulants, so they were spared. She woke up sufficiently to hear Valerie voting in a further 10 per cent increase for the Widdershins Walk budget and that some query from the Charity Commissioners had been satisfactorily parried. She did not comment.

The next day Dr Simmins took Tyler into London for a further consultation with Dr Marlene Patstock at the New Beginnings Private Clinic, or NBPC, in Harley Street. They travelled in the Mercedes. Leda had offered to drive and Dr Simmins had accepted the offer. Nobody liked driving into central London any more. Better leave it to the professionals, RoSPA-accredited as Leda was.

But at the last minute Valerie had insisted on coming too – to keep Tyler company in the hour of his decision, though so far as Ruby could see the decision had been well made already, and what Valerie really wanted to do was torment Leda. As it happened Dr Simmins saw no sign of anything untoward going on between them. The glass partition between chauffeur and passengers remained firmly closed. Leda's neck, shoulders and head did not seem unduly tense – with any luck the Prozac was working.

Tyler was looking particularly pretty in a white cotton dress splashed with large red roses and not his normal jeans and t-shirt. Very much Tayla.

Traffic was light all the way to Crawley. Dr Simmins told Tayla more about her surgeon, Dr Marlene Patstock, the rather oddly-named surgeon who was herself an MTF, then a Michael not a Marlene, who had been a one-time colleague of Ruby's at the North London GRC before starting the NBPC.
'So many initials,' complained Tyler.
'It's as well to learn them', said Dr Simmins. 'GRC – Gender Reassignment Clinic, MTF – male to female, FTM – female to male. Cismale – born contentedly male, cisfemale – born contentedly female.'
'Don't teach the cisgrandson how to suck eggs,' Valerie chimed

in, laughing merrily. But now she was snuggling up to Tyler, her hand under his skirt and on his knee or even further, Dr Simmins suspected, but didn't like to bend her head and look down to check.

'It's all such a new world to me,' Tyler was saying. 'Like, not the way I expected, not really. A spot of trannyism was lovely. But all this is so – kind of – full on!'

'Get over it,' said Valerie, and Dr Simmins felt like murmuring that it was a bit late for Tyler/Tayla to worry, but thought it was wiser to say nothing. It was hard, even for the good doctor, to keep up with the world of gender-correctness where definitions changed so fast.

But she did think that through the glass she saw Leda's shoulders stiffen and her hands tighten on the steering wheel. There was no visible mirror, but in a bullet-proof armoured Mercedes S600 there was probably some camera device which enabled the driver to see what was going on in the backseats. When Dr Simmins drove the vehicle she revelled in its comfort, and ignored all unnecessary gadgets.

Valerie Valeria, the bitch, was wearing her normal Balmain distressed slim-leg biker blue jeans, ivory Moschino t-shirt, and some other notable-label magenta cashmere cardigan, and Tyler's dress was not only pretty, but looked extravagantly expensive. Valerie and Tyler had been shopping together at Harvey Nichols only the week before, which Valerie had taken care to mention as she hopped aboard today. Tyler had wanted to drive on that occasion, it seemed, but Valerie had insisted on taking Leda in her standard IGP Security uniform of navy blue nylon, paler blue piping and peaked cap to do it, presumably the better to hurt her by canoodling with Tyler in the back seat amongst the shopping bags. Such a subtle sadist, Valerie! Even Dr Simmins, who had seen and heard just about everything, had been taken aback.

At Croydon traffic began to thicken and move slowly. A discussion started about dates, and further surgical procedures. Major gender realignment surgery would be in early October and the more minor cosmetic improvements, labiaplasty or vaginoplasty, would wait until late November.
'What's the difference?' asked Tyler.
'Labiaplasty is making the outside more attractive and vaginoplasty tightens the inside,' said Valerie.
'Which would you chose? I've never cared to look.' Tyler sounded quite anxious.
'Men – don't know, don't care!' exclaimed Valerie. 'You know so little about female bodies. Anyway, you can always have both. By New Year's Day and the World Widdershins Walk, you'll be fully Tayla, complete at last, working your way up to the very top of the IGP and heir to the She Devil. They do so love you at the IGP! You and Lady Patchett really must process together at last. How the media will love it!'

Yes, and the She Devil's got to go sometime, thought Dr Simmins, bitterly. Probably in the next couple of years. By which time you'll be married to your Princess, never have to worry about money again, and can still keep Leda for a bit of fun. Lesbians of the world, rejoice!

Brixton was almost blocked. Valerie seemed anxious to give Tyler all the details of the major surgery, normally a three-hour

operation in which the testicles were removed and the skin of
the penis used to form a vagina and the sensitive tip of the glans
inverted to create a clitoris: 'Rather like peeling a banana,' Valerie
said, 'and bending it back. Just being careful it doesn't snap.'
'Honestly! Oh Please!' said Tyler. 'Valerie! Please! I don't want
the details. I just want to be put under and wake up a girl and
still have orgasms.'

Vauxhall Bridge was a nightmare of gridlock. Dr Simmins
explained that a labiaplasty was included in the normal GRS,
and a vaginoplasty later might be needed but might lead to
complications and excessive bleeding but no doubt Dr Patstock
would advise.
'Complications?' asked Tyler. 'What complications? Valerie
said it was like peeling a banana.' At which Valerie told Dr
Simmins to stop being such a downer and trying to scare Tyler.
Dr Simmins was not a surgeon but a hormone specialist so
what did she know about any of it anyway? What was three
hours out of a lifetime when the result would be so magnificent? To go to sleep as a man and wake up in the delight and
sensitivity of womanhood? Dr Simmins should just shut up.

Park Lane was jammed. Dr Simmins refrained from saying that
IGP was paying for the three-hour op. If Tyler went to Thailand
he could have the six-hour version, and come out of it with
even more delightful female sensitivity – if he came out at all.
But it would cost double, and presumably IGP funds wouldn't
stretch to the expense. The She Devil must have argued that
case, and won. Dr Simmins just shut up.

But when they got to Harley Street with five minutes to spare

Valerie did not go in to Dr Patstock's clinic with Tyler and Dr Simmins but said she would wait outside in the limo with Leda. She didn't want to interfere with Tyler's right to choose and knew she might be tempted and so cloud his judgement. 'You're a really good person, Val,' said Tyler, taking her hand. And he really believed it.

August

An informal meeting of the Board was called for the 23rd and all were invited to attend. Wine and cakes would be served. Venue: canteen. Time: 4 p.m.

All crowded in and there was much excitement and merriment. An engagement between Ms Tayla Patchett and Ms Valerie Valeria was announced. The date of the wedding was to be the 1st of December. The happy couple would lead the Widdershins Walk round the High Tower with the She Devil on New Year's Day. Tayla and Valerie embraced. Leda from Security walked out. Tayla didn't even notice. Dr Simmins wondered if perhaps she should switch Leda to one of the newer and more potent SSRIs. The She Devil was the first to toast the happy couple-to-be.

As she was leaving Dr Simmins thought she overheard a rather heated discussion between Ms Bradshap and the Luxuriettes, Ms Sidcup hovering, about today's cakes being a disappointment. Ginger slices had been served and not the lemon-drizzle and profiteroles ordered. Something about 'no specials until the bill for the real cream for last December's éclairs had been met'. Ms Bradshap, Dr Simmins concluded, was not one to give in easily, especially about trivia. Forgiving and forgetting was not her strong point. In some individuals SSRIs could magnify rather than soften an initial temperament.

Dr Simmins was gratified to see that Ms Octavia seemed more cheerful without ropinirole and with estradiol, though still somewhat hyper and impulsive, noisily if vainly demanding that the canteen install a gambling machine to cheer everyone up; 'Oh, the thrill of the dancing lights,' she'd cried, 'the surge of the tumbling coins!'

'Just fancy,' she confided to Dr Simmins that evening, snuggling up to her. 'All this and a dear little baby too!' Ms Octavia might be confused but at least she was happy.

The very next day the sleepy peace of the High Tower in high summer was broken by a furious ciswoman at the gates demanding to see Tyler Finch Patchett. She screamed and ranted, but had no appointment, so Leda was having to stand four-square in her way. Leda was civil, as High Tower Security was trained to be, but stood firm, as the stranger battered away with little fists into her sturdy flesh.

Others in the Security team watched from the window as their Leda, their leader, coped with the situation and they were proud. '*Her strength is as the strength of ten because her heart is pure*,' said one, quoting Tennyson's *Sir Galahad* – they learned sections of it by heart in their induction classes. Leda was popular. She suffered but was brave. No one in Security liked Valerie, who had caused Leda such pain. They saw Valerie as Elaine, the wicked lily maid of Astolat. They blamed Valerie for their uniform, and the dent in their budget created by the quite unnecessarily expensive armoured Mercedes, the Iron Maiden. Security went down en masse to help Leda.

All this Leda reported later to Dr Simmins.

'If you mean Tayla,' Leda was saying, dancing round to avoid the blows, 'be aware that you're misnaming her as Tyler. It's seen as very rude. But I can call through and see if she is receiving guests. What name can I give?'

'Bullying cow!' shouted Tyler's visitor. 'Irresponsible, sacrilegious bitch! I'm his therapist, Matilda Eavens. His mother was right! You're keeping him prisoner the same way you kept his grandfather. I'm calling the police!'

While the crew restrained the attacker Leda called through to the Lantern Room to ask if Tyler wanted a visitor named Eavens, and after a short pause and a scuffle and shuffle or two Tyler said he would prefer not to, not just at the moment: but, ever polite, he asked her to please give Matilda his regards and thank her for visiting. Leda passed on the message but it provoked Matilda to further fury.

Leda had been looking forward to a better future. She assumed that Valerie was there in bed with Tyler, pursuing her elusive orgasm. She had stopped being jealous of Tyler once she realised how much she, Leda, was needed for Valerie's sexual fulfilment. She would win in the end. The power of the orgasm was great. The realisation that only she, Leda, would do, had given her comfort. That, and possibly the anti-depressants. What Valerie found with Tyler was the satisfaction of aesthetic lust, but what Valerie had with Leda was fleshly and spiritual completeness. Leda could wait. Valerie would come back sadder and wiser. Lesbians should stick to lesbians, and not go wandering. Hasbians were despicable.

The visitor continued to hammer and shout in an unreconstructed way, so Leda felt it sensible to call Dr Simmins to come down and deal with her. Dr Simmins, known as Dr Pill Popper, and popular with all down at the security gate, came at once. At the sight of her Matilda calmed down and became quite reasonable. Dr Simmins was able to lead her to 3CC/4 without incident, where she made a nice cup of tea for both of them. Nothing stronger was needed.

'You have to make a fuss with these people,' the therapist said. 'Violence and noisy objection are the only language Security ever responds to. And the women are worse than the bloody men.'

As it happened, the good doctor knew Matilda Eavens quite well. Eleven years back Matilda had set up shop as a psychotherapist in St Rumbold's. She and Dr Simmins had frequently exchanged patients. Dr Simmins saw Matilda as a bright and intuitive healthcare assistant, while doubting her qualifications. Anyone can put up a brass plate, claim to be a therapist, and stand or fall by the results. At the same time she knew that Matilda had written a rather good book on the Narcissistic Mother Syndrome. It had sold well: these days everyone who was anyone claimed to have had one, a selfish mother on whom they could blame all inadequacies, failures, addictions, poor self-esteem leading to sexual excesses and so on. 'Narcissistic mother' was fast climbing up the blame stakes, along with 'bullied at school' and 'mental health issues'.

For her part Matilda saw Dr Simmins as a totally irresponsible if licensed purveyor of psychoactive substances. St Rumbold's had not perhaps been the best place for either of them to start practices – the villagers on the whole being pre-Freudian feelers and thinkers, and suspicious of anyone who tried to interfere with their bodies let alone with their minds. They were not much prey to self-examination.

'So it's you,' said Matilda as she sipped tea in Dr Simmins' smart new clinic. 'You disappeared. I thought you must have been struck off. What's all this about Tyler changing sex? He's as male as Mike Tyson, only nicer.'
Dr Simmins said mildly that Tyler thought he'd do better in life as a woman.
'Take no notice! He's a drama queen. Tyler loves attention. He has a narcissistic mother. That's all that's wrong with him – and those sisters! I suppose the wicked old grandma got her hooks into him? It's what they do.'

Dr Simmins said it was not quite like that, and might be a bit late to worry. The op was in a couple of months and pretty much an optional extra anyway. Tyler was indeed on his way to Tayla, under proper medical care. At this information Matilda switched to shrieking mode and beat upon the wall – she had a very unstable personality, Dr Simmins thought.

'Proper? You? Proper?' Now Matilda was laughing hysterically. Between gasps and gulps Matilda told Dr Simmins she was disgraceful and that Tyler was totally frivolous. Tyler liking to wear his sister's nightie and a spot of impotence was no justification for gender reassignment. She would call the police. Dr Simmins said calmly she would call the High Tower Security and they would get there first.

Matilda responded well to that, as to a slap on the cheek. She became more reasonable, and said she had treated lots of genuine trans people and it was a really painful affliction; it disrupted people's whole lives, it destroyed them. It often ended in suicide. To live with the mind of a woman in the body of a man, and vice versa, was social and personal hell. To change gender because you wanted a new dress was an insult to seriously suffering people. Tyler had never shown signs of being worried by his sexuality, indeed he could be accused of rampant heterosexuality as a rebellion against the narcissistic mother. So much had become evident to her in their weekly family therapy sessions, on which she had been basing much of her book, *The Pain of Malehood and the Mother*, already commissioned by her publisher.

She was speaking more and more quickly, as if afflicted by glossolalia. Dr Simmins wondered if Matilda herself was not the daughter of a narcissistic mother: speaking but not listening, the better to drown what she heard as the Mother's voice. Yes, bipolar. And probably too much Ritalin.

'I've moved in with her,' Matilda chatted on. 'I should know. I'm able to record most of it. The whole family make such excellent copy.'

Though Dr Simmins often thought she was beyond surprise she again found she was not. Tyler and his mother and sisters bled emotionally dry just to furnish a book!

Matilda had set herself up in Nicci's front room and was already seeing clients. The new housing estate was a much richer source of neuroses than St Rumbold's had ever been. It was working out really well at Nicci's. Bed and board and all for free!

'And sexual services?' asked Dr Simmins.

'Of course not!' cried Matilda, indignantly. 'What do you think I am? I'm a professional in an unequal power relationship, I couldn't possibly. Rent in exchange for therapy, that's all. Anything else is in Tyler's imagination.'

Dr Simmins said Tyler had seemed disturbed by his under-standing of the fact that his mother and his therapist were in a sexual relationship. Matilda said that was absurd, but typical of a reverse transference, and only to be expected from one of today's lost young white males. Tyler was borderline paranoiac, insecure in his own sexuality and overcompensating. Tyler's mother Nicci, as it happened, was in a fulfilling and permanent relationship with a property developer who had bought her a four-bed detached house in the best part of a fancy new estate, but was not averse to letting her children imagine she was a deviant. It kept her young and radical in their eyes. Not that one used the word 'deviant' these days. *Delete, delete.* Just part of Matilda's research – a longitudinal case study into an intergenerational narcissist trope – which was bearing theory out very nicely.

It was with triumph that Matilda declared that Tyler's grand-father on the paternal side, Bobbo (the one whom the grandmother had been keeping locked up and hidden away, and then buried in the garden to boot – typical!), had also had a narcissistic mother who had made the little family live in hotels. Dr Simmins pointed out that if it was a matter of epigenetics, a change in phenotype without a change in genotype, surely a single generation would do to prove what she wanted? Matilda ignored her.

'So that was what it was,' said Matilda in a quiet moment. 'The reverse transference! Tyler driving off into the night over a little thing like that! He couldn't take a joke. Men are so bad at jokes, don't you think?'

'Depends on the joke,' said Dr Simmins, sourly.

'And then poor Tyler falls straight into the trap of the grand-mother. No wonder – it's the kind of terrible thing that happens!' cried Matilda. 'It's always, always the grandmother! The She Devil loses her own child so she goes for the child's child. And she wants a daughter rather than a son and will stop at nothing to get it. Nothing. Can't you do something?'

'Too late,' said Dr Simmins briskly. 'The process is under way.'

Matilda switched again. Her position of rest became that of a concerned adult speaking to a recalcitrant child. Matilda Eavens said Tyler had really let her down by missing so many sessions and then springing this sex change thingy on her when frankly she hadn't anticipated it. Perhaps he'd see his way to repairing the damage he had done? She could already see a sequel. *Brother or Sister? The Doubt of the Mother.* She'd put it to her publisher. Provisional title, of course. And by the by, Tyler should know that the woman at the Jobcentre was really fed up. Miss Swanson, one of Matilda's clients too, was finding it difficult to make any decisions. Tyler was in real danger of being sanctioned if he didn't turn up soon. Miss Swanson said she could cover for him so long, but only so far. Could Dr Simmins let Tyler know?

'Of course,' said Dr Simmins, and added: 'But I don't believe for one moment Tyler is changing his gender to please a narcissistic mother, monstrous though she may be. He's doing it because he knows he'll have a better life as a woman than a man.'

Matilda peered at her sharply, as if hearing her for the first time, and, what was more, looked suddenly sane.

'You're all so convinced,' Matilda said, 'that you're not just equal to men but better than them! I see it now. You're radicalised, the lot of you. You're religious extremists. There's no getting through to you.'

Dr Simmins, exhausted, saw Matilda to the gate and got her through Security without further incident. What could the girl be on? Ritalin, almost certainly. Bipolar, yes, and far too heavy a dose. But not her responsibility, thank God.

Dr Simmins found the strength to look in on Tyler to see how he was getting on. Valerie had just left the Lantern Room and Tyler was putting on some kind of helmet to play a computer game, presumably joining a world in which his avatar was the heroine; and from the occasional loving deep male growl she guessed the game must involve Tayla with a romantic hero. She looked at the box. *Blade & Bliss*, an MMO. Massively Multiplayer Online, she supposed, a role playing game.

Oestrogen warred with testosterone. The sound track, though also interrupted by gunfire and explosions, was unmistakeably David Bowie's *Heroes*. Something about a king and a queen? Taylor must identify with the queen. Probably after the wedding, the handsome man would go and there would be two beautiful girl partners on screen.

Dr Simmins, satisfied, slipped away. Testosterone had been put back in its rightful place.

September

Dr Simmins was happy. Tyler was looking very much like a girl, at least from the back. All the good doctor's other charges were well and content. Demand for SSRIs had flattened out. Ms Bradshap's diet kept them healthy no matter how much they all complained, and actually Ms Bradshap, now on 20 mg Seroxat, seemed more open and trusting and less suspicious of what others found normal. She allowed crème brûlée with the breakfast cereal, and apricot jam in the breakfast yoghurt.

Such a warm Indian summer! The tower seemed to doze in tranquil sunshine. A group of IGP-ers would go down to the little cove at the foot of the High Tower to skinny-dip in the sea, allowing themselves to giggle and laugh and throw their scrawny wrinkled bodies around, careless of observation. They would keep their flip-flops on because the rocks could be sharp. They were surprisingly free with their language, too, fucking this's and shitting that's. They were nuns on Prozac, the lot of them. Well, at least these days, thought Dr Simmins, they were happy. Most of them had no children: too busy all their young lives setting the world to rights, more concerned with the future than the present. Perhaps that was what the SSRIs did, disinhibited you, allowed you to live in the present, singing, splashing, swearing. She was doing them a favour.

It occurred to Dr Simmins that the IGP-ers were not merely just modern nuns on Prozac but like the cloistered sisters in a mediaeval Carmelite convent. Were not all at the High Tower sustained by the asceticism of comparative solitude, manual labour, chastity (at least amongst the older ones) and sisterly charity, hiding themselves away from the temptations of the outside world? Was the High Tower not the modern equivalent to an ancient convent? They might not acknowledge what they were doing, not see themselves as nuns, but they were treading the same human path as those who went before.

Their Mother Superior was the She Devil. Valerie was an ambitious novice trying to persuade discalced nuns to move from the second to the third order of the Carmelite sisters. She was trying to empower them to become uncloistered and fraternise with like-minded men: to become lay nuns, in other words, not obliged to practise chastity, but to move about the world as normal if virtuous women. In which case, 'No Blame Attached' – as the I Ching would say. Valerie was driven not by malice but by history, concluded Dr Simmins. She would have to be forgiven.

The High Tower itself played a part. Perhaps because it was the place where a small group of Carmelite novices were known to have taken shelter in 1646, escaping from religious persecution. They had come from Brussels and were on their way to the new Chichester Carmel, twenty miles down the road (ironically, as it so happened, on the Manhood Peninsula). Here they were no longer in fear for their lives. Perhaps something of their delight and relief had permeated the walls, and the High Tower looked to repeat its performance.

Or perhaps the High Tower had aspirations of grandeur; saw itself as the convent of San José in Spain and the She Devil as St Teresa of Avila (comparisons could certainly be made) with her constant self-inflicted pain – '*I bore these sufferings with great composure, even joy*' – doubts from friends and clerics as to whether the visions were diabolic or divine, the same protracted theological disputations through the night, the agonised self-reproaches and always the pain, the pain: the suffering to be endured – if St Teresa suffered the better to experience God, the She Devil had suffered to achieve the grace that was sexual attractiveness. The one achieved her goal, the other lamentably failed. But running the race is the thing, isn't it, not the prize? Or so they say.

Dr Simmins wondered how it was she herself had got so far in her life without bearing any children who would cluster round her bedside when she died. Even old Bobbo had managed a grandson, thanks to Samantha, who may have been supremely idiotic but whose heart was in the right place. Recently, Dr Simmins realised, she was feeling more generously to others than she used to. Was she perhaps overdoing the Prozac?

She was only sixty-four – perhaps she could computer date? She and Leda got on well but Leda was such a gloomy guts, and when it came to it Dr Simmins did not fancy women. All that love and romance business, long ago, scarcely discovered and then, so early on, out the window! She had taken offence at her own life; sulked and skulked and bitten men's heads off ever since just in case they turned out to be another Stephen. If only SSRIs had been invented then. She might now be loved and not respected and have a family round her when she died and not a cluster of IGP-ers. Though she was becoming very fond of them.

She'd read in one of her mother's despised Mary Fisher novels way back – a blue-eyed blonde soldier with cleft chin off to war, kissing a slim doe-eyed beauty with tumbling red hair and the rest – that in order to be loved you had to learn first how to love, and she had never managed. She felt tears welling in her eyes. She hated these 'if-only' thoughts. You always ending up a self-pitying wreck, the kind of patient she most abhorred. There'd been all that silly nonsense about the High Tower being haunted by Mary Fisher's ghost: a patch of good weather had wiped it all away. She should sit in the sun more often. Or take more Vitamin D.

Or perhaps it was just the old man being dead and buried and safely out of the way that had made the difference. It was true that sometimes she seemed to hear breathing when there was no one else about there to breathe – she'd be sitting quietly in the clinic when the hairs on the back of her neck would stand up for no apparent reason – but whatever it was, it was benign. Now she could hear, drifting out of a clear sky, long ago and far away, a song they'd made her sing at primary school. She hadn't wanted to sing it at the time. It came true, that was the trouble.

> I lean'd my back against an oak,
> Thinking it was a trusty tree.
> But first it bent and then it broke,
> So did my love prove false to me.

Of course she had been sulking ever since. Sex didn't make you miserable and jealous. Love did.

It was in this soft mood that Dr Simmins was driving the Iron Maiden through St Rumbold's when she came across the silly carer Samantha whom she had encountered in the bad days of the High Tower, nursing the abominable Bobbo – as he was referred to these days, if at all. Amethyst Builders had now shovelled so much earth on top of him there was no fear he would rise again.

Samantha was looking slim and smart and pushing a vintage Silver Cross pram and in it was a moon-faced baby. Dr Simmins stopped the car and admired the pram while avoiding any mention of the baby. She preferred not to lie if it was possible. Samantha told her that now she was a mother she wasn't going back to work. The family had come into money and been able to put in a new kitchen and bathroom and add a conservatory to the back of the house.

Dr Simmins congratulated her and said she was a very lucky girl, and Samantha said it wasn't luck, she had earned it. She'd done important work for the She Devil. Dr Simmins expressed polite surprise. Samantha said it was way back in January. The She Devil had asked her to go over to a bank in Switzerland and take a suitcase out of a safe deposit vault.

'And you must have been so pregnant at the time,' said Dr Simmins, sympathetically.

That had been the whole point, apparently; no one suspected pregnant girls. She'd gone over as Samantha Patchett, Lady Patchett's granddaughter, with documents to prove it. She'd brought the old battered suitcase with chrome locks back to the High Tower, crossing Europe by train on the way back. She'd got through customs all right at Harwich. It had been very exciting! She'd peeked into the suitcase on the ferry and it was crammed full of £50 notes and important-looking documents. The suitcase was now down in the Archive Room.

'So you see,' said Samantha. 'The dear old gentleman was right all along. There was all that money. To think that no one ever believed him!' She had gone to put flowers on the grave but you couldn't quite see exactly where it was any more, there was so much new wet earth over everything. 'Funny place to work in, that Tower. The vibes always too light or too heavy. Never could make up its mind. Forces clashing, that kind of thing.'

'The ghost of Mary Fisher, I daresay,' Dr Simmins heard herself saying, 'flitting to and fro. Certainly didn't do much for the weather.' And she drove off.

An extraordinary thing happened as Dr Simmins did a wheelie at the gates of the High Tower, the better to swing into the courtyard and park. Security would normally come out and drive the car into the garage, the better to record miles driven and so forth – Valerie's doing: one had to be accountable, apparently, for the sake of the books – but this time they didn't.

Where Bobbo's grave had been, Samantha was quite right, were now just piles of wet earth. A particularly high tide must have managed to lap entirely round the High Tower. Indeed as she looked the tide was creeping round the corner towards her, dragging soil with it as it took its one step back in order to take its two steps forward. She sat in the Iron Maiden and watched, fascinated. The ground seemed to be churning. It was as though dinosaurs were heaving away just below the surface, waiting to break through. It had to be a trick of the light, surely.

And what the hell was this? Two big ugly-looking pink-faced men in dark suits and ties were walking towards her. Men? An unusual sight around the High Tower, and not the kind to be nuns' priests – '*so grette a nekke, and swich a large breest*' as Chaucer put it – who used to accompany nuns when they went on pilgrimage abroad. Rather these were pallid of face, narrow of neck and sloping of shoulder, though with the unmistakeable and disagreeable air of those who come from authority to upset one's apple cart.

They approached the car, asked Dr Simmins to get out of it and take her personal belongings with her. She did. They then showed her court documents to the effect that due payments had not been made to a leasing company called Marianne Limousines: the vehicle was being re-possessed.

They got into the Iron Maiden and drove it away.

PART FIVE

Apotheosis

Nurse Hopkins Reflects

Well, that was a turn-up for the books! I can watch things indoors through windows but what goes on underground I have had to deduce. Obviously I haven't been able to deduce sufficiently well, or this débâcle wouldn't have come as such a surprise to me. I've looked over Ms Belinda's shoulder while she's typed up the minutes in her office, 3CC/4 – how annoying these room numbers have been. I hope whoever runs the High Tower next will devise a simpler system. Perhaps even the minutes haven't been sufficiently informative. Mary Fisher, with all her irritating *wooo-h, wooo-h*ing, did rather better than me when it came to working out what was going on. And the world through Dr Simmins' eyes turned out to be rather, shall we say, prescription-drug enhanced?

Since sharing the Treasurer's job with Ms Sidcup Valerie Valeria has managed to run up bills with local tradespeople over and above annual income to the tune of some £742,000. Believing as she does that the end justifies the means, her end has been the smooth running of the High Tower. And the means? Why, the spending of other people's money! Marianne Limousines has had to repossess the Iron Maiden, which Valerie had sold to them, leased back then not kept up the payments. Amethyst Builders, Luxuriette, Femina Electrical and so forth have all been driven to litigation. The IGP, far from being wealthy, is struggling to survive. The success of the brochure has been very largely wishful thinking.

Someone at the Charity Commission has noticed that B. Patchett had suddenly become T. Patchett – changed from a shaky old hand to a bold strong one, very arresting, with swirls and arabesques in purple ink – without due notification. A few major discrepancies were then discovered in the very scatty accounts, and now the Charity Commissioners are asking questions. Ms Sidcup is at death's door in a hospice, and is in no position to answer them. She was taken poorly very suddenly. They have given the High Tower three months to sort itself out. Valerie says everyone is panicking, three months is more than enough. The gravity of the situation has been kept from the She Devil. The poor old dear deserves at least that.

I blame my failure to notice what has been happening on the problem I have seeing through masonry walls. Momus should surely find a solution. A rock fall or a landslide, something like that. I need to have a look at Valerie's accounts, get into the Archives. A prayer to him seems advisable. He has left me in this pickle and so should in all reason oblige. Not that he's very hot on reason, as we know. But here goes:
'Dear Momus, Great God of Narrative, Teller of Tales, High Lord of Mystery and the Whole Fictional Universe, hear my prayer. Do what is needed at this juncture, hear my prayer. A rock fall perhaps or a landslide to make a hole or two in the basement would help me bring this story to fruition. Hear my prayer. I know you're busy and beset by your own deadlines but hear my prayer. Your power is undoubted, your blessing on this project most earnestly sought by your humble servant.

Just let me fucking see what's happening! (Delete. Sorry, just slipped out. But I am rather desperate.)' That should do it. Momus goes for a bit of grovelling. Dodgy bloody shuffler.

I take it back.

He's done it. In his own way, of course, not mine. Nothing dramatic, not an earthquake, a volcano or a rip tide as he sometimes does when approached in prayer – and perhaps just as well for he can be terrifyingly impetuous – but I hear a kind of electronic crackling. Then, when I stare at the stone wall I don't exactly see through it, but instead a kind of second-hand version of what is going on, I suspect edited at his own caprice, on a porridgey black and white old-fashioned screen. The sound at least comes through clear as anything. Okay. On we go. Thanks be to Momus.

'*Wanker, aresehole, scum,*' I feel like saying sometimes under my breath. Foul-mouthed in life, foul-mouthed in death, that's me. Alarming, how deeply ingrained is this habit of darting ill wishes at animate people and inanimate objects in others, outrunning even death. '*Look at me,*' one is saying to a recalcitrant universe. '*Look at me! Still furious but functioning!*' I thought I heard Bobbo's fading '*cunt, cunt, cunt!*' as he was sucked up into the infinite, but I may have been mistaken. I digress. Back to doing Momus' work for him, the blighter.

The edited scenes on the spectral TV screen:

Valerie sits at her desk in 3CC/2 when Dr Simmins comes storming in. All around are unopened letters, but also wads of £50 notes.

Dr Simmins: What is all this, Valerie, what is all this? Have you not been taking your pills?

Valerie: People have so little understanding of the important things in life, let alone how great minds work. The important thing is to go forward with the plan. Money matters are so trivial!

Dr Simmins: But all these unopened envelopes – the bills?

Valerie: I've been so busy I've hardly been down here. But here *(she hands over a few hefty wads)*: this should cover the Iron Maiden: take this to Marianne Limousines: it will bring us up to date. Tell them they're lucky I'm not suing. But we must have our Iron Maiden, mustn't we. You're free to use it any time, Dr Simmins, without going through Security. Your need is greater than mine. And take this *(more money)* too for Luxuriette – we have the wedding to think about. But their behaviour has been so reprehensible – there is such a thing as trust! I'll see to the rest of the bills now I know about them.

Dr Simmins: So Ms Sidcup lost her grip some time ago?

Valerie: I will not have Ms Sidcup blamed. She did what she could, poor old dear. I take full responsibility. That's what I'm like. Stop panicking, Dr Simmins. You have been such a boon to all of us! Perhaps take another pill?

The scene changes. Valerie is taking the lift down to 1HT/3, the Archive Room. She goes inside and opens the old suitcase with the chrome locks and takes out a big pile of notes – which, however, scarcely diminishes the amount visibly remaining there.

Valerie (to the world): Enough – and for everyone. Fate is so totally on my side!

Another scene: The Lantern Room. Tyler, to all effects Tayla, except he still has his willy, is entwined with Valerie.

Valerie: Our great day together, Tyler, tomorrow. I so love you. Do you love me?

Tyler: Of course I do, Val. But couldn't we just go off to the Bahamas or somewhere? The money's mine, Grandpa said so.

Valerie: He was dead when he said it. It might not hold up in a court of law.

Tyler: But why an actual marriage? It's so last century. You know what men are like.

Valerie: You're a girl. All girls adore weddings. I'm the husband so I'm wearing a penguin suit – ironically. And your dress is fabulous. Stop panicking. And only a couple of weeks to go and you'll finally be *all* girl, not four-fifths girl. And we'll live happily ever after with nothing penetrative to stand in our way. Isn't that wonderful?

Tayla (gives up): Yes dear. Yes dear.

The scene changes. The Lantern Room is being made ready for the wedding, paint brushes wielded, chairs unstacked, bunting pinned up, a wedding cake borne in, glorious wedding hats brought out of retirement. All is completed, the guests (including a scattering of men, one of them being Tom Brightlingsea, at whom the She Devil scowls) are seated. The registrar is Wendy Singh from the local Register Office. Nicola, Matilda and the girls are there in various stages of dress, alarm and disbelief. Enter the wedding couple to the Wedding March. The bride is in virginal white with all the trimmings, the groom in a penguin suit: a very good-looking and happy pair indeed.

Dr Wendy: Do you take this woman to be your wedded husband?

Tayla: I do.

I had a good view of the wedding reception: it was held in the Lantern Room. There was a large window area, so I didn't have to rely on the screens. Nicci managed a little reunion with the She Devil before Matilda dragged her away in fear of contamination.

The She Devil more or less apologised saying she had done the best she could within the limits of her own nature. Nicci said she supposed she could say the same about herself and now Tyler was a Tayla they might have an easier relationship. Would her mother please give him/her – Tayla – his/her mother's best wishes for the final procedure? Madison and Mason, cautious, thanked their grandmother for her offer of jobs at the High Tower, but said they were already sorted for jobs.

Nicci asked if Bobbo had left her any money, and the She Devil, seeming a little surprised, said no, he'd died penniless and a dependent, mentioned that the IGP, who'd done the supporting, was a co-operative into which she'd paid all her own wealth. After that the meeting was a little cooler.

The cream meringues were excellent, the oyster patties superb. Luxuriette had been paid.

The Charity Commissioners would be arriving on the 3rd of January to examine the books but Valerie said there were no worries; she had everything under control. They had three whole months! The charity that was the co-operative that was the IGP was in thriving financial order. Cheques, postal orders and BACS payments were pouring in. All IGP members could rest assured that their money was safe. She was believed.

A little later I look at the screens, and what do I find in one of the committee rooms? Valerie come to ask Dr Simmins for a top up of Ritalin. In the days after the marriage Dr Simmins and Valerie seem to be getting on rather well.

> *Valerie*: He says he doesn't like being Mrs Valeria. He thinks people are laughing at him. But it's such a nice name. I don't see what's so good about being called Patchett. It's so sort of anyone's.
> *Dr Simmins*: It was his grandfather Bobbo's name and he honours him.
> *Valerie*: Well, he's the only one who does.
> *Dr Simmins*: He'll feel much more relaxed about everything after the final op: more amenable. Passing post-wedding doubts are pretty normal. And poor girl, she'll be having pre-op nerves.
> *Valerie*: Not that I've noticed And I love her to bits and I still can't orgasm with him. Do you think that's going to get better? Is it the penetration that puts me off?

This is getting far too personal. But what does one expect if one eavesdrops? Bugger Momus. Anyway, Dr Simmins says she hopes so after all this, and perhaps it is that Valerie's still feeling guilty about poor Leda. Valerie says she's never felt guilty in her life and she's totally given up Leda. Dr Simmins hopes she isn't lying. Valerie is now Dr Simmins' patient: the latter ups the lithium to even out her bipolar swings, and the Ritalin to counteract her depression.

When procedure day, the 6th of October, dawns bright and fair, I watch as Leda drives the Iron Maiden out on to the London

Road. Tayla, Dr Simmins and Valerie are in the back. Of all of them Tayla seems the most relaxed. She's wearing the pretty red-flowered dress again. Five hours later they come back but without Tayla. From their faces I can tell that the operation has gone well.

On the 8th an ambulance brings Tayla back. She's a little pale but rejects the offered wheelchair, and walks on through Security to cheers from a gathered crowd. The She Devil is there and applauds politely. Tayla goes through to the canteen, takes up her guitar and sings 'She's a Woman' by the Beatles. She finishes. Valerie goes up to her and says:
'Wife.'
'Husband,' says Tayla.
They embrace. Cheers all round. The She Devil goes to her room. I can't see the expression in her face – which is probably just as well.

Two weeks later I look in to Dr Simmins' surgery and Valerie is there and she is crying. I almost turn off the sound out of respect, because I think I already know why: M to F has made no difference. Dr Simmins is writing out another prescription. Perhaps she fears suicide.

Tayla has been spending too much of his time on his computer with a headset on playing noisy and violent virtual reality games. I actually thought I had a glimpse of nasty old Bobbo staring in the Lantern Room window – perhaps he *is* still around after all, trying to stir up the old Adam in the new Eve? And using musical taste to do so! In which case double bugger bloody Momus! I just knew he was playing games with me, not allowing me the whole story. That transition did go suspiciously well. Not even any need for dilation – when the urge of the body simply to close up after a wound is so strong!

But no sooner was Bobbo there than he was gone. Just in a flash. Will the old dinosaur never give up? He's so wily. Oh Momus, what have you done, with your gift for upsetting apple carts? I thought we were friends? I thought we were going for a happy ending?

But when I look in on Tayla in the Lantern Room myself, I feel comforted. She is wearing some kind of helmet and staring into a computer and looking so pretty and innocent. No harm done. It might have been my imagination. What they call a third-person action game, presumably, when you use avatars to do all the dirty work. I believe they can be addictive, and Tayla certainly seems intent. But I'm sure she has strength to resist the old Adam anyway.

And later, when I look in through Housekeeping's window there are the three of them, the She Devil, Valerie and Tayla, all girls together, dressing up for the Widdershins Walk ceremony. Tayla is trying on a laurel wreath, and the She Devil is actually holding her hand, while she herself is having a fitting for the old red dressing gown, transformed with ermine and gold trimmings into a truly regal cape; Valerie looking on. All is well.

It's all so exhausting for me – running a successful internet business was nothing compared to this. But then work was always a piece of cake compared to friends and family. I doze right through the Christmas season and wake up with bells ringing in the New Year, at least I think that's what it is: the ragged sound is overtaken by the noise of the wind.

Don't ask me how I hear it, having no actual ears, but I just know, as I know what I see without actual eyes. Ask Momus, whose press-ganged servant I am; his reporter, some kind of unreliable cosmic, comic journalist. Why me, I cry, why me? Because I spent those years with Ruth and then failed to keep in touch? Well, I did all right, didn't I? Humble mental nurse makes good! I'm not a bit-part player in the She Devil's life, any more than she's a bit-part player in mine. I ask Momus – why should I deserve this? I have no choice but to trust you, but do you actually know?

Down there at the foot of the High Tower it's mayhem. A dreadful dawn is breaking on New Year's Day: the day of the Widdershins Walk. Stupid Valerie, so sharp she cut herself! Anyone could have told her it was unlucky: many did, actually.

They'd all been working down there through the night – the sound of voices, little piping squeaks from all the women, stentorian tones from the FTMs in Security, mixed with hammering and the clanking of scaffolding poles and everything lit by full moonlight.

A romantic scene is brought to a sudden end.

Faster than is possible a twisting tornado approaches over the sea from the horizon. It heads straight for the High Tower.

A banshee wind so strong, nothing like Mary's gentle *wooo-h, wooo-h, wooo-h*: more like Momus himself, blasting away and laughing.

The Powers have been saving up their energies for this for months and it shows.

All goes dark.

The searchlights go on – at least they are ready and prepared, in spite of Valerie's inefficiencies, thanks to Leda. Valerie was all froth and bubble. Leda was for real. Dark-coated shapes at the bottom of the High Tower move about on the rocks. They are trying to salvage aluminium tent poles, rescue torn awnings, hold down the podium for the speeches. The high tide is receding fast but that's no great comfort: it's probably drawing back only in order to return in tsunami-like form and overwhelm everything. The searchlights go off. The power has failed.

What were those flames running round the wooden walkway? Fire, in this weather? There's been no lightning strike? Or arson? But there was no time for that. The elements seem determined to wipe the High Tower off the face of the earth. The emergency power goes on. Bless Leda again, ever forethoughtful!

I watch the great garage doors at the foot of the Castle Complex slowly open and the Iron Maiden ease out. In the front, revealed by the rapid swishes of the great central windscreen wiper, sit Valerie and Leda. It is Valerie for once who is driving. Leda sits beside her, beaming, in the passenger seat. Valerie, as ever, exudes brightness and confidence. They are running away, rats leaving a sinking ship. The New Year's Widdershins Walk was obviously cancelled and the Charity Commissioners were due on the 3rd.

The honking, piercing yar-hoo, yar-hoo, yar-hoo of emergency vehicles is approaching.

Then the scene closes down on me. Fucking Momus again! He's got his cliff-hanger, that vulgar bastard...

After The Ball Is Over, After The Break Of Morn, After The Dancers' Leaving...

Though the rain had stopped, water still dripped in slow heavy drops through cracked windows onto the inner sills of the Lantern Room. An ominous peace had descended on land and sea. The sense that the weather was merely holding its horses for something worse was very strong.

In the High Tower the lights flickered: the reserve generators were struggling to keep up with demand. Ms Bradshap's store of emergency candles had been ransacked. Ms Bradshap had broken an ankle when the walkway collapsed and been taken off with the others in the fleet of ambulances: fifteen injuries, but no fatalities.

At the foot of the High Tower all was quiet, ambulances and fire engines had left, guests had departed. A few girls from Security kept an eye on burned timbers, charred rocks and a fast retreating tide. Bobbo's body had surfaced again, the stray arm reaching up to heaven once again, and had been removed to the cold store on the fire chief's say so, to await collection by the local morgue in the morning. Dr Simmins had signed all appropriate forms without argument, upset as she must have been, thought the She Devil, at seeing the Iron Maiden escape before her very eyes.

Bobbo's body was in surprisingly good condition: the fire chief observed that sand was a great absorber and filter of bacteria and pathogens, and could act as a preservative. Ms Octavia was even able to retrieve her shroud, and when the electricity came back on it would be laundered well, of course at the IGP's cost, and replaced in her cupboard.

The She Devil had watched the great garage doors slide open and the Iron Maiden nudge forward into the drive, Leda in the passenger seat, animated by excitement and happiness: no longer glum, Valerie at last all hers. Leda's resolution and perseverance had paid off. It had been hard for a moment to recognise her.

The She Devil wondered if the fires had been set on purpose and the lightning strikes had been pure coincidence. What Valerie would think, did a little arson matter? The ends justified the means. She had set the scene for her departure, used panic and confusion the better to get away with all her ill-gotten gains. It was in the nature of the High Tower to attract conspiracy rather than coincidence, and buildings, like people, had their own souls.

True, as Dr Simmins would warn, the old had to fight against paranoia, but even so it was clear enough that Valerie had chosen Leda as the more reliable partner, filled the 350-litre boot of the Mercedes to the brim with unbanked cheques and postal orders from the membership, set a fire and absconded, scarpered. There'd been no one to check that she'd actually banked them – all those unopened envelopes – and she was tempted and she gave in, true to her own nature if not the principles to which she pretended.

Good no doubt that Leda – older, wiser, sadder – had found happiness and completion with Valerie, or at least Valerie with Leda, and were off to South America or who knew where. Somewhere where names could be changed and new lives begun with such untraceable funds as they had purloined. Very Thelma and Louise.

The She Devil found herself amused and almost admiring, instead of angry. A case of the Stockholm Syndrome, of falling in love with one's kidnapper?

But oh, the elegance! The chutzpah! The style! The timing!

Oh, Valerie Valeria!

The She Devil Comes To A Decision

The She Devil, Ruth Lady Patchett, finally divested of the sopping wet red velvet cloak and green victor's wreath that she'd donned to go and help her women with the clearing up, but a damp red skirt still down her ankles, followed her granddaughter Tayla up the stone stairs to the Lantern Room, arthritic legs aching, eyes blurry from exhaustion. She wore the costume prepared for the Widdershins Walk that would never take place. She was their Queen, their leader.

She was weighed down by the leather suitcase with the chrome locks. She had been down to the Archive floor to retrieve it and found it open. Obviously some cash missing, but more than enough was left. Valerie had at least had the grace to leave the suitcase behind.

It was the same suitcase she had carried when sent off to boarding school all those years ago. She'd been seven. She could scarcely carry it then and she could scarcely carry it now. Then it had contained the few light belongings of an unhappy little schoolgirl, now it held stacks of £50 banknotes, bonds, the deeds of properties bought forty years ago – what had once been reckoned in thousands would now be reckoned in millions and even a diamond necklace, all held in Bobbo's safe for decades, in trust, stolen by little Elsie

Flower way back then and retrieved lately by a very pregnant Samantha Travers.

Poor Bobbo, thought the She Devil. No wonder he'd gone on waving his fist and pinching bottoms from the grave. Ten years in prison and all her fault. But she'd been so angry!

Tayla, ever genial, relieved the She Devil of her burden and leapt ahead undaunted up the stairs on good, strong, long legs, female enough, if perhaps a little muscly round the calves. The ballet flats seemed a good size 10, and did not flatter. Well, if you lived on the ninth floor with no elevator from the third, a girl's passion for drag-queen heels might well get discouraged.

Once in the Lantern Room Tayla went immediately to her desk and switched on her desktop PC. The She Devil sank down onto the antique white velvet sofa, which always seemed to her vaguely familiar, though she could no longer remember why, to recover and catch her breath. The suitcase stood between them.

'I need to talk to you, Tayla,' she said. 'Valerie has gone, and many things have changed rather quickly.'
'That's one way of putting it!' said Tayla, in the voice that was still Tyler's. She looked longingly at her screen as the computer booted up, then back at her grandmother. 'Okay. I'll pay attention.'
'I am going to retire,' said the She Devil. 'And what will happen to the IGP then? How will you manage now Valerie has gone?'
'I'll manage,' Tayla said. 'Bunch of old ladies. It hasn't been too difficult so far. Val sorted everything out financially. She told me so before she left with her diesel dyke.'
So they'd all three of them worked it out between them, the She

Devil realised. That was a turn up for the books. To hell with it. Good for them.

'And I have you to advise me,' Tayla added, prudently.

'But I'm going to die,' said the She Devil. 'What then?'

'Not for a long time, Grandma,' said Tayla, piously. 'There's life in the old girl yet. Let's worry about that when it happens.'

The She Devil clicked the chrome locks of the suitcase, held open the lid and Tayla's lovely black-fringed blue eyes widened. 'This will be all yours when I die,' said the She Devil. 'There's rather a lot of it. The IGP has my money, but this is your grandfather's. What will you do with it? Bail the IGP out, because it will need a lot of bailing, no matter what Valerie told you? Or what?' Tayla thought for a moment, eyes darting to and fro, finally speaking.

'If it goes to me I'd better carry on in your footsteps,' Tayla said in his man's voice. 'You were the first Lady of the High Tower and I will become the second. I will carry on in your footsteps.'

It was what the She Devil wanted to hear, but she knew better than to trust a grandchild to speak the truth when it came to matters of inheritance. It might be true but it might not.

The She Devil asked Tayla if she minded if her old Grandma put her feet up and had a little rest. Tayla said fine, go ahead, did the She Devil mind if she, Tayla, went back to her MMO game?

'MMO?' enquired Lady Patchett.

'Massively Multiplayer Online,' replied Tayla. Tayla's voice was pleasant enough – at least tenor not baritone – the voice of a young man with an amiable disposition who saw no need to bark, control or intimidate, but still an octave lower than a girl's would be. The She Devil said of course she did not mind, and Tayla slipped a helmet on to her pretty head which effectively removed her from the outside world. Odd that, to look at, Tyler had seemed so Bronze God like and awesomely handsome, and now Tayla was merely pretty.

But the hands that put the helmet on were strong and competent. The helmet curved down round Tayla's Adam's apple – which Tyler had decided when she was still a he to keep intact – making it more pronounced and wobbling when she spoke. The MMOG she was playing, according to its box, was *Slaves of Blood and Savagery* and in smaller font below: *See girls struggle! See the blood flow!! Have a laugh!!!* Tyler's choice, not Tayla's?

The She Devil decided she could not call him Tayla any more. He was Tyler and that was that. Testosterone would always win the battle over oestrogen, male progeniture over mitochondrial succession. Play about with the genitals as you might, change the hormones to suit a new society – the old Adam would always rise again.

The She Devil sank down upon the white sofa – these days thought was enough to exhaust her – and contemplated past and future.

With Valerie Valeria's departure, it seemed to the She Devil, a kind of miasma was clearing from her eyes. Valerie had managed to convince her she was old and worn out, fit to die, and the sooner the better. But she could see herself clearly now. She was worth something. She had achieved something. She had spent her early years struggling to make things fair between pretty women and plain women, but it hadn't worked, so she'd turned her attention to the prosaic – equality of pay and opportunity – and lo! the IGP was born! That was good. Valerie, seeking to stand on the She Devil's shoulders, fiddling about with body and soul, had sought justice by turning men into women, only to be thwarted by greed and her own base desires. Which was not good. The She Devil wished she wasn't so old.

The bangs, crashes, screams and metallic chords of *Slaves of Blood and Savagery* had fallen silent. Tayla had turned the sound off, but played on, helmeted, cut off from human contact. She seemed happy and relaxed. Valerie had been relegated to just-another-girlfriend status. More fish in the sea, no doubt lining up for rich, gorgeous, important Tayla, the She Devil's heir. Hermione had already been up at the High Tower once or twice, selling her wares. The young put so little store on fidelity.

Under Valerie's influence she had madly believed that the man-woman, the woman-man could become the norm and that would be the end of the gender wars, and with that so many ills. That Tayla/Tyler was the great prophesying energy. She doubted it now. He/she was a false prophet.

And she was the one who had let him in, let him share her crown, given him dominion over all her lands. She realised, and it was a horrid realisation, that in the war between the sexes, the gender war, men had just won a decisive victory. Finding themselves despised and derided, they had won back control. They had lied and cheated, plotted and planned. Feminist Man, in pretending to be an ally, was the most dangerous enemy of them all. She'd been right. The Tom Brightlingseas of this world were the very thin end of the wedge: Tyler might have tucked away his manhood but it was a small sacrifice in a greater cause. With Tyler in charge the nunnery in no time at all would be the monastery. The needle would swing back; women would be despised and derided once again. In her folly the She Devil had betrayed her gender.

All this she thought while she recovered her breath, and Tyler's helmeted head bent to his game. All was silent. Now the lights went on at the foot of the High Tower. The main power was back on. She could see a few female shapes still moving about down below. Most women were probably in bed and asleep. Dark rocks and lapping waves reflected back light. A moon flickered in and out between racing clouds.

As if on cue noise suddenly blasted from the loudspeakers: the game's sound track, noises of warfare, terror and rapine synthesised to make a jolly jape. Tyler looked up briefly and smiled but did not turn the sound down. It was a message. He was telling her something. Tyler had declared the war between the genders over, claiming the privileges of both – while opening hostilities on another and quite unexpected front. It was worse even than she had thought. War between those who loved noise and those who hated it, the strong against the weak, the quick against the slow, digital against analogue.

It was a war between the young and the old. Energy would always trump wisdom. With Tyler on top the young would win.

Now she could make out the lyrics through the racket: the squelching of flesh, the slicing of knives, the sobs of victims, the moans of the ruined: not nice or meant to be: the glory of chaos and damage, the power of want over ought. *B-doong, b-doong, b-doong.* '*I am the rapist!*' *B-doong, b-doong, b-doong.* '*I am the greatest!*' *B-doong, b-doong, b-doong,* '*Wild!*' *B-doong,* '*Wow!*'

She thought she heard Bobbo laugh.

The Assumption

Ruth, the She Devil, rose from the white sofa with some difficulty – her stiff knees and weak thighs made rising from any low chair difficult. It was the same sofa, though she had forgotten this, where once Bobbo had lain with Mary Fisher and all the trouble had begun. She picked up the suitcase, oh how heavy: she trembled – and went to the wooden door which opened onto the narrow stone stairs leading up to what seemed to her to be the phallic glans, the very top of the Tower where the aerials spurted forth. Few ever came up here.

Dusty, flakey walls closed in on her as she climbed, the space narrowing and the steps growing steeper as she approached the top. She dragged the suitcase behind her, the thump as it rose each time sending pain shooting through wrist and knee. She took her time. There was no hurry. Tyler had not noticed her leave; his game was addictive. Ruth wondered whether he had chosen a male or female avatar – men often chose women anyway for reasons known only to psychologists – but she suspected he saw himself as the predatory male. Her breath came in short gasps.

When she pushed the door open and heaved the suitcase outside the force of the gale took her breath away altogether. It was ferocious. Wind snatched off her black wig and carried it

344

far, far up and away. It did the same for her full red skirt, so she had to stand there in her knickers, poor bald old granny with scarred and skinny trembling bare legs. The wind eased to let her drag the suitcase to the edge of the parapet. A full moon showed itself briefly between clouds.

'*I see the moon and the moon sees me,*' she sang, looking up at it, not that anyone could hear her. Moonlight caressed her. She was glad that at least she had her knickers on. She felt like a child again.

Rain, sleet and hail had stopped. Down below the little ants of people still worked away under searchlights, making good, fighting desolation, chaos, entropy, as was human custom. She felt great affection for them. She had tried to make things better for them, and failed.

She had got the suitcase out of the future She Devil Tayla's clutches, but now what was she to do? The wind decided for her, swerving from northwest to north, cyclonic again. It howled, grew icy, burst the case open, and flung its contents far off to a stormy sea, whereafter they were of no value to woman or man.

Looking up, the workers down below thought they saw a disturbance on the top of the High Tower. Some swore they'd seen the She Devil standing there naked and as she had been in her youth, magnificent and glittery eyed, arms stretching up to heaven, demanding justice. Others said they'd seen a lightning bolt. Perhaps that had consumed her, for when the Security girls got up there to investigate they found nothing but an old, empty suitcase.

Some assumed she'd jumped into the sea – but why would the She Devil do such a thing? She had disappeared, and was never to be seen again.